IF

—

A NOVEL

RANDI COOLEY WILSON

Published by SECRET GARDEN PRODUCTIONS, INC.

Edited by Liz Ferry | Per Se Editing

Cover Design by ©ByHangLe | Hang Le

Book Formatting by Type A Formatting

IF (A Novel)/Randi Cooley Wilson

Printed in the United States of America

First Edition December 2018

ISBN: 9781791884666

For the boy who stole a piece of my heart,
And the man who never gave it back.

No matter how much pain it has caused,
no matter how many tears have fallen,
sometimes love isn't meant to be,
leaving the *ifs* to linger.

CHAPTER 1

I close my eyes and take a few deep breaths, attempting to regain my composure. The crisp evening air fills my lungs but does nothing to soothe my soul. The truth is, tonight, nothing is going to keep me calm—except maybe copious amounts of alcohol.

The brisk fall weather isn't unusual for this time of year in New England. Cooler temperatures hang in the air, chilling even with a jacket. This evening, though, there is another reason for the icy presence deep within my bones.

I shiver and stare at the closed double doors in front of me, knowing what's waiting behind them. Tears threaten to burn the back of my throat. Suddenly, I miss California.

My safe place.

Far away from the memories.

I exhale slowly, staring at the scene in front of me. The plain white church sits unassumingly on the grassy hill. Like most buildings in Massachusetts, it has a rich history and longstanding secrets. The steeple stands tall against the dusk-colored sky glowing with crimson and auburn hues.

A breeze passes over me, carrying with it the whispers of the ghosts who've passed through the sacred doors. Blue hydrangeas frame the front of the historic building, popping off the white clapboards, which look like they've just received a fresh coat of paint. It's picture perfect. On the outside. What's inside is anything but perfect.

"You ready, Emerson?" a gentle voice asks.

I unglue my gaze from the church and turn my attention to the tall, handsome man beside me, Jake Irons. When my eyes meet his, he smiles effortlessly.

How does he always appear so completely at ease all the time?

It's a gift. It must be. One that I don't possess.

My gaze roams over the tailored black suit he chose for tonight. It's flawless.

He's flawless.

"Ready," I force out, focusing on how handsome he looks.

Jake is easygoing. Calm. Steady.

Exactly what I need to keep me composed.

To keep my façade firmly in place.

He reaches for my hand with his larger one. "You okay?"

No. This is the first time my two worlds will collide, and it's impossible to be *okay.*

Lifting my gaze, I give him a watery smile and nod. "Just happy," I lie.

Jake studies me for a moment before squeezing my hand.

He's always so perceptive.

It's unnerving.

But even he has no idea what we're about to walk into. I've kept it from him, because I don't want my complicated past to tarnish my future with him. I know he senses the sadness at times, the void, but he never pushes. Never asks. He doesn't try to fix the broken pieces or make me whole. He simply accepts that this is the way I am.

With a slight tug of encouragement, he guides me toward the entrance. And with each step closer, my heart lodges itself farther in my throat. The panic crawls underneath my skin, threatening to break through the surface as I try to convince myself that my world won't fall apart the moment I step into the church.

The doors open and a friendly face greets us. "You guys made it!"

Relief crosses my friend Josh's face, and I can't help but smile at his energy.

"Sorry we're late." I step into his warm embrace.

Josh has always been my favorite boyfriend of Kennison's. The three of us went to college together—part of a larger group of friends. And while they've had their ups and downs, it really does make me happy to see the two of them getting married this weekend.

"Where is Kenz?" I ask, hoping to see my best friend.

"With the wedding coordinator, going over some last minute details. She'll be out in a minute. Come in. Everyone is already here." Josh steps to the side, letting me by so that he and Jake can shake hands and do their guy greeting thingy.

The moment I enter the church, the air around me jumps with electricity. My chest begins to cave in and my skin feels too tight all over my body. The weight of *his* stare is on me, and my skin heats under it. My head swirls and chaos grips me. I take a deep breath, trying to control what I knew was going to happen the moment I saw him again.

Lincoln Daniels is impossible to ignore.

We are impossible to ignore.

When my gaze lifts, it tangles with a set of steel-gray eyes.

And with one look, I'm gone.

Lost in the memories and heartache.

The *ifs* lingering between us.

CHAPTER 2

FRESHMAN YEAR OF COLLEGE

Heading to class, I ignore the tiny drops of water falling from the dark gray sky. For early September, it's cold. And wet. All around crappy out. I growl under my breath and make a mental note to move somewhere warm and full of sunshine after graduation. It's been two days since I started my freshman year at the private college I'm attending in Massachusetts, and both days have been full of nothing but dreary weather.

With a sigh, I rush up the cracked brick stairs and head into the oldest building on campus. Unfortunately for me, it's also the farthest building from the freshman dorm. The heavy double doors slam behind me as I rush down the corridor trying to find my lecture hall. Once I do, I stumble into the room and take a seat in the middle row of the auditorium. With a heavy exhale, I slide off my backpack and place it down next to my feet.

Chilled, I snuggle into the oversized jacket keeping me warm. It belongs to my boyfriend, Lucas. We had an amazing summer together, which ended with an ugly reality—we were leaving for separate colleges. In a pathetic attempt to hold on to what we thought was love, he sent me on my way wearing his varsity jacket. It keeps me warm, I'll give him that.

After a few minutes, a tall slim older woman walks in, taking her place at the podium in the front of the class. The handful of us who made it on time fall quiet and listen.

"Good Morning. You are in English 101, Writing Rhetorically. If you are not supposed to be in here, now is your chance to escape. I'm Professor Landry. This semester we will be focusing on intensive practice in composing persuasive texts, while exploring various rhetorical writing techniques. My TA will be handing out the syllabus shortly," Professor Landry announces. "I will not be taking daily attendance. You are adults. I expect you to show up and do the work. If you do, your grades will reflect the effort."

"Hey." A guy pokes me in the shoulder with his pen, whisper-shouting.

Turning, I meet his gaze. "What?" I whisper back.

"Do I know you?" he asks.

My gaze runs over his face before I shake my head no. I haven't seen him before.

He glares at me in disbelief. "Where did you get that jacket?"

My eyes drop to my chest before they return to the brown ones staring at me.

"It's my boyfriend's."

The guy grins widely. "I went to that prep school." He tilts his head so he can read the name on the sleeve. "Lucas and I are high school buddies. You're his girl?"

"Yes." I turn my attention back to the professor, trying to focus on the lecture.

A second later, a commotion to my right pulls my focus as the stranger slides into the empty seat next to me, leaning into my space. "When did you two start dating?"

Without facing him, I sigh heavily. English is my favorite subject and, to be honest, his inquisition during class is starting to grate on me. "This summer. He's the cousin of a good friend of mine from high school. I met him at her graduation party."

He presses his lips together in contemplation. "I'm Tyler Hamilton."

"Emerson." I keep my focus forward, hoping he'll get the hint that I'm here to learn.

He doesn't. "So, Emerson, did you go to many of Lucas's baseball games?"

"A few Cape League games over the summer," I mutter under my breath.

A light chuckle falls out of him. "We played high school baseball together. He's an amazing pitcher. Really talented. He's on scholarship at Boston College, right?"

Turning, I look at him. Tyler's baby face is framed by short curly dark brown hair. Freckles dot his innocent expression and his friendly gaze screams beloved hometown baseball player. He's definitely someone I can see Lucas being friends with.

"Yeah. He's playing ball at BC."

"Good for him. He's got a solid chance at the minors," he replies with admiration.

I give Tyler my best polite smile. I spent endless hours sitting in bleachers this summer watching Lucas play. Let's just say, baseball is not my favorite pastime.

Holding my eyes, Tyler dips his chin. "I'm on the baseball team here."

I nod, fighting off my overwhelming sense of irritation. "That's great."

Tyler finally gets the hint and falls silent for the rest of the class. When Professor Landry releases us, I stand and begin to leave, but he suddenly appears at my side.

"So, here's the deal, Emmie. Back at prep school, the players looked out for one another's girls. Since Lucas and I are good friends, that extends here to college as well."

I throw my bag over my shoulder and narrow my eyes, not following. "What?"

Tyler stares at me like I'm amusing. "Consider me your big brother slash bodyguard for the semester. Where you go, I go. It's an understanding we have with our teammates."

"You two aren't on the same team anymore," I point out. "And it's Emerson."

He cocks his head. "Brothers are brothers. No matter who or what team we play for."

"Look, I know you're being nice but, I don't need a . . ." I motion up and down. "You."

"Have you seen you?" He takes my elbow and gently pulls me toward the door as he falls into step with me and we walk together. "You totally need a . . . me."

"What is that supposed to mea—" I start, but he cuts me off.

"Come on, pretty girl. Let's not be late for our next class."

Furious, I glare at him, but he brushes it off, as if I'm simply amusing to him.

During our walk, Tyler goes on and on about our friendship and how things will be. He chats with me the entire way, telling me all about his classes and baseball schedule as if we've been friends our entire lives and he's merely filling me in on things I should already know. When we finally get to the building my next class is in, he makes a point to walk me to the door and then strangely hands me a bottle of water from his backpack before returning my own bag to me, which he insisted he carry the entire way here.

His motions his chin toward the bottle of water. "Hydration is key to health."

I blink at him. "Right. Listen, Tyler, Lucas is my boyfriend, so . . ."

"I'm not hitting on you. I have a girlfriend."

"You do?"

"Yeah. That isn't what this is about."

"It's not?" I frown, confused.

"Teammates take care of our own. It's what we do, Emmie."

"Emerson," I correct.

He smiles brightly. Realizing he's not leaving until I walk in, I shake the bottle at him.

"Thanks. For this. And carrying my bag," I exhale.

"Anytime. Have a good class."

"You too, Tyler."

"Oh, and Emmie? I'll be outside in an hour to walk you back to the freshman dorm."

Before I can protest, he winks and walks backwards toward his class.

And that is how Tyler Hamilton came into my life, and ruined it.

CHAPTER 3

My heart pounds in my chest as I make my way down the crowded corridor, which is on the second floor of the freshman dorm. The stench of beer and marijuana permeate the air as I follow my roommate through the sea of bodies partying around us. Even with the wide hallways, people are shoulder to shoulder, hanging out, laughing, and drinking.

Voices blur, mixed in with the music as students lean into each other's ears so they can hear and talk, their arms flailing with dramatic gestures as they try to communicate over the noise.

"Stay close!" Kennison shouts over her shoulder, guiding me forward.

For a quick moment, I lock gazes with some guy who winks at me as I pass by him. I roll at my eyes at the blatant way he's checking me out, unimpressed by the attractive dark-haired jock. He reminds me of Lucas, and even Lucas isn't impressing me these days.

We've been at school for an entire month and he's called me twice. And when we do talk, our conversations are entirely focused on him. Or baseball. Nothing about me.

Ignoring another guy who smiles at me in the hallway, we push our way through the throngs of drunk freshmen toward Tyler's suite. As we stumble in, a heavy cloud of smoke hits me in the face. It's settled around the room and reeks of marijuana mixed with booze.

I look around. Everything here screams panic-attack trigger and safety-rule breaking.

"Hey!" Tyler brightens when he sees us. "You ladies made it."

"We did." I wince when his beer-scented breath hits my face.

Tyler's bloodshot eyes meet mine and then slide to the pretty blonde girl by his side. "This is Julia, my girlfriend," he shouts proudly, before leaning into Julia's ear. Julia's new. Last week, it was Rebecca. Tyler changes girlfriends often. "This is Emmie, a prep school teammate's girlfriend, and her roommate, Kennison," he slurs.

"It's Emerson," I correct for the hundredth time.

Julia gives us a polite smile and quick wave before she slips away, over to her friends.

"Booze is in the back left corner. Other shit to the right!" Tyler winks at us.

Uncomfortable, Kenz and I watch as he follows Julia like a puppy dog over to a group of large-chested blonde girls. They're surrounded by members of the baseball team. I shake my head at the way they're all drunkenly flirting with one another without shame.

My roommate meets my eyes with a knowing smile and we both laugh.

After we met at orientation, Kennison and I became instant friends and requested to room together. I watch as she throws her curly chestnut hair up into a clip and I can't help but be grateful she's here. She's from a small town not too far from campus, and like me, she's lived a pretty sheltered life. We're definitely both out of our element tonight.

She tilts her head at me as I stare at her. "You want to stay or go?"

"We can stay for a bit," I reply, knowing she wants to.

"You sure?"

I shrug. "This is part of the college experience, right?"

"Right." She nods once.

Suddenly, the air in the room shifts. The electricity

bouncing off the haze of smoke pulls my attention to a guy who appears in the doorway across the suite. Relaxed and unaffected by the throng of people in the tiny space, he strolls in and the crowd parts.

Everyone seems to give him space to swagger in, as if he's some kind of celebrity. I stare, because he is impossible to ignore. He makes his way over to a group of people, acting as if he owns the world. Lean muscles stretch under his sun-kissed, tattoo-covered arms as he crosses them casually over his broad chest, hidden under a white T-shirt.

My breath hitches as I watch the corner of lips lift at something the guy in front of him says. Whatever it is seems to mildly amuse him. After a minute, he lifts a hand and brushes some of his messy short blond hair off his forehead before running the same hand over the light scruff on his jawline.

Captivated, I watch as the entourage surrounding him hangs on his every word. He speaks with confidence and yet gives off a casual ease—like a wolf in sheep's clothing.

Without thinking about what I am doing, I take a step toward him but stop abruptly when Kennison's face suddenly appears in front of mine. She's eyeing me strangely.

"Em?"

"Mmm?"

"You okay?"

"Fine." I meet her questioning gaze.

She looks at me with an odd expression. "What are you doing?"

"What do you mean?"

"You were walking off as I was talking to you."

"I was?"

"Are you sure you're okay? You're acting weird."

I shake off whatever odd spell I seem to be under. "Sorry. Um, yeah. I'm fine."

Her eyes hold mine for a moment, filled with judgment, before she looks over her shoulder at the blond guy, and then back at me with an understanding sly grin. "Ah."

"What?"

"He's cute."

"Who?" I act like I have no idea who she is talking about.

She rolls her eyes. "Jill and Kylie just arrived. Let's go say hello."

I nod, distracted. "Let me grab a drink first."

"A drink?" she repeats, surprised. "You want a drink?"

I don't drink at parties. She knows this. "Yeah. Do you want one?"

An amused smile crosses her lips. "I'm good. I'll meet you over there."

My gaze slides over her shoulder and lands on the blond guy again.

He's standing in the middle of what appears to be an all-female fan club.

"M'kay," I reply absentmindedly.

"Em?" Kennison attempts again, but I step around her.

"Be there in a sec . . ." I trail off, walking away.

I walk by him as I casually make my way over to the corner of the room. The keg and other booze are over here, surrounded by a bunch of loud, obnoxious guys funneling beer.

For a moment, I stare at them, impressed by their gulping skills.

A smooth voice at my ear sends shivers across my skin. "Need a drink?"

I suck in a sharp breath through my teeth before lifting my gaze, only to look up into the most beautiful eyes I've ever seen. They're steel gray, like the color of the sky right before an unexpected storm. Unable to speak, I stand and stare at the guy I'd seen from across the room. He's so close, I can feel his breath as I take in the perfect angles of his face. Everything about him is sharp, pointed and—underneath his breathtaking façade—maybe a little bit dangerous. He smells like cigarette smoke and freshly cut grass.

His gaze doesn't stray from mine, and he seems amused at the way I'm regarding him.

"Your eyes are ocean blue," he says with awe. "They're fucking beautiful."

My lips part at the velvety sound of his deep voice as it wraps around me.

"Thank you," I breathe out.

"You're flushed," he points out, looking at my cheeks.

"Am I?"

"Did I embarrass you?"

"No." I shake my head.

A sly grin falls across his lips at my response, and his eyes roam over me. With each passing moment, I try to remember how to breathe. There's no denying that being this close to him is a bad idea, but for some strange reason I can't bring myself to move away.

"So?" he prompts.

"So?" I repeat on a breathy exhale.

He cocks his head. "Did you want a drink?"

"Y-yes," I falter. "But, I-I was hoping for something with a sealed cap."

"Sealed cap?" he repeats, frowning.

"I, um." I take a small step away from him so I can think more clearly. "I don't drink anything at parties from an open cup. Girl safety rule number one: always open the bottle yourself and hold your hand over the top when not drinking out of it," I explain lamely.

He nods, considering my words as some of his hair falls over his forehead.

When his eyes meet mine again, they seem to get darker. "You like safe?"

I hold his intense gaze and feel like his question runs deeper than beverages.

"I like safe," I reply.

Suddenly, I'm shoved from the side and pushed into his arms.

He growls and looks over my head. "Hey! Watch what you're doing, asshole."

"Sorry, Daniels," the kid mumbles, and quickly moves away from us.

"Come on," Daniels says.

He grabs my hand, pulling me toward a closed door in the back corner of the common area. I look around and realize he must be one of Tyler's suitemates. I know the sports teams here all have suites with four private rooms and a common area connecting them.

I watch as he slides his hand into the front pocket of his jeans and produces a keycard before slipping it in the lock and opening the door. Flipping on the lights, he motions for me to enter. Biting my bottom lip, I contemplate whether I should follow him for a minute before he smiles and lifts his chin to someone behind me.

When I turn, I see that Tyler is watching us with narrowed eyes, but he isn't making any efforts to stop me, which is good. Kennison is next to him, holding up her cell, and I touch my back pocket, double checking that I have mine before nodding to her it's there.

Facing him again, I hesitate for the tiniest of moments.

I have a feeling the moment I step into his world, everything in mine will change.

Forever.

CHAPTER 4

I look around his semi-clean dorm room as he makes his way over to a small fridge in the back. Baseball gear and some clothes are strewn around the bed and floor. Some books, an iPad, and a few other items are sitting on his desk. It all looks normal. He opens a mini-fridge in the back corner and pulls out two bottles of beer, then grabs a bottle opener.

With a cool swagger, Daniels makes his way back over to me and hands me a bottle and the opener. This guy oozes sex and rebelliousness, and I force myself not to sigh or roll my eyes at his attempt to suck me in. He cocks his head to the side, considering me.

"I'd offer to open your beer for you, like a gentleman, but you strike me as the kind of girl who prefers to open your own beer bottles," he jokes with an amused challenge in his tone, given that I've already informed him of my capped-bottle preference.

I lift my chin, taking the bottle and opener from him. "You would be correct."

Once I get my bottle open, I hand him back the opener and he opens his own bottle, then throws the opener on the bed next to us. I take a long drag of my beer, trying to do something other than stare at him.

"I'm Lincoln. Lincoln Daniels," he says. "But everyone calls me Daniels."

"It's nice to meet you." I hold his eyes. "Lincoln."

He smirks at my purposeful use of his first name, taking a sip from his bottle.

"And you are?" he prompts.

I shrug. "Does it matter?" I motion with my chin toward the Lincoln Daniels fangirl club watching us with annoyance from across the party. "Do you know all their names?"

Lincoln's expression tightens. "*Yours* matters. Not theirs."

I take a breath and let it out slowly. "Emerson Shaw. Everyone calls me Emerson."

Amusement softens his eyes and face as he chuckles at my words and I smile at him.

Lincoln clinks the top of his bottle to mine. "It's a pleasure"—he pauses—"Em."

As I smile, I try not to show how much he's affecting

me—how his intense gaze makes me want to melt into him or the way his velvety voice has this insane lulling effect on me.

"How do you know Tyler?" he asks.

It's an innocent question. But I panic, remembering Tyler is friends with Lucas. Lucas, my boyfriend. *Shit! What the hell am I doing flirting with this guy?* I look into his eyes as he stares at me. "Tyler is in my English class," I answer, sounding more calm than I feel.

"That so?" he asks, but it's more of a challenge. Like he can see through my vagueness.

"That. Is. So."

Inexplicably drawn together, we just watch each other with a magnetic intrigue.

Lincoln takes a step in my direction and lifts a strand of my long wavy hair. "What color is this? It's not really brown, but it's not blond either. I've never seen it before."

"Ash brown. With blond highlights." *God I'm lame.*

"Ash brown." He twirls it between his fingers. "It's pretty. Soft and silky."

Lincoln steps closer, his smile carrying a hint of sensuality. I take a sip from my bottle and step around him, taking my hair with me, needing to put some distance between us.

When I see his textbooks, I exhale. "Are you a sports medicine major?"

Suddenly, I feel his hard chest pressed against my back as he looks over my shoulder, down onto his desk. At his closeness, all the blood rushes to my head and starts pounding.

"I am. What about you?" Lincoln's beer-laced breath tickles my cheek.

My stomach does small flips at his nearness. After a moment, I look up and meet his eyes, and he grins playfully, like he knows he makes me feel all spastic and crazy inside.

"I'm not into sports," I manage through a dry throat.

"What *are* you into, Em?" he whispers, holding my gaze.

Slightly unsettled by his question, I swallow. "I'm undecided."

"Yeah?" His eyes twinkle.

I nod. "I haven't decided . . . on a major yet."

"Well," he says, his eyes darkening. "Let me know if I can help you . . . *decide*."

Feeling hypnotized and light-headed from his scent, I tear my eyes away from his and take a step away from him, determined to find something safe to look at or talk about.

Something that doesn't turn into a weird intense sexual energy or subtle flirting between us. I have a feeling that is going to be an impossible task. Walking toward the left side of the room, I pick up his team jersey and turn to face him, holding it up to him.

"How long have you played baseball?"

"My whole life. I'm on full scholarship here because of it."

"What position?"

"Third base."

I smile and shake my head. "Of course you do."

"It's my favorite base." He winks and I raise a brow at him.

"Not a *home run* kinda guy?" I tease.

"Sometimes being close, without actually *scoring*, is just as rewarding."

Lincoln throws me a roguish smile and I melt. I'm way too attracted to this stranger for it to be normal. Or healthy. *What is happening to me?* I toss his jersey back down because clearly baseball is off-limits. Nervous, I continue my tour of his personal space.

As I look at shelves and furniture, I notice something odd.

"No photos?" I question. "From home, I mean?" I look over my shoulder at him.

He arches an eyebrow. "Are you asking if I have a girlfriend at home?"

I hold his stare. "I was asking why you don't have any personal photos or items."

Lincoln nods his understanding, but there's a flatness

27

to his response. "I've never needed photos to remind me of people who are important. And I like things . . . uncluttered."

I frown at his odd response. He seems edgy. I decide to shift the conversation.

"So, no girlfriend at home pining for you, then?"

"Nope." He takes a long pull from his beer, swallowing while holding my gaze. "Or here." My insides light up with excitement at his admission, even though they shouldn't.

"Why not? I mean . . ." I pause. "Have you seen you?"

That earns me another chuckle. "I'm not boyfriend material."

"No?" I challenge, then turn and lean back on the empty nightstand. "Why is that?"

Lincoln stares straight into my eyes, his voice void of emotion when he speaks. "I'm not the kind of guy that girls want to—or should—bring home to meet Mommy and Daddy."

I tilt my head, hating that he thinks that. "What kind of guy are you, then?"

"The kind of guy that will fuck you in a dark hallway when you're trying to escape your sheltered life, or want to piss off your parents." He holds my eyes in an intense stare as he stalks toward me. "The kind of guy that you let touch you, even when you have a boyfriend. I'm the kind of guy who brings darkness into your world as I destroy it. And you." I hold my breath as he takes a final step into my space and dips his mouth toward my ear, whispering, "I'm the kind of guy who isn't, and won't ever be, good for you."

Something inside me wants to tell him that he's full of shit. Even though I don't know him, I sense that there is more to him than this bad-boy persona he's trying to give off.

A loud knock on the open door has Lincoln slowly backing away from me to reveal Tyler. He's standing in the doorway watching us with a scowl on his face, holding his cell. He glances back and forth between us, so I quickly shoot him a *what's up* look.

"Everything okay in here?" Tyler asks, with a bite to his tone.

"Fine," Lincoln says casually. "I was just getting to know your friend Em."

"Emerson," I push out quickly.

I don't know why I clarify what my full name is; it's not like he's been using it this entire time, but for some reason letting him use *Em* in this moment seems inappropriately strange, given I'm always correcting Tyler for trying to shorten it in a cute way.

At my correction, Lincoln's grip on his bottle tightens, and his knuckles become white.

"What do you need, Hamilton?" Lincoln asks Tyler, but keeps his attention on me.

He's doing it again. Looking at me in a way that makes me feel naked and vulnerable.

Tyler steps closer to us, holding up his cell to me. "Lucas called looking for you."

"What?" I unglue my eyes from Lincoln and meet Tyler's scolding expression.

"He's been calling and texting you. When he couldn't reach you, he called me to see if I knew where you were," he explains. "I said you were with me and I'd have you call him."

"Who the fuck is Lucas?" Lincoln asks rudely, causing my eyes to cut back to his.

In my peripheral vision, I see Tyler frown. "Her boyfriend, asshole."

Lincoln exhales a long breath, slowly lifting his face to look at me. "Boyfriend?"

I fall silent. Oddly, his eyes are full of hurt, and all I can do is stare at him curiously.

"Lucas is a friend of mine from prep school," Tyler states.

Even though I don't really know Lincoln, he somehow looks like he is in a world of pain at this information. His eyebrows are furrowed and his breathing is slow and shallow.

"Em, you have a *prep* school boyfriend?" His voice is cold and distant.

I stare back because I'm confused at the change in his demeanor. He's intimidating. Angry. Watching me as if I should be giving him an apology, or explaining myself.

I place my bottle down on his nightstand and stand to my full height.

"It was nice meeting you, Lincoln." I drop my tone, ignoring his question.

Tyler takes a step back, giving me space to slip out the doorway, but before I can even take a step, Lincoln reaches out, grabbing my elbow. His gentle hold forces me to stop.

Annoyed, I look at where he is holding my arm, because even through the cotton of my sleeve, my skin burns under his touch. "What do you want, Lincoln?" I whisper.

"I don't know," he replies quietly.

For a moment, I squeeze my eyes shut and try to drown out the smooth sound of his voice as it slides over me, setting off every nerve in my body, warming me. With a deep inhale, I open my lids and look up at him from under my lashes.

As he looks down on me, his expression turns soft and tender.

"Do me a favor and take a step back," I croak.

To my surprise, he does. With every ounce of willpower I have, I walk past Tyler and toward the open doorway to escape whatever insane moment we've been sharing.

As I leave, I hear Tyler's cool voice. "Emerson belongs to someone, Daniels."

"You're right, Hamilton. Em does belong to someone. Just not who you think."

CHAPTER 5

I don't bother to look up when the seat across from me moves and Lincoln folds his body into it. Instead, I keep my head down, focusing on my reading as he unpacks his stuff and settles in, like he does every Tuesday. This weekly study date began a few days after the party. One Tuesday afternoon, I came into the library and there he was, studying.

Even though I had no right to be, I was annoyed I hadn't seen him in days. Instead of talking to him, I ignored him and picked the farthest table from his, then set about getting comfortable. Fifteen minutes into what I thought was a clever dodge, he packed up his stuff and my insides filled with disappointment that he was leaving. Sulking, I turned my full attention to my schoolwork, which is why I didn't notice his approach until he pulled out the seat in front of me. When I looked up, his eyes sparkled with delight and held mine as he wordlessly sat down, opened his textbook, and then proceeded to ignore me.

Since that day, this is our Tuesday afternoon ritual.

We don't speak.

We just sit in silence, studying.

"The library is quiet today," he mumbles.

My breath hitches at the sound of his voice. Keeping my head down, I try to ignore him for as long as possible, but when I look up, he's watching me, his mouth turned up in amusement. Our eyes lock and he smiles at me with one of his panty-dropping, charming expressions and that's it. With one look, I'm gone. Consumed by him. He's that good.

"I'll alert the media." I try to sound bored.

He chews on the pen in his mouth and smiles before placing a folded note on my book.

My focus drops to it and then back to him. "What is this?"

"Open it."

I do, and frown when I see that it's blank. I eye him curiously.

"There is nothing written on it," I point out.

"I know."

"I don't get it."

"Here's the thing. I was going to write *I'm sorry* on it. But after I thought about it, I'm not sorry. I have nothing to be sorry for. I'm not sure why you're pissed off at me."

"What makes you think I'm pissed off at you?"

"It's been weeks since we've spoken."

Sitting back in my chair, I wrinkle my nose while my eyes drink him in. He's right. Aside from being slightly rude and put off because I didn't tell him about having a boyfriend, he didn't do anything to merit whatever crazy emotional bender I've been on.

I shake my head slowly. "I'm not pissed."

He blows out a long relieved breath. "Then what's the issue between us, Em?"

Looking around, I lower my voice. "It's complicated."

"We're complicated?"

"It. It is complicated."

"Why?"

"I'm not going to sleep with you."

A slow smile creeps across his lips. "I haven't asked you to sleep with me."

I lean forward. "Not with words."

"Not with words," he nods and repeats at the same time.

I wave my hand at him. "Your seductive looks, hot tattoos and sexy, indifferent attitude toward me, and life in general, aren't alluring. And don't pretend you don't know what I'm talking about."

A light chuckle falls out of him. "Your unresponsiveness toward me is noted."

"I mean it, Lincoln," I bite out. "This"—I point between us—"can't happen."

"I'm not trying to get in your pants, Em."

"You're not?"

"No. I'm trying to be friends with you."

"*Friends?*" I repeat, disbelief lining my voice.

"Friends."

"The way you flirt?"

"For the record"—he leans in closer so his breath washes over me—"you flirt back."

Holding my breath, I stare at his lips. They're so close to mine. If I lean forward the slightest bit, mine would brush his. The truth is, I think the realization that I might actually like this guy and want to spend time with him is making me far more skittish about a possible friendship with him, because right now, all I want is to devour his mouth.

Lincoln's eyes meet mine. They're calm and serene, but if you look deeper, you can see the untamed wild darkness that swirls like a cloudy storm in their steely depths.

"Emerson," he whispers, and I shiver. "Do you want to be friends?"

My full name on his lips sounds different. Like I'm some sort of special and mystical creature to be revered.

And I like it. I like the way he makes me feel. And that's really bad.

"What if . . . I say no?"

"What if . . . you say yes?"

My insides heat, because apparently I have a thing for his voice. It's husky and warm, slow and teasing. Velvety and smooth, like silky hot chocolate on a cool fall day.

"Do I really have a choice?"

"Nope."

My skin prickles with reluctance. "Then I guess we're friends," I give in.

He sits back in his chair, watching me with a curious expression. "Good. Now, tell me about this prep school tool you're dating, who clearly isn't good enough for you."

CHAPTER 6

The harsh fluorescent lights above me hum quietly in the empty room, while the clean, fresh smell of laundry detergent mixed with fabric softener curls around me. From my seated position on the dryer, I look up and across the aisle to check how much time is left on my washing machine before shoving my nose back into my book to finish my chapter.

A few minutes later, a shadow crosses over me, prompting me to look up.

"Hey," I say, taking my earbuds out.

"Hey yourself," Lincoln replies. "Laundry night?"

I nod. "I like to come down here late so I can study. It's quiet and warm."

"Warm, huh?" He looks around the dorm's basement turned laundromat.

"From all the dryers," I explain.

"Not a fan of the cold?"

"Nope. Warmth is my jam."

"Your jam?" Lincoln laughs. "Well, if it's your *jam*, Em."

He places his full basket on the dryer next to me while preparing a washing machine to use across from us. For the longest time, I just stare at the shirts sitting on top of his dirty clothes, curbing the desire to curl up in them because I know they'll smell like him.

When he clears his throat, I realize I've acquired some serious stalker tendencies.

"Did my shirts offend you?"

"What?" I look at him.

"You're giving them a dirty look."

"Am I?"

"It's as if they've mouthed off to you or something."

An odd sound falls out of me. It's half laugh, half groan. "No. Sorry."

Lincoln's eyes search mine and he gives me a strange look I don't quite understand before shrugging it off. Turning my attention back to my book, I pretend to read, but every so often, my gaze lifts and I watch him separate out his clothes and throw them into the top machines. His height allows him to reach them without issue. I'm envious; my five-foot frame only allows me access to the bottom washers, and for whatever reason they take longer than the top ones do to run through the wash and rinse cycles.

With his back turned, I openly stare at his broad shoulders and solid muscles. He looks like he's been working out more. Every time he lifts his arms, the thermal he's wearing slides up, giving me a peek at his toned and tanned lower back right where the top of his jeans meets the bottom hem of his shirt. It's an amazing view. Stunning really.

And those damn jeans. I'm unable to tear my eyes away from the way they hug his ass in the most perfect way. I don't realize he's turned back around and is watching me until he clears his throat again. I summon the courage to look at him, knowing I've been caught.

I blink like crazy, doing my best to pull my shit together around him.

A mischievous glint flashes in his eyes. "Are you checking me out?"

"No." The word comes out of my mouth too quickly.

Lincoln cocks his head to the side, considering me. "Sure you weren't."

"I wasn't," I state, a little too firmly. "I was checking the time left on my machine."

He steps away from his empty basket on the floor, walking toward me before he stops directly in front of me. "This is a different look for you," he says. "More . . . casual."

I look down at my favorite long sweatshirt, yoga pants, and fuzzy slippers.

"It's laundry day," I say, as if that explains my frumpy look. "And midnight."

"Not many girls can pull off *just rolled out of bed* and still look cute as hell."

"Your point?"

"You can."

I squint my eyes at him. "You're flirting again."

Lincoln gets a faraway reflective look on his face before he shakes it off. "Sorry."

Some of his hair has fallen back into his face and it's all I can do not to reach over and brush it away. I bet it's soft. I scold myself. *What is it with me when he's around?* It's like he drains me of all my common sense and proper etiquette, making me look and act crazy.

He touches my textbook, lifting up one side so he can look at the cover.

"You contemplating declaring architecture as a major instead of walking around all . . . undecided?" His charming smile is back, firmly etched on his lips.

"Probably not. It just sounded like an interesting lecture."

"Is it?"

"Yeah. I like it so far. I mean, I'm not sure if I want

to spend the rest of my life designing buildings, but it's a cool class and it takes care of my art science credit," I reply.

"I need to find something to cover that requirement."

"I recommend it." I smile brightly. "It's not an easy A, but it's stimulating."

Lincoln smirks at me, and all of his usual sharp edges soften a bit, making him even more attractive. I lick my lips and his gaze drops to my mouth before he steps closer.

"Truth be told, Em, I'm not interested in something easy," he says in a low, rumbling voice that vibrates straight through me. "I prefer challenges and . . . stimulation."

Silence quickly falls between us, our eyes catching and staying locked on one another. My skin feels all flushed and heated, as if the dryers all turned on at once and raised the room's temperature. Thoughts and feelings run wild through me, all blurring together and stupefying me, because whatever it is that my heart is doing, it can't be good. At all.

An impish grin sharpens his features as he leans in a bit closer. "Want to play a game?"

My eyebrows pull together, confused at the topic change. "What kind of game?"

"Truth or Dare."

"What?" I laugh nervously.

He slides himself onto the dryer next to me and points to his empty basket. "I have a tub of detergent pods. We'll each take a turn trying to get one into the basket. Whoever makes the shot gets to pose truth or dare to the other person. Then they have to answer the question, or perform the dare. It'll be a fun way for us to pass time while we wait."

"You're joking, right?"

"Scared?"

"No. It's just . . ." I trail off, trying to come up with a reason not to play.

Looking over at him, I try not to seem unnerved, when in actuality I am so out of my comfort zone with him. He always makes me feel so unhinged and disjointed.

Lincoln hands me a pod and winks as I roll my eyes at his childish excitement.

"I promise not to ask to see your panties," he announces. "Unless you want me to."

"If you want to see my panties, Lincoln, all you have to do is look up. They're tumbling in the washing machine in front of you." I smirk when he swallows and tries not to look.

"Ladies first," he says, distracted, pushing his sleeves up.

My eyes roam over his tattoos before I throw the

44

pod. In one shot, I get it in. That's when I realize the basket is way too close for either one of us to actually miss. Interesting.

He rubs his hands together. "I'll take truth."

My eyes slide to his. "Truth, huh? Scared?"

He scowls at the wall of washers, avoiding my eyes. "I think I actually am."

"Don't be," I say, softening my voice as he meets my gaze again.

For a moment, I actually forget what we're doing. We just stare at each other in silence, like we are waiting for something or trying to figure something out. It's weird.

Lincoln looks at me with unguarded eyes. "So, what do you want to know?"

"Where are you from?" I start with the easy stuff.

"Trenton. It's a shitty little town about an hour from here."

"What's so shitty about it?"

He waves the pod at me. "My turn."

I watch as his pod slips into the basket and his expression fills with excitement.

"Truth," I grumble.

He laughs. "What do you want to be when you grow up?"

I frown. "I told you. I'm undecided."

"I don't buy it."

"No?" I ask in disbelief. "Why not?"

"Everyone wants more. To be something, someone, or somewhere different."

I cross my arms over my chest, my expression twisting and becoming tight with tension. "Maybe I'm already who, or where, I'm supposed to be," I reply dryly.

"You aren't." His gaze runs over me and he pushes a hand through his hair.

Watching him, my heart squeezes. No one has ever asked me what *I* want. Not ever.

My family has a plan for my future—*their* plan. I've never been given a choice.

"It's silly, but sometimes I daydream of moving to California," I admit. "Basking in the warmth of the sunshine. Meeting new people. Making it on my own . . ." I trail off.

"That isn't silly," he says, focused on our conversation.

"No?"

"Not at all. I can see you relaxing under a blue sky with the sun kissing your skin."

I like the picture Lincoln paints. And I like him.

I throw another pod into the basket. "Truth or dare?"

"Truth."

"What's your family like?"

"My dad is dead. My mom is remarried to an

asshole. I have a lot of cousins. I also have a half sister, but we aren't close. I don't spend a lot of time with my family, or at home."

Suddenly, I feel like a jerk for asking about his family. "That must suck."

"Don't do that."

"Do what?"

He points to my sympathetic frown. "Everyone does that. Don't be like everyone else, Em. I accept my life. It doesn't matter where I come from, or what shitty hand I've been dealt. Life is about getting back up, no matter how many times you're kicked around."

I clear my throat. "Have you been kicked around a lot?"

He works his jaw for the longest time. "Every damn day of my life."

My gaze floats over him and I can see the darkness seeping through the cracks.

And it's that darkness that draws me to him, because in a way, it's just like mine.

Two pods land in the basket, shifting my attention, and I narrow my eyes at him.

"You just asked me for two truths," he explains. "I get two now."

I take in a deep breath. "Dare." I switch it up on him.

He flashes me a wicked smile and his eyes go all

naughty, and I know I'm screwed. I immediately regret my decision when he leans into my personal space, caging me in.

"I dare you to let me in. To show me the parts of yourself that you hide from everyone else. The ones behind this . . . façade of control and perfection you work so hard to maintain."

I study him for a moment. "You think I'm hiding something?"

"I think you're hiding a lot."

Lincoln moves closer, the heat from his strong, solid body seeping into me as he leans into my side. I exhale, hating myself for *wanting* to show him those parts of me.

"And if I am?" I whisper.

Gradually he lifts a hand, tucking my hair behind my ear before holding his hand still with his thumb on my cheek. My breathing ceases at his touch. Ever so slowly, his thumb runs across my skin. I know I should stop him, but every part of me savors the intimate way he's touching me and the glimmer of desire in his eyes.

"Those secrets you hide, you do it because you don't want the world to see them. You don't think they'll accept them. I get it. More than you know. But here's the thing—under all your layers of perfection, I see the real you," he whispers. "Just like you see me."

Something ignites within me, knowing he sees through my armor. It's unsettling, but even more, it's exhilarating. Being near Lincoln is an addictive feeling, and I want more.

Taking a breath, I lean closer, only to stop the moment the washing machine beeps. Its high-pitched sound pulls me out of my lust-filled fog. I turn away from him, slide off the dryer, and walk to the machine. Leaning down, I open the door, putting my wet clothes into my own basket. When I'm finished, I turn around to see he's been watching me the entire time. Ignoring him, I head over to the dryer I was sitting on, open the lid, and start shoving my clothes into it, trying to remind myself I can't like him, and I certainly can't kiss him.

I can't get addicted to him. He isn't mine to get addicted to.

Without a word, Lincoln's hand snaps out and his long fingers curl around my wrist. The heat of his touch forces me to look at him. When I meet his soft expression, I shiver.

This heightened awareness of him is driving me insane.

"I can't do this," I whisper.

"Can't do what, Em?"

"Whatever this is we're doing."

"We're playing a game. Getting to know one another."

"No. We aren't." I slam the cover down and turn on the dryer with an angry snap. "Getting to know one another is learning about each other's favorite foods and colors." I step away from him, my skin feeling itchy. It's too tight, because he sees through it.

Right into my soul.

I love it.

And I hate it.

His brows lift. "You want to have a superficial friendship with me?"

"Yes," I reply quickly. "No. I don't know," I exhale, tripping over my words.

Lincoln frowns at my response as his eyes dip and focus on my trembling hands.

"Green," he pushes out, in a deceptively calm voice.

"What?"

"Green is my favorite color." His voice is matter-of-fact. "I love Italian food. Not so much the pasta, but I'm a fan of the chicken dishes, like piccata. I'm not big on sweets. I love ice cream, though. I got my first tattoo when I was fourteen. It was something to hide a scar my shithead of a father gave me during a beating before he died. I like to sleep in and stay up late. I love beer but hate tequila. I'm a sports medicine major because I can't imagine not being around a baseball field. I'm not good enough to play professionally, so my major will still keep me tied to it. I'd love to coach someday, maybe little league. I don't really want to be married. Or have kids. I love to laugh, so comedies are my favorite movies, and I try to read but don't do as much as I should. As for music, Pearl Jam is my favorite band." He pauses. "And I like hanging out with you, Em."

"Why?" I whisper.

"Why what?"

"Why do you like hanging out with me?"

Lincoln runs his hands over his face before pinning me with a look. "Because you calm my storms. I don't have a lot of people around me I can depend on." His voice drops. "I like depending on you. Maybe more than I should. Because you should know that eventually, I'll fuck up and ruin this. Whatever it is."

The depth of sadness in his voice is suffocating, and my throat tightens. When our eyes meet, the storm that is usually in his is gone, leaving them eerily vacant, as if he's no longer behind them. Suddenly, I want to be everything to him. Heal him. Hold him.

With a small step, I stand between his knees, reach out and touch his forehead, gently caressing his brows as I whisper to him, "Yellow is my favorite color. I like Mexican food because I love heat and spice." I hate that my voice is small. "I would love to get a tattoo, but I have no idea of what. My parents are country club assholes. I've been told what to do, and who to be friends with, my entire life. I'm only expected to succeed, not fail. That means you can't ruin this, Lincoln, because I won't let this fail. I have you. I promise."

When he closes his eyes, his long lashes touch his cheeks. Taking a breath, I lean closer to him. Using both my hands, I run my fingers over his forehead and temples, down his cheeks and over his jawline. I'm surprised at how soft his stubble is under my fingertips. His expression relaxes under my touch. Slowly his hands come up and with the lightest of touches, his fingers wrap around my waist, pulling me closer to him.

"I don't know what I did to deserve your placement in my path, but I am so fucking grateful, Em. You're exactly what I need. You're becoming . . . important," he rambles.

I clench my jaw at the sound of his gritty voice.

It's sinful and sexy.

The beeping of his phone has his lids fluttering open. As if coming out of a fog, he shakes his head and sits up straighter, pulling his face out of my hands and leaning away.

When his fingers quickly disappear from my waist, I take a step back.

Without a word, he slides off the dryer, pulls out his phone and shoots off a few texts.

Then his preoccupied gaze meets mine. "I, ah . . . I-I have to go meet someone."

At this hour? Something in the way Lincoln said *someone* sets me on edge.

"Oh," I manage, confused at the sudden change in him. "Okay."

He's distant and acting like he can't escape the laundry room, or me, fast enough.

He looks around and pulls his bottom lip into his mouth. "You okay here, alone?"

I wrinkle my nose and nod. "Fine."

He drops his chin and begins to walk toward the doorway. "Don't worry about my stuff; I'll come back in the morning to finish it up."

"Sure," I reply, not knowing what else to say.

Lincoln's lips flatten as he makes his way toward the door. "See you soon, Em."

I stand here for I have no idea how long, watching his back as he disappears, wondering what in the hell just happened between us. Regardless of his strange exit, it's clear the novelty of our relationship—whatever it is— hasn't worn off yet. In fact, I think it's growing and morphing into a slow fiery burn. One that at some point, will spark a raging fire.

And that terrifies me.

A fire that burns this hot is bound to leave lasting scars.

CHAPTER 7

There are days, like today, when nothing is clear. Things become fuzzy and dark around the edges. No one knows, because I've gotten good at concealing it. I hide my daily struggle for control. I hide the constant pressure inside my chest.

I hide the shaking and darker thoughts that sometimes run through my head.

Some days, my inner turmoil takes over. Normally, I can fight it, but not today.

Today, everything feels so much bigger than it really is. So much harder.

More closed in and suffocating.

Outside, the snow falls in a steady stream. The storm is the reason classes have been cancelled. Being stuck inside all day has me feeling trapped and on edge, causing my anxiety levels to spike. I try to remain calm and not have a full-blown panic attack.

My breath catches when a hard bang on the door startles me. I make my way over to it and swing it open to find Lincoln on the other side. He's casually leaning against the frame. I look around the hallway nervously, because I can't deal with him today. I don't have the energy to push away the darkness when it's standing in front of me, wearing jeans and a gray Henley. At the sight of him, the panic grips me tighter.

The last time I saw him was in the laundry room. Scratch that. I saw him two days later, making out with some girl in the quad. He had his tongue down her throat in broad daylight for everyone to see. Including me. It was an epic sight to behold. Truly.

"Kennison left her wallet in my suite when she left with Josh. I thought I'd return it in case she might—" He stops, the expression on his face falling as he studies me. Lincoln narrows his eyes, taking me in and standing straighter, pushing off the frame. "What's wrong, Em? You're white as a ghost. Are you okay?" he asks, pushing me back and stepping into the room, taking up the last bit of air that was left in here.

I stumble a few steps back as he closes the door. All of a sudden, his form becomes blurry and I struggle to breathe. The blood rushes to my head and the heavy thudding of my heartbeat echoes in my ears. I feel hot and cold at the same time.

"Em," Lincoln says, calmly throwing Kenz's wallet on her desk before grabbing my upper arms and dipping his chin so he can look into my eyes. "Hey, you need to breathe."

I try to nod and pull air into my lungs, but his voice sounds far away, like he's talking to me from inside of a tunnel. Sounds rush around in my head, swirling and mixing in with the dark spots, threatening to take over as everything inside me shuts down.

Vaguely, I realize I'm suddenly on the floor, on my knees, and Lincoln is in the same position across from me. It takes every ounce of strength I have left to throw myself against him and curl my fingers into his shirt. The pulse at the base of his neck jumps against my temple as I cling to his familiar scent. Strong arms wrap around me, holding me to a hard chest. I claw at him, trying to crawl inside of him to survive my attack.

"Don't let go," I slur almost incoherently.

"Never." Lincoln's shaky hands run up and down my back as he whispers in my ear, "It's okay. I've got you. Just listen to my voice. Can you do that, Emerson?"

He's said my full name before, but this time, it's said in a raspy voice filled with worry that wraps around the panic and somehow makes it stop torturing me. I try to pull my thoughts back into order as he holds me, bringing me back from the brink of a breakdown.

I latch on to him like a lifeline as he soothes me, calming me down as I fight my way back from the confusion and disorder that was churning in my head. I focus on the way he smells, the broadness of his shoulders, the feel of his fingers as they run along my back.

"Did you know that banging your head against a wall for one hour burns 150 calories?" he asks. "It's true. There is the potential for brain damage, but at least you'll have burned off your morning donut. Also, pteronophobia is the fear of being tickled by feathers. And in Switzerland it is illegal to own just one guinea pig," he rattles off. "I read a lot when the team travels. That leads to knowing a shit ton of useless information. Like, bees sometimes sting other bees. And space, it smells like seared steak," he goes on.

"You're making all that up," I mumble into his shoulder.

"Am not," he whispers. "It's all true. Google it."

Lincoln just holds me until I come back to myself. I have no idea how long it takes before I can breathe again and focus on my own without him talking me down, but I do.

After a long time, I release my grip on him and sit back a little on my heels.

"I'm okay," I lie.

Lincoln's brows pull together as he lifts his hands to my cheeks, holding my face between his palms. With a gentle touch, he wipes away tears that I hadn't realized had fallen with the pads of his thumbs. Concern radiates off every line of his tense body.

"Are you sure?"

I blink a few times and take in an uneven breath. "It's just a panic attack."

"You're still shaking. And you're on the fucking floor crying, Em," he growls.

"I'll be okay," I whisper.

"Has this happened before?"

"Sometimes. I haven't had one in over a year."

Lincoln's mouth tightens as he pulls back and climbs to his feet. When he reaches out his hands for me, I take them and allow him to help me to my feet before he guides me over to my bed and helps me sit down. Once he sees I'm stable, he walks over to the windows, yanking them open, allowing fresh air to float into the room before he takes in a sharp breath and turns around, cutting me a look out of the corner of his eye.

"Who else knows about your anxiety?" he asks with a hoarse voice.

I don't want him to see me like this, raw and hurting on the inside, so I remain silent.

"Not even Kennison?" he catches on.

I shake my head no.

"What or who fucking triggered it?" His voice is lower and huskier than usual.

My lips part to speak, but I'm too embarrassed. Nothing comes out.

Lincoln bristles, giving me impatient side-eyes as he waits me out.

"Pressure. Anxiety," I admit in a quiet voice. "Feeling trapped."

"You're claustrophobic?"

"I can be, if my anxiety levels are higher than normal," I find my voice.

"Which they are right now?" he prods, trying to figure me out.

"Yes," I admit, ashamed of my weakness.

Lincoln walks over and squats down in front of me. With an intense expression, he looks up at me, his jaw working back and forth. "You scared the shit out of me, Em."

"I'm sorry." I stare at his shoulders, which are bunched with tension.

Feeling the distance seeping in between us, I go into protection mode and put my walls back up. Lincoln says nothing for the longest time as he studies me in silence.

"Now I understand the safety–control freak thing." He stands to his full height.

I look up at him and narrow my eyes. "I am not a con—"

"Don't even try to deny it."

I clear my throat. "Why are you here again?"

"I dropped off Kennison's wallet," he reminds me.

Right. "She's outside building snowmen and women. With Josh."

A sly expression crosses his face. "Guess that means you're free to hang out with me."

"I don't need a babysitter," I groan, standing. "I'm okay now."

"Maybe I need one. It's snowing out and boring as hell. Let's watch movies and eat leftover Chinese food." He shuts the windows before we freeze to death.

"I don't have Chinese food." I cross my arms over my chest protectively.

"I do. I'll go grab it and be back. Pick a movie. And do NOT pick a chick flick."

"Lincoln," I say to his retreating form as he opens the door.

He turns and faces me. When he reaches up to grip the top of the doorframe, it's all I can do not to start weeping hysterically at his soft, concerned expression.

"Thank you," I whisper.

"For what, Em?"

"For telling me that space smells like seared steak."

He smiles. "I'll always have you, Em." He disappears, only to return a few minutes later with three bags of food, drinks, and a bunch of random crap, like a blanket and pillow.

"Moving in?" I ask as he closes the door.

"Is that an invitation?"

"What's with all the bags?"

"I need to be comfortable if we're watching movies all night," he says, throwing his pillow and blanket onto my bed before sliding onto it, settling in on top of the covers.

"Um." I stand in the middle of the room, arms crossed. "All night?"

"Breathe, Em. You're turning blue. Kennison is staying with Josh tonight."

"Oh," I sigh. "Can you at least move over to her bed?"

"I'm not sitting on her bed."

"Why not?"

"I don't know her well enough to sniff her sheets."

"She's practically living with Josh in your suite. Wait, sniff her sheets?"

"That doesn't mean I want to smell like her."

"Fine. I'll sit on her bed."

"No."

"Why?"

"I don't want you smelling like her either. I like you smelling like . . . you."

"You're weird."

"Come over here and sit down with me. It's cold in here."

An eyebrow arches at the suggestion and I remain glued to the floor.

"We're just watching movies. I'll stay on my side."

Making an exasperated sound, I walk over to my bed and slide onto the top, putting a throw blanket over my legs, keeping a sliver of space between us as I get comfortable.

Lincoln turns the movie on as he munches on an eggroll. On my bed. Ew.

"This is awkward," I pout, and chance a look at him.

The side of his mouth curls up the tiniest bit. "It's only awkward because you're making awkward. No talking during the movie. Eggroll?" He passes me the container.

I lean over to snag one as his scent hits me. "Why do you always smell like cigarettes?"

Little lines appear between his brows. "Why are you sniffing me?"

I groan. "I'm not. You just have a certain . . . *smell* to you."

"Are you saying I stink?"

"No. It's just, I've never seen you smoke, but there is always this strange smoky smell lingering beneath the scent of your soap and remnants of your cologne," I point out.

He licks his lips, eyes cagey. "Occasionally, I need a cigarette to take the edge off."

"The edge of what?"

"Life," he says, his voice terse.

"Smoking is bad for you."

"I'm an adult, Em. I can smoke if I want to."

"Okay, fine. We were talking smells, I was just asking." I shift my focus to the movie.

I must have fallen asleep halfway through, because when my eyes open, it's dark outside and dimly lit in here. The white Christmas lights that Kennison hung around the top of the room are on, and the television is casting shadows across Lincoln and me.

Stretching, I roll over onto my left side. When I snuggle my face into my pillow, I notice Lincoln sleeping on his right side, facing me. He looks so relaxed and peaceful. For a moment, I creepily watch him sleep, and as I do, my feelings begin to sink in.

My attraction to him isn't fading. In fact, my feelings are getting stronger. I was an idiot to think they would go away while I was living in the same building as him, running in the same circle of friends, breathing in the same air. At some point, I need to stop lying to myself, because I don't think my attraction to him is going to fade away anytime soon.

"I think I have feelings for you," I admit so quietly, even I can barely hear myself.

Without thinking, I lift my hand and run my fingertips over his face, down his cheek and across his jawline, before I let my thumb run over his lips. They're warm and soft.

I close my eyes and stupidly imagine how they would feel pressed against mine in a searing kiss. When I open them again, his stormy gaze is on me, staring at me with an intense burn that twists and knots my insides and makes me want to curl up to his side.

"You have *feelings* for me?" The way he draws out the word causes me to freeze.

I take in a deep breath, studying his fierce features. He licks his lips, holding my gaze the entire time, and my stomach drops into a freefall. I just lie here, petrified that I've ruined whatever this is we're doing, because being this close to him is pure heaven.

Lincoln's breath hitches, but he moves closer, pleading with his eyes.

"Say it again," he demands hoarsely.

"I-I have feelings for you," I whisper.

We stare at each other, each of us waging an internal war that I am certain neither of us will ever win. When he leans in again, his lips brush mine with the lightest of touches, and my entire body ignites with need. I whimper into his mouth and clutch the soft fabric of his shirt. He leaned back, looking into my eyes again, silently asking my permission. I responded to his unspoken question with a small nod. He grabs the back of my head and pulls my mouth harder against his as his lips devour mine. There is nothing gentle in this kiss. It's raw and demanding.

His tongue invades my mouth while he slowly slides the hand that isn't holding the back of my head up my side, edging it higher until his palm is covering my throat, pushing me back gently. I roll onto my back and he shifts on top of me. Trembles wrack my body as a dizzying mixture of fear and desire runs through me. I curl my fingers into his shirt harder, twisting the fabric, pulling him closer, afraid he'll let go as our lips dance across each other's in an intoxicating and all-consuming way. He pulls away, just far enough to stare down into my eyes, but close enough that I can still feel every one of his breaths on my lips. When he looks at me, I become paralyzed by the flashes of desire and lust swirling behind his eyes. Warmth floods me and an ache settles between my thighs as he closes his eyes, lowers his head and slowly drags his lips across my cheek, before he drags them back over my cheek and brushes them lightly over mine again, but he doesn't kiss me.

His voice is husky when he speaks across my mouth. "Do you want me to stop?"

My heart sinks with sadness at the idea of him stopping. "No."

Exhaling with a deep rumble, he fills my mouth with his tongue and I fall into a euphoric haze as he kisses me harder and deeper. I surrender to his touch and lose the ability to think—all thoughts escape me. As his mouth devours mine, the sighs and whimpers drifting out of my lips beg and plead for more with every stroke.

I drown in him, breathing him in.

His leg slides between mine, pushing them apart, and his jeans brush against my core, causing me to squirm under him. Lincoln removes his hand from the back of my head and runs it down the side of my body. I arch under his touch, needing more. After a few minutes, I release his shirt and move my hands to the top of my sweatpants, lifting my hips and pushing them down as far as I can until I need my legs to do the rest of the work.

Lucas was my first. And yet, none of his touches or kisses felt anything like this.

Lincoln is all-consuming.

With one touch he renders me boneless, dominating me.

Even though I should, I don't push him away. I don't say no. I just want to burn in his flame. I move my hands back to his chest, but he quickly snatches them and pins them above our heads, interlacing his fingers with mine. I squeeze his hands hard when his leg moves and brushes against my clit. Everything he does feels insanely amazing.

He moves one hand, locking it with both of mine as his other hand moves to my leg, squeezing my inner thigh hard enough to make me whimper into his kiss. I slip further into ecstasy when his finger languidly glides back and forth over the damp spot on the front of my panties, coaxing and teasing, luring me into a mindlessly numb blissful state.

When he pulls away again, I stare into Lincoln's stormy eyes, wondering what the hell I've gotten myself into with him. He presses his thumb against the thin material over my clit and traces a lazy circle as he watches me, his lips hovering over mine.

It's unrushed, rendering me powerless as he savors every one of my whimpers.

I shake under him as he watches me like he's memorizing my responses to his touch.

I resist rocking into him for more as his breathing becomes ragged.

"Do you want me to make you feel good?" His husky whisper pulls me in.

"Yes," I hiss.

"You're going to have to let go of that control you love. Can you do that, Em?"

Unable to speak, I nod, and he licks his lips, staring deep into my eyes.

Nobody has ever looked at me like he does, like he's claiming me.

And I know in my heart that no one ever will.

The muscles in his jaw jump as he slowly slides down my chest and stomach, finally stopping between my legs. His hot eyes are on me the entire time, never wavering.

I push up on my elbows, watching as his thumbs hook into the sides of my panties and pull them off with an aching slowness that almost has me falling apart. When the black fabric clears my ankles, he throws them on the floor next to us before placing his tongue on my right leg, licking, tasting my skin. Humming the entire time he edges back up.

When he reaches my core again, he looks up with a hunger I've never seen in another person. It's crazy unnerving. All I can hear is my own heavy breathing as I watch him.

"Lie back," he orders.

"What are you doing?" I pant, my nerves buzzing.

"I want to taste you," he growls against my leg.

Oh god. "Wait," I plead.

He stills, looking at me, waiting for my permission.

"I-I've never. No one has ever . . ." I trail off.

Lincoln's brows pull together. "You've never. . ." He prompts me to explain.

"I mean, I have. Just not . . ." I motion to his mouth.

"Oral?" he finishes.

"Lucas doesn't like it." I swallow my words when I see how pissed off he looks.

"Because it's not about him," he snarls. "He's a fucking tool. Lie the fuck back, Em."

"Wait. We're really doing this?" My stomach dips.

Instead of responding, he slides his hands over my thighs as his head disappears. I've never seen a more beautiful sight in all my life than Lincoln Daniels between my legs.

"Oh, my god," I pant.

Lincoln's warm breath hits the oversensitive flesh before he drags his tongue up the length of my lips, sending sparks of pleasure up my spine. "Holy shit," I growl.

In response, he hums against me and I drop my head back at the sensation. Blood rushes through my veins as soon as his mouth covers me. His fingers sink into the flesh of my thighs as his tongue laps at me, causing me to release a guttural moan.

The sensations he's creating cause me to lose all

sense of decency. My hips jerk, demanding more. It's too much and not enough. He laces his fingers over my hips, pushing them down, holding me in place so I can't slip away from his fierce assault.

I want it over, and yet, at the same time, I never want it to end. He works me with his mouth, his tongue diving deep, tasting me with a hungry appreciation. I curl my fingers around his wrists and squeeze hard, writhing under his skilled movements as primal sounds fill the room. If I weren't under the influence of his tongue, I would be mortified.

When Lincoln trails the tip of his tongue up to my clit and teases me, I cry out so loud, I barely recognize my own voice. The muscles in my thighs tighten as he gives my clit long, circular licks full of pressure, followed by sweet, soft kisses. My head spins.

I feel high on a rush of emotions. As he drives me to intense wetness, my legs shake and I ache with the need to come. With his tongue, Lincoln focuses on my clit as two fingers enter me, then he sucks hard, finishing me off, sending me straight over the edge.

Everything blurs and I grip his wrists tighter as I scream out his name. I come harder than I ever have. Shivers race across my skin as tiny aftershocks run through me with each of his gentle touches as he helps guide me back down. It takes me a while to return back to reality and catch my breath.

When Lincoln's face appears above mine, there is a hint of cockiness in his smile that makes me almost want to smack it right off him. Instead, I start giggling and cover my face with my hands, partly in mortification at my response to his oral talents, because holy shit.

"Hey, don't hide from me," he rumbles, grabbing my wrists and moving my hands so he can look me in the eyes. "Seeing you like that was fucking amazing, Em," he rasps.

"Really?" I ask shyly, my heart pounding so hard in my chest, I think I might die.

He laughs, a deep reverberation that slides its way down my spine. "Really."

I'm still trembling under him as I catch my breath. "That was insane."

His eyes remain locked on mine as he drags his knuckles across the blush on my cheek.

"You okay?" he asks.

I nod as I try to put together a coherent thought, but Lincoln just looks at me like I'm a brand new game he's discovered. One that he likes playing. A lot. His eyes are dark and dangerous. My fingers run over his shoulders and down his arms.

Right before they reach the button on his jeans, he shakes his head twice. "No." One of his hands covers mine, stopping me. "Not tonight. That wasn't what this was about."

Rejection hits me hard, and my cheeks heat with embarrassment as I look away.

"Look at me," he commands, and my gaze slides back to his. "It's not that I don't want to rip off your clothes and ravish your body in other ways. Because trust me, I want to."

"You do?" I whisper.

"More than anything," he growls. "Tonight, I want this to be just about you."

"Why?"

His voice is low and direct as he looks at me with sincerity. "Anyone who refuses to take care of you, and make you feel the way I just did, with their mouth and tongue, doesn't deserve you. Do you understand?" He stares down at me.

Goose bumps crawl over my flesh at the fierceness behind his words. My skin feels hot and feverish. I suck in a breath as my mind tries to catch up with my erratic pulse.

"I understand."

"Good."

I touch each side of his face with my hands as I caress his jaw with my thumb.

Lincoln closes his eyes and leans down, kissing the corner of my mouth.

"Let's get some rest," he says quietly, settling back down on the bed.

After covering us with blankets, he pulls me against him, tensing his arms around me.

I nestle my face into his neck and shut my eyes, trying to savor the feeling of being in his arms like this, knowing someday all I'll want is to live forever in this moment again.

CHAPTER 8

My fingers brush over the two words written in black pen on the tiny piece of paper. I found it resting on the empty spot where Lincoln had been sleeping the night before. When I woke up the next morning, he was gone. In his place was this small note that reads, *what if.*

Kennison taps her pen on my book, gaining my attention. "Midterms."

I fold up the piece of paper and attempt to focus on studying. "I never thought I'd say this, but honestly, I'm glad to be going home for winter break," I mutter under my breath.

"Me too," she sighs. "It's been a long December. This semester was hard."

"In more ways than one," I add, and chance a look at her.

She throws me a sympathetic look. "You still haven't heard from Lincoln?"

I shake my head. It's been weeks.

"If it makes you feel better, I haven't seen him either. Then again, since breaking up, Josh and I aren't exactly on speaking terms." She frowns and lowers her lashes. "It hurt seeing him kissing some random girl. I mean, he was *kissing* her, Em. Full-on, tongue-down-throat lip sucking. In public. Near food," she quietly shrieks.

A few days ago, Kennison decided she didn't really want a full-time boyfriend in college. Josh was hurt, but he understood. Then she saw him sucking faces with another girl in the dining hall, which is out of character for him. Of course, Kennison had a bad reaction to their PDA and has the visual committed to memory. Now she wants him back.

"I know it sucks, but I have a feeling things aren't over between you two."

"Well, even if it's not, he won't find me waiting, pining away for him. Asshat." She sits back in her chair. "I don't want to talk about it anymore. Let's talk about the moody, broody, smoking hottie that gets under your skin and makes you do naughty things."

I make a face at her description. "I don't want to talk about Lincoln."

"What's going on between the two of you, anyway?" she asks, ignoring my protest.

I lift a shoulder and let it fall in a half-hearted shrug. "Nothing."

"I wouldn't call what happened between you two *nothing*."

"One minute, I'm his sole focus. The next, I don't exist."

She tilts her head to the side as she looks at me. "Why do you let him do that?"

My grip on my pen tightens as I consider her words. I like him. It's that simple.

"He needs someone to depend on," I mumble.

"That someone doesn't have to be you."

"Maybe I'm the only option he has."

"I just don't want to see you get all wrapped up in this guy."

"Trust me. I have no intention of getting wrapped up in Lincoln Daniels."

———

The door swings open and Lincoln stares at me for a moment, surprised. He blinks at me with wide eyes, as if he can't tell if I'm really standing in front of him or not. I don't say anything, because I'm too busy staring at his bare chest, which has little drops of water on it. In some places, they're crawling over his tanned skin before rolling across the muscles on his stomach and landing on the knotted towel wrapped around his waist.

"Em?"

"Hey," I croak, and lift my gaze back to his.

"Hey."

"Is this . . . a bad time?"

He stares at me before it occurs to him that he's half naked. "Sorry. I just showered."

I nod, suddenly feeling like I'm intruding. "I can just . . ." I motion over my shoulder with my thumb. "I can come back. Or leave." Yes. Let me slip away in my humiliation.

What the hell was I thinking coming here tonight?

Lincoln shakes his head and steps back from the door, gesturing for me to enter.

I take a few steps into his room before facing him. "Tyler let me into the suite."

When he closes the door, I realize that I haven't been in here since the night we first met. It looks the same, except for the two duffel bags that it looks like he's in the process of packing for winter break, which starts tomorrow. Guess he's a procrastinator. Like me.

"Packing?" I ask lamely, motioning to the bags.

"I am. You packed yet?"

"I am." I shift, uncomfortable.

"All done with finals?" he asks, rubbing the back of his neck.

"I am. You done?"

"I am."

Lincoln forces a smile, and I can see he's working hard to keep the conversation light.

A long pause stretches between us before I exhale slowly. "This was a bad idea."

I take a step toward the door, but he jumps in front of me, blocking my exit.

"Don't go," he says, with a desperation that causes a lump to form in my throat.

"I don't want things to be weird between us," I mumble.

"They aren't."

"They are."

"Em."

Slowly, I lift the folded piece of paper between us. "What does this mean?"

Lincoln focuses on it, like he's expecting it to explode or something.

"For the past few weeks, I've been staring at it," I admit. "Obsessing. Like a crazy person. I've replayed every moment of that night in my head in some lame attempt to make sense of it and what it means. We . . . and then you disappeared on me. Again."

My body shivers at the memory of how his touch made me feel.

"I didn't mean to disappear. School and baseball kept me away, and busy."

"I've been busy too, Lincoln. Obsessing over what these words mean."

"They mean . . ." He exhales, holding my eyes.

"What?" I ask, irritated.

"You've become a need I can't explain."

My lips part and I blink at him, taking in his words. The second we met and shared the same air, I changed. I felt it deep within my soul. I guess he did too. It takes every ounce of willpower I have, but I refuse to let him off the hook with an easy explanation.

"I need you to use more words," I whisper.

"I'm stuck in this place where I can't remember my life before you. It's only been a few months, and yet, you're everywhere. In every thought. Every breath. I wrote that after watching you sleep all night. I kept thinking, what if?"

"What if what?"

He runs his hands over his face. "What if you weren't with Lucas? What if I wasn't so fucking broken —such a fuckup? What if . . . what if we belong together?"

He looks away from me and searches the room until his eyes lock with mine again.

"What if you were meant to be mine?" he finishes in a quiet tone.

Rendered speechless, I can't take my eyes off him or turn away. Nobody has ever said anything so incredibly beautiful, and yet, at the same time, heartbreaking to me. Ever.

"Is that the only reason you're here tonight? The note?"

The small amount of space between us disappears with one tiny step I take.

"I-I also wanted to see you again. Before we leave for break."

"Why?" His jaw tenses.

"I don't know," I admit quietly.

"I'm not buying it."

I lean back and look into his eyes. "Because you make me feel—"

He leans closer. "Tell me," he orders.

"You've changed something inside of me. And I-I want—"

"What do you want, Em?"

"You," I manage to say. "I want you." My voice is small and unsure, hesitant.

My heart pounds in my chest as he looks at me with surprise, before his eyes soften. I swallow and hold my breath. Lincoln leans down, pressing his lips against mine in a delicate, slow kiss. I part my lips, letting his tongue find its way to my mouth. When it does, I sigh, finally able to breathe. After a few moments, he tries to pull away.

I don't let him.

Determined, I kiss him impatiently.

Trying to show him with my lips what I can't say with words.

"We shouldn't be doing this," he growls against my mouth.

"I need you to touch me," I plead, as my lips dance with his.

At my words, any reservations he has vanish. His mouth takes mine, harder and more eager. With one smooth move, he lifts me and I wrap my legs around his waist. My fingers run down the length of his back and edge up again, settling behind his neck in a forceful grip that I'm sure will leave bruises. Lincoln clutches me tightly against him.

His lips part and his tongue brushes mine. I release a pleasured sigh at his familiar taste. I lose myself in the feeling of my lips moving against his as he walks us backwards.

Lincoln's breath quickens along with mine. He groans as he pulls me against him tighter. His hands slip under my shirt, clutching my lower back as he caresses my skin.

Something about the feel of my body pressed against his and the intensity of our kiss ignites a powerful need.

One that lingers under my skin as I drown in his taste and touch.

I tighten my grip on his neck as his fingertips caress me. His hands edge higher until he's pulled my shirt up completely. He breaks our kiss for a second so he can yank it over my head and toss it onto the floor, then reclaims my mouth in a deep, searing move.

My thighs tighten around him when his hands travel down my back again and slide into the gap in the back of my jeans, gripping my ass hard. I moan into his mouth, which urges him on. He spins us around, bends over, and gently lays me down on the bed.

Our lips slow and then still as he pulls back, staring down into my eyes, and I almost stop breathing completely when I see the intensity swirling in his gaze. All I can do is stare into his deep stormy eyes as he pants and his breath tickles my swollen lips.

"Are you sure?" he speaks softly.

"I've never been more sure of anything," I whisper.

We stay in this position for a moment, taking each other in, my arms tight around his neck. One of his hands rests on my waist, the other leaning on the bed by my head. In the quiet, our heavy breathing seems to intensify the raw need in each of us.

"You're so fucking beautiful, Em," he says hoarsely, as if in pain. "I just want to remember you like this." His eyes rake over me. "With your hair splayed across my sheets and your scent screwing with my head. Nothing will ever be better than this moment."

At his words, I release my grip on his neck and slide my hands down to his sculpted chest. I'm awed at the perfect contradiction his body is—hard muscles and soft skin.

With each of my touches, Lincoln's chest rises and falls, his breathing heavy. I trace every defined crease of his abdomen. He lets out a deep groan and sucks in a quick breath when I run my fingers along the V at the bottom, lingering and teasing him.

My body instantly responds, and I sigh when he brings his mouth to my neck, his lips trailing down my skin. He slides one hand under my back and undoes the clasp of my bra. My head drops back, giving him more access to my neck as I arch my back so he can release the strap. Nipping and sucking behind my ear, he lets his fingertips slide over my shoulder, pushing down the strap, then repeating the motion on the other side.

I close my eyes, reveling in his touch. My hands slip into his hair, tugging gently as he removes the pink material, pushing it away. With a deep exhale, he runs his hand over my stomach, up to my breast, cupping it and teasing the nipple.

I arch against his warm palm, because it feels so good.

Sensing my need, Lincoln glides both his hands

down my sides, heating my skin before he undoes the button on my jeans. Gripping both sides, he slides them off, along with my panties, pulling them down my legs. Once they're gone, his palms find my knees again and I let out a long faltering breath when his hands slide up the insides of my thighs.

His face appears above mine again, and his lips take mine in an unrushed kiss that seems to go on forever. My knees twitch when his fingers wander between my legs. I shake with each skilled movement. My hips arch into his touch. He's being gentle, but there is an edge to the way he touches me, and the way he bites and nips, tasting my skin.

I dig my nails into the flesh on his back as his fingers begin to caress and tease me in the most painfully beautiful way. Everything inside of me is overheated and shaking.

He kisses me hungrily as he lowers himself down so our chests are pressed together. The feel of the weight of his body on mine causes my nipples to pull tighter and my legs to shift restlessly against his hand. His fingers move with purpose. Each touch makes me feel breathless and overwhelmed. The muscles on his back flex under my fingertips, and I feel the heat rising as his thumb draws circles over the most sensitive part of me.

The impressive bulge under his towel presses into my stomach as he releases my mouth. The tip of his nose skates down my neck and across my clavicle, before I feel the rush of his lips dancing across the crest of my breast. Suddenly, everything feels too much.

I gasp and quiver as his fingers bring me to a quick and hard orgasm. I squeeze my eyes shut. As I tremble, he moves up and over me, placing his knee on the edge of the bed next to my hip and helping me move higher onto the bed. I melt at the way he looks at me and I sink into the way he makes me feel—like I'm special and important.

Eagerly my hands find their way to the knot at the top of his towel and quickly I undo it, pushing it to the side before admiring the sight of him. Breathing hard, he sits back and reaches for the top drawer of his night-stand. He pulls it open, grabs some foil packages, and slams it shut before throwing a few onto the bed near my head. I grab one, ignoring the crackling sound it makes as I tear the package open with my teeth.

Lincoln places a hand next to my head as his face hovers over mine. The stormy shadows normally present in his eyes are gone; in their place are promises.

He stares down at me as I roll the condom over him. Nerves overtake me as I take in the length of him. He senses my worry and hesitation, a knowing grin tugging at the corners of his mouth. He leans down, placing the lightest of kisses on my lips, and speaks across them,

"You can take all of me, Em. I promise. I've got you." His voice is rough.

I peer up at him, his eyes intent and soft as I trail the fingers of one hand up the line of his spine and my other hand slides over his face, cupping his cheek. His hands are gentle as they skim over the surface of my over-heated skin. He wraps one fist around his shaft, and a second later I feel his body press slowly and steadily into mine.

My breath catches and his eyes drift closed as his forehead falls to mine. I ignore the slight ache of discomfort as I stretch to accommodate his size, instead focusing on the pleasure that suddenly erupts within me at the feel of him inside of me. My thighs tighten around his hips, and he kisses me again as he slowly moves in and out of me.

"I've wanted you for so long," he breathes against my mouth.

That bit of knowledge makes my body ache.

"Oh god . . . Lincoln . . ." I moan.

He buries his head in my neck, pausing to catch his breath. Impatiently, I raise my hips, and he growls, pushing into me harder. The sounds he's making low in his throat and deep in his chest cause goose bumps to form all over my skin. Scorching heat races through me. It is familiar, but new. With Lincoln, this is so much bigger than this moment. It's more intense than I've ever felt. He slides in harder and deeper, and I eagerly meet him with each thrust. With every sensation, my body is swept up in the feel of him.

Lincoln's mouth meets mine again, swallowing my cries as I lose control and clench around the length of him deep inside of me. He falls apart with a long, deep groan. When he collapses on top of me, breathing heavy, he lifts his head and looks into my eyes.

"I was wrong," he says.

"About what?" I pant, staring at him.

"I thought I was going to destroy you. It turns out, you're going to ruin me."

CHAPTER 9

I lie awake for hours, listening to the sound of Lincoln's soft breaths. He demanded I spend the night. I've tried to fall asleep, but can't. I keep replaying all the moments that happened between us last night over and over in my head while I stare at the ceiling.

My eyes slide to the clock on his nightstand and I groan at the time, thinking about how uncomfortable things will be when the morning light shines through his windows.

Six weeks is a long time not to see each other. My eyes close with the reminder of all the promises of a future that swirled around in his eyes last night as he looked at me.

An icy blast of reality hits me.

I have a boyfriend.

And I just slept with Lincoln.

My lids snap open in horror.

What I have done? How could I be so stupid and irresponsible? I never let myself lose control, but last night, I did just that. I need to end things with Lucas as soon as I get home. Regardless of whether he's been a shitty boyfriend or not, he doesn't deserve what I'm doing to him with Lincoln behind his back. And when, or if, he finds out, he'll hate me for it. I swallow the lump in my throat and my stomach clenches. I cheated on him.

I maneuver out from under Lincoln's arm and quietly get dressed, so as not to wake him. Grabbing my shoes, I see the note on the floor and pick it up. Staring down at his sleeping form once more, I exhale and place the note gently on the pillow next to him.

And like a child, I run away.

By the time I get back to my dorm room, my entire body is exhausted. I feel cold and empty. I close the door behind me and in the dark, slide down it, sobbing into my knees.

Lincoln's scent is lingering on me. It's on my clothes, in my hair, and seeping out of my skin. I suck in a deep, grounding breath and manage to stand and make my way to my closet to grab all my shower stuff and fresh clothes. I rush to the bath-room, turn on the hot water, and step into the shower stall, still trembling despite the scalding water.

The tears don't stop. They mingle with the dripping water as I scrub my body. But no matter how hard I try, I can't wash away the memories of how he tasted as he kissed me, or how he felt inside of me. And god help me, I don't want any of it to wash away.

Closing my eyes, I let the hot water run over me, staying in the shower until it turns cold, then wrap myself in a towel and get dressed so I can finish packing for break. As soon as I step back into my room, my cell buzzes again. It started going off an hour ago.

Every five minutes it buzzes and jumps off the nightstand.

"Em," Kennison groans from her bed. "Answer your damn phone!"

I reach over and silence it, then close my suitcase, putting it with my other bags.

"Why are you up so early?" she grumbles, sitting up and rubbing her eyes.

"My dad's driver will be here soon. I wanted to get an early start."

She pouts. "Why are you in such a hurry? I thought you were dreading going home?"

I shrug noncommittally. "We have to go, right? Might as well rip the Band-Aid off."

"What's really going on?" she asks quietly.

"Nothing."

"Bullshit. Tell me what's wrong!"

I close my eyes, forcing the tears that have pooled in them down my cheeks, before reopening them and meeting her panicked and worried expression.

"I slept with him," I whisper.

"Who? Lincoln?"

I swallow and nod.

She clenches her teeth. "Was it bad?"

"No."

"Was he rough? Did he hurt you?"

"No."

She sighs. "Is he like, super tiny?"

"Kennison!"

She rolls her eyes. "Jesus, Em. Why all the dramatics, at this hour?"

I blink a few times. "I don't know. I just . . . panicked."

Kennison tilts her head, considering me. "You're all wrapped up in him?"

Nodding, I drop onto her bed, and she wraps her arms around me.

"I warned you," she scolds.

"I know."

The display on my cell lights up again, and with a growl, she leans over and grabs my phone off our shared nightstand, thrusting it at me. "You have to call him. You have to at least tell him you're okay, Em. He probably woke up and freaked out that you were gone."

I take my phone from her and stare at all the missed calls from an unknown number.

She's right; Lincoln's probably freaking out.

My fingers hover over the screen, trying to figure out what I am possibly going to say to him to make myself seem less crazy, when a pounding on the door has both of us turning our attention to it. With a heavy groan, I stand and toss my phone onto my bed.

Another hard pound has me hesitating with my hand over the handle. I look over my shoulder at Kennison. She's motioning at me to open the door. With a slow exhale, I pull it open and instantly, I wish I hadn't. The sight in front of me has me speechless.

"Lucas?"

"What the fuck, Emerson? I've been calling you all fucking morning."

My lips part in shock as I stand in the doorway staring at him.

Without an invitation, Lucas huffs and storms around me into my room.

His movement causes me to turn around and watch him as he stands in the middle of the room and throws daggers at me with his eyes, apparently pissed off with my lack of speech and movement.

"What are you doing here?" I ask.

"Your father sent me to pick you up. Why the hell haven't you answered your phone?" he snaps. "What is it with you and not answering my fucking texts or calls?"

"My phone was on silent," I point out. "It's early."

"No shit," he bites out.

"Your number came up as unknown."

"I got a new number. If you ever bothered to call me back, you'd know that."

Kennison slips out of bed and steps between us. Trying to defuse the situation, she holds her hand out to Lucas. "Hi. I'm Kennison. Em's roommate. It's nice to meet you."

Lucas grunts at her and turns his attention to my suitcases. "Is this all your stuff?"

"Y-yeah, it is," I stutter, because he's being uncharacteristically rude.

"I'll take it down to the car and let you say your goodbyes. We have an hour drive, so don't be long," he snarls, and grabs my stuff, heading out the door without another word.

"He's charming." Kenz doesn't hide her sarcasm. "*This* is the guy you've been dating?"

"He was nicer this summer," I mumble, confused.

"Well now, he seems like a complete jerk," she counters.

"Em?" Lincoln's deep voice curls around me from the open doorway.

Kennison's eyes widen as she holds my gaze before I spin around.

"Lincoln."

Fury is etched all over his expression. It's mixed with hurt as he stares at me with a challenge in his eyes, leaning against the door frame with his arms crossed over his chest.

"You just leave and don't say goodbye?"

"I'm going to go brush my teeth," Kennison announces, grabbing her toiletry bag.

She quickly slips out of the room and as soon as she does, tension settles in around us.

"I—" I begin, but he cuts me off.

"You what? Regret what happened?" His voice is lined with hurt.

"No."

"Did I hurt you?"

"No, Lincoln. It's nothing like that."

With a relieved exhale, he steps into my room. When he's close enough, he takes my face between his palms, drops his chin, and looks me in the eyes. "Then what is it?"

My brows pull together. "It's just . . ."

"I thought you were coming?" Lucas barks from the doorway, and Lincoln freezes.

I try to step back so Lincoln's hands will fall away from my face, but he holds me still. A flash of surprise crosses his expression before he glances over his shoulder at Lucas, who is scowling at us both. I'm sure the fact that Lincoln is touching me is the reason.

"I see what it is," Lincoln says.

When Lincoln's focus returns back to me, his eyes lock with mine and he throws me a dangerous smirk. My mouth opens to speak, but suddenly, Lincoln's lips are on mine in a dizzying kiss. He groans loudly and pulls me to him as his hands leave my face and grab my ass, pushing me against him, as if he's claiming me, stealing me away from Lucas.

Annoyed, I push at his chest and take a few steps back. "What's wrong with you?"

"What the hell is going on here?" Lucas shouts, moving between us.

The amusement in Lincoln's face makes it all too obvious he's enjoying this. He turns his attention to Lucas and cocks his head to the side with a wicked gleam in his eyes.

"Who the fuck are you?" Lincoln asks calmly.

"Lucas. Emerson's boyfriend."

"*Emerson's* boyfriend?" The way he says my full name has a harsh bite to it.

"That's right, asshole."

"She never mentioned you," Lincoln goads him.

"Lincoln," I warn, and take a step toward him, but Lucas pushes me away.

I don't know if it's because Lucas pushed me, or because he put his hand on me, but Lincoln sees red, grabs him by the shirt, and tosses him to the side. Lucas falls onto my bed as Lincoln grabs my hand and yanks me behind him protectively.

"Don't ever fucking put your hands on her like that," he spits out, pointing at Lucas.

Lucas chuckles and stands, fixing his shirt. "She's my girlfriend. I'll put my hands on her all day if I want to. I don't know who the hell you are. Emerson, get over here."

"Stop it. Both of you," I yell, and try to step around Lincoln, but he doesn't let me.

"Em isn't going anywhere with you," Lincoln says to Lucas.

"Em?" Lucas mocks. "Tell your trashy friend good-bye. We need to leave."

Finally managing to slip out of Lincoln's vise grip, I jump in front of him as he advances on Lucas again. Pushing on his chest, I look up at him, pleading with my eyes.

"Stop," I whisper. "Lincoln, please."

His heated gaze falls to mine. "Tell me you're not going with him?"

I fall silent.

Lucas huffs and storms toward the door. "Five minutes, Emerson. Then I'm leaving."

We watch as he storms out of the room, slamming the door behind him.

"He's an asshole," Lincoln says darkly.

"Lucas may be an asshole, but he's my boyfriend. I owe him an explanation."

"You owe him nothing."

"I do. And you and I both know it."

Lincoln shakes his head. "I can't let you go with him. He put his hands on you."

"He isn't dangerous," I assure him. "He's upset. And he has a right to be."

"Is he why you left this morning?"

"No. I didn't know he was coming here."

"I don't like it." Lincoln shakes his head. "I don't like him."

"It's not for you to like. It's my mess and I need to clean it up. It's that simple."

"Trust me. Nothing about this is fucking simple, Em."

Lincoln's gaze focuses on something over my shoulder. The hard lines of his jaw pop as he clenches his teeth, trying to control his temper and annoyance at the situation.

"I have to go," I whisper. "He's waiting."

After a minute, he steps away from me. "Fine."

I step toward the door, but he grabs my elbow, stopping me.

Twisting, I look up into his hard gaze. "Let me go."

"Not so fast. If you leave with him, we can't go back to being . . . *us*."

The air rushes out of my lungs.

I try not to cry.

Pissed off or not, his ultimatum cuts deep.

"Then it's a good thing we were never an *us* to begin with." My voice is flat.

With an angry glare, he lets go of my arm and motions to the door. "We're done."

My eyes sting. With each step I take away from him, my heart feels heavier. Right before I'm about to step into the hallway, his cold tone hits me hard, causing me to falter.

"He's not the guy for you, Em."

"Turns out, neither are you, Lincoln."

CHAPTER 10

A heavy beat vibrates through the walls as I take the stairs two at a time. Once I'm on the second floor, I fling open the stairwell door and I'm met with loud music as I walk down the hall. Doors are cracked open, laughter and conversations spilling into the hallway. I have no idea what I am doing or why I am doing it, but it's been six weeks since I've last seen Lincoln. Over break, he didn't return any of my calls or texts.

The need to see him is overwhelming. We left things on such ugly terms that the second I got back to the dorm and unpacked, I was out the door and making my way to his suite—without taking a moment to think about what I was doing. Pushing through the throngs of students celebrating being back on campus, I push my way into his suite and find myself beelining toward his closed door, drawn to it like a magnet.

Before I reach it, though, Tyler steps in front of me, cutting off my path.

"Emerson!" he greets me, pulling me into a tight hug. "Welcome back."

"Hey, Tyler." I shift and try to focus on him. "How was your break?"

"Boring as fuck," he groans. "I'm glad to be back."

"Me too."

"Need a drink?" he asks, stepping back and winking at me.

"No, thanks." I look around. "I'm actually . . . um, I'm here to see Lincoln."

A frown turns Tyler's mouth before he looks over his shoulder at Lincoln's door.

He stares at it for a long moment before returning his attention back to me.

"I'm not sure you seeing Lincoln is such a good idea tonight," he says.

"Why not?"

"Daniels has been a little unhinged since before break."

My brows pull together. "What do you mean?"

He exhales hard. "Honestly, it's just not a good idea to get mixed up with him."

Music echoes in the hallway behind us as more laughter spills into the room.

After a moment, I smile at him while trying to sidestep him. "I appreciate you looking out for me, but I'm a big girl, Tyler. I think I can handle Lincoln and his bad mood."

"No." The word comes out clipped as he steps in front of me again.

"I just need to see him."

"I can't let you."

"Move," I order.

"Listen, I know you and Lucas ended things over break. I can't say that I blame you. He and I hung out over the holidays, and he's turned into a grade A asshole. And I know you and Lincoln started to get close before we left." He stops, choosing his words.

"No offense, but Lincoln and I are not your business," I point out.

"You're a nice girl."

"What does being *nice* have to do with anything?"

"I still feel responsible and protective of you."

"You don't have to. I can take care of myself."

"I know but—"

"But what?"

"I don't think it's a good idea for you to be mixing yourself up with Daniels."

"That's not your call."

"Lincoln," he lowers his voice, "comes with a reputation."

"A reputation?"

"He's known around campus. Everyone wants to be around him, or *with* him."

"So?"

"Have you ever asked yourself why that is?"

My brows knit together, because the truth is, when it comes to Lincoln, I have tunnel vision. Tyler is right. I don't know him. Not really. Not the way Tyler does, anyway. And for some reason, this bit of clarity makes me feel unsettled and apprehensive all at once.

Lincoln's door swings open and I freeze as he stumbles out with a leggy, gorgeous blonde girl, who is making a show of flirting with him. She's wearing jeans and a half shirt that shows off her belly button piercing and tattoos. He laughs at something she says as she skims her fingers up and down his arms, over his tattoos. *What the fuck?*

Jealousy surges through me as I watch them. It takes every ounce of willpower I have not to go over there and rip her away from his side. As if he can feel me watching him, Lincoln suddenly looks away from her and searches the room until his eyes lock with mine. There is a flash of surprise on his face when he sees me.

Inhaling through my nose, I try to shift behind Tyler's large form, but it's too late.

Lincoln saw me.

And now, he looks really pissed off.

He blinks several times, as if trying to clear his vision.

"Em?" he says.

"Hey . . ." I force myself to breathe.

"You're back?" he asks, as his blonde friend's cold gaze slides between us.

I clear my throat. "I'm back."

I can't help but notice how bloodshot his eyes are. They're glazed over with a far-off look in them as he stares at me. The way he's looking at me is nothing like how he used to. Instead he looks confused and lost. Like he can't decide if I'm here or not.

"Actually"—Tyler steps between us—"she's here to see me."

"No shit?" Lincoln growls.

"No shit," I lie, because the way he is acting has me second-guessing my visit.

"Daniels," the girl next to him coos. "Aren't you going to introduce us?"

Lincoln holds my eyes. "Yeah," he replies absent-mindedly.

Steeling myself, my fingers curl into my palms until my knuckles ache.

"Emerson, this is my girlfriend . . ." Lincoln's voice trails off.

Girlfriend? Refusing to show any sign of hurt, I dip my chin at the girl.

I try to push away how dumb I feel. Ashamed that I know nothing about a guy who only a few weeks ago had his body buried in mine. A guy who has consumed my every thought and breath for months.

Lincoln's gaze drops from mine to hers and I struggle to pull air into my lungs.

"I have a name," she giggles. "I'm Shayla," she slurs, stumbling toward me.

Tyler puts out his hands to catch her before she can get too close to me.

"Easy there, Shay. Maybe no more drinks for you," he announces.

"I am so drunk," Shayla giggles again, and I wince.

Tyler guides her away from us. "Let's go find you some water."

"Water?" she hiccups.

"Hydration is key to health." Tyler winks at me. "And hiccups."

Once they're a far enough distance away, I look back at Lincoln, who is staring at me like he can't decide if I'm real or not. Taking him in, I notice he's swaying a bit and I can't help but wonder if he's also had a little too much to drink. Or is it something else?

Anger in the form of heat fills my cheeks. "Girlfriend?"

Straightening, Lincoln's gaze drifts up me slowly, leaving a familiar wake of heat behind with each look. I can't help but shiver, because when his eyes return to mine, the old Lincoln is back. His expression softens and that fierce look he has for me is present.

I cross my arms over my chest, hiding myself.

"It's new." The corner of his lips tips up.

My eyes narrow. "Congrats."

He bites down on his lower lip, his eyes piercing me. "How's Lucas?"

"I broke up with him. On the car ride home. It was extremely awkward. If you'd bother to return a call or text, you would have known that." I stare at him angrily.

Lincoln doesn't answer. His eyes widened only a fraction of inch, but his grin slips.

"I'm glad. He wasn't the right guy for you, Em."

"No. He wasn't," I state, trying my hardest to hide the shakiness of my voice.

"He didn't deserve you. He wasn't good enough . . ." He trails off.

Trying to hold in my disappointment at how this is going, I stare at the crease that has appeared on his forehead. I can't tell if it's a result of confusion or being pissed off.

"Neither am I," he adds, and my heart sinks.

"I guess you aren't."

"Some things are just not meant to be, no matter how much we wish they were."

Two days. That's how long it took me to stop crying. To stop mourning the death of my heart. I'm not sure what I expected that night from Lincoln, but I know it wasn't for him to rip out my heart and step all over it the way he did. Then again, I suppose I'd been the one to push him away first. Regardless, the scars he left are deep and ugly.

Looking out the small circular window, I swallow, trying to keep the tears at bay. Little did I know it then, but my return from break set off four months of an awkward semester between the two of us. Lincoln was everywhere. Our friends were all connected.

We ran into each other almost daily.

Breathing anywhere near him became an impossible feat most days.

When the anger finally dissolved between us, we tried being friends.

Not our best idea.

No matter how hard we tried to be normal, we just couldn't pull it off. At some point, he broke up with Shayla, but the damage had already been done. What started as a small tear soon became a gaping wound. In the end, Lincoln was right. Some things are just not meant to be. No matter how hard we try to make them so, or how much we want them.

I settle back in my seat just as the pilot is about to announce our descent into Heathrow Airport. During the first month of school, I'd applied for study abroad. I was told there was a two year wait list. After mono hit our campus this spring, the wait list dwindled and I was able to slide into a two-semester program in London, England.

After I declared architecture interior design as my major with a focus in interior design, my advisor was able to extend the program for two additional semesters, which will be less focused on practicums. Instead, I'll be earning work-study credit by interning at a top design firm.

As hard as it was to leave Kennison, she knew I needed to go.

I needed distance.

And now, here I am, ready to land and put the last year behind me.

Start fresh and forget everything.

Including Lincoln Daniels.

CHAPTER 11

SENIOR YEAR OF COLLEGE

Two years later . . .

Normally, I despise waking up at the asscrack of dawn. However, my body is still on London time and hasn't adjusted back yet. I squeeze my eyes shut, then pop them open, roll over, and glare at my digital clock. It's only three o'clock in the morning. Ugh.

Tossing off the covers, I slide out of bed and stumble out of my bedroom toward the kitchen, tripping over several boxes in the process. Each clumsy stagger will no doubt leave ugly bruises on my skin. Groaning, I keep stumbling until I finally reach the kitchen.

"Shit!" I whisper, trying to locate the light switch on the wall in the dark.

Once I find it, I flip it on and then groan as the lights

blind me. Immediately regretting my decision, I shut them back off. With a sigh, I feel my way into the kitchen with my hands until I reach the handle on the refrigerator door. Yanking it open, I find the interior light less assaulting. I grab my half-empty Starbucks java chip frappuccino and sip on it, willing the extra shots of espresso to work their magic. Time changes are hard.

When I'd first arrived in London, adjusting was difficult, but over time, I came to realize that studying there was the best decision. Over the past two years, Kennison visited me every chance she could, so we remained really close. During her last visit, she mentioned finding an affordable, two-bedroom apartment off campus for senior year. I was beyond thrilled.

After living on my own for two years, I hated the idea of moving back into the dorms. Luckily, I had been working at the design firm in London while studying, and they paid well, so I saved up enough to afford it without having to dip into my trust fund.

I squint my eyes and take in all the boxes. Since I'm awake and our furniture is supposed to be delivered later today, I should probably start unpacking and moving stuff out of the way in preparation. That way it's organized for Kennison's arrival.

A few hours later, most of my junk is as put away as it's going to be without furniture. With a smile, I look out through the sliders that lead out to the balcony. The soft colors of the sun rising and awakening the morning skies ease me into the day. Feeling energized, I decide to try to bring all of the empty boxes down to recycling before I shower.

Placing the flattened boxes in a pile, I tie them up with a string, attempting to keep them together, and drag them to the door. Fighting to get it open, I make several attempts before I back out, dragging the boxes behind me. Just as I'm about to make it, the string breaks and my bundle falls apart. The boxes slip and get stuck in the doorframe, causing me to have to try to yank them out, which is impossible, since they're so wide and the doorframe is so tight.

Hot and sweaty from the effort, I growl into the empty apartment, only to hear some asshole behind me chuckling at my predicament. With a sharp exhale, which pushes the strands of long hair out of my face, I give up and face whoever thinks this is amusing.

"Something funny?" I ask, spinning around.

The moment I turn, my eyes tangle with a familiar steely gaze. My heart pounds harder and beats faster as my lips part. I stare, riveted to the stormy swirls in his irises.

Lincoln Daniels.

He looks the same. And yet different.

My chest heaves with deep breaths as a mix of anger and intense yearning clash inside of me. The gray in

Lincoln's sparkling eyes is striking as he takes me in. His hair is a bit longer on the top but still looks perfect and soft to the touch. And he still has the light bit of scuff on his jaw, but it makes him look even more good-looking, as if that were possible. He looks older. More filled out. Hotter and just all-around . . . remarkable.

Even his shoulders and arms look wider under his shirt. Without speaking, I take in every inch of him. As I do, that all too familiar lump of emotion forms in my throat, making it hard to swallow. No matter how much time or distance we put between us, the sight of him still draws me in, possessing me with an ache that only belongs to him.

"Em?" He lets out a slow breath.

When I meet his eyes again, a playful smile falls across his lips. He stares at me for a few seconds before standing up straight and approaching me slowly, as if not to scare me.

I open my mouth to respond, but nothing comes out. I'm actually speechless.

"Holy shit. I never expected to see you here," he says.

I squeeze my eyes shut and try to drown out the smooth sound of his voice as it slides over me, warming me in all the places that only Lincoln can reach. When I open my lids again, he eyes me hard for a few seconds, then tilts his head slightly forward and arches an eyebrow, probably at my lack of speech or movement. I can't help but just stare at him.

When he looks back at me, his gaze hides nothing, and everything.

"Do you live here or are you visiting?" he asks.

"Yes," I say simply, not able to manage much more.

He smiles and dips his chin. "Yes, you live here? Or yes, you're visiting?"

When I don't reply, he just continues to stare at me until I come to my senses.

I clear my throat. "I, um, I . . . live here. With Kennison."

"You live here?" he says, more to himself than to me.

"I . . . live here." My voice wavers over the words as I repeat them.

"Since when?" he counters. "I mean, Josh and I have been here two years and—"

"Wait, *Josh* lives with you?" I interrupt, coming back into focus.

"Yeah. After freshman year, we moved out of the dorms and in here."

"Where is Tyler?"

"He's still in the dorms."

Josh. Of course. Now it all makes sense. Josh is why Kennison was so excited about finding *this* apartment. He lives across the way—with Lincoln. Ever since she broke up with Josh freshman year, she's made it her life's mission to win him back. Damn it.

"This is . . ." He takes a step forward, so he's close enough to whisper. "I don't even know what this is, Em. I mean, you're here. And . . . *living* across from me now?"

Every single part of me tenses as I meet his unfathomable stare once more. I shift uncomfortably, because he's making me feel all weird and awkward. The way Lincoln has always watched and studied me makes me feel like I'm some sort of confusing piece of artwork on display. One he's trying to figure out if he likes or not.

"My study abroad ended. I'm back for senior year," I blurt out.

Lincoln takes in a calming breath and nods absentmindedly. "Seven hundred and eighty-five days ago, you left. Without so much as a goodbye. You just . . . disappeared."

My heart stutters in my chest and my breath hitches at his words.

"You counted the days?" I ask, swallowing the thickness that just swelled in my throat. My lips mash into a straight line while I dissect the meaning of his words.

His eyes move slowly over me. "You ran away. You took the easy way out."

I look at the floor for a moment, letting the weight of his words settle in.

"I didn't run," I lie. "I picked a major and immersed myself in it."

When I return my gaze back to his, hurt crosses his face before it disappears.

"A major?"

"Architecture. With a focus on interior design."

Lincoln's jaw clenches. "I'm glad you finally made a *decision.*"

He may not have meant for that to come out like a double-edged insult, but that's exactly how it sounded. Silently, we just stand here while this weird energy floats between us. It's filled with all the what ifs that could have been, had there been some semblance of closure between us, instead of this lingering awkward . . . whatever this is that's left.

He clears his throat, rubbing the back of his neck with his hand. "Is this going to be weird for you? Living across from me? You know, because we hooked up a few times?"

I stare at him, waiting for him to laugh or show any signs of joking. He doesn't.

"Not sure you can call what we did *hooking up*, Lincoln," I whisper.

His body becomes rigid for the first time as he gives me an unyielding look.

Lincoln nods. "You're right," his voice is voice of emotion. "Every second of us together is burned into my fucking memory. Haunting me." He rubs his hands over his face. "And now? Here you are." He motions to me. "Living across from me."

The air becomes thick between us. The silence is suffocating.

He's looking at me expectantly, like he's waiting for me to say something. To answer some question of his. Two years and thousands of miles of distance between us suddenly disappears. As if they never existed at all. Once again, he's everywhere.

After a long silence, he scoffs as if something is funny and takes a step back.

Lincoln looks behind me and lifts his chin. "Do you want some help bringing those boxes down to recycling? I'm heading to practice and can take them down for you."

I shake my head slowly. "Thank you, but I'm good on my own."

His eyes hold mine for a moment, turning a bit hard around the edges.

"I guess you are." Something unspoken settles in his eyes and maybe even his voice.

I can't help but feel this exchange has nothing to do with empty moving boxes.

He pauses at his front door, waiting to see if I have a comeback. I should say something, but I have no idea how to respond. Everything that comes out of my mouth just sounds wrong. Instead, I do my best to ignore the way he makes me feel.

My first mistake, of many.

Lincoln Daniels isn't someone you ignore.

He is everywhere.

In everything.

Whether I want him to be or not.

"I need to get to practice, so," he interrupts my thoughts. "If you're good?"

He glances over me and his eyes feel like warm hands, running over every inch of me.

"All good." My voice cracks. "Thanks." *God I hate this.*

With a quick wave, I turn back to my apartment and start stacking the boxes.

Behind me, Lincoln remains glued to the floor. I know this, because I can feel him.

"Em?" His voice sounds hoarse.

"Yeah?" I stop stacking boxes, but don't look at him.

My teeth clench together and my breath halts as my body becomes tense.

"Welcome home," he whispers, and I shiver.

Home.

Not welcome back.

Or welcome to the building.

Welcome *home.*

As his footsteps fade toward the elevator, I realize Lincoln will always be home.

CHAPTER 12

I stare at the computer screen, watching my mother attempt to FaceTime with me. We do this every week. She still has no clue that she needs to move the camera back so I'm not looking directly up her nose. You'd think a Yale-educated woman would understand how technology works. Sadly, that is not the case with Emily Shaw. After a few more seconds she finally gets things positioned the way she likes it before frowning as she stares at me.

"You look tired." She arches one of her perfectly manicured thin brows.

"I'm fine," I lie.

I'm anything but fine. I haven't been fine since bumping into Lincoln the other day with his soft and sexy golden-blond hair, mesmerizing steely eyes, broad shoulders, and hot scruff lining his firm jaw. I inhale through my nose, ending thoughts of him.

"Emerson Katherine Shaw, are you listening to me?" my mother screeches, when she realizes my thoughts have floated off and I'm no longer giving her my full attention.

"Yes, Mother. I'm listening to you." Another lie.

Not only am I back in the States, but I'm back to lying to myself and others.

"Have you started to think about design firms here? It's important that you intern at a top one before graduation. You'll want to be sure to secure your first choice before classes get started. We have some friends at the club who know people, if you need help."

"I've got it covered." I don't, because I'm a procrastinator.

She throws me a pointed glare that screams disbelief. "Covered?"

"My boss in London is helping me out." Or at least she will, when I ask.

Emily frowns and the space between us grows. I've never been close to my mother. She isn't the maternal type. I'm an only child and was raised by a nanny, while my mother chose to focus her attention on being a judge's wife. Even though she went to Yale Law, she prefers the life of a socialite rather than being in courtrooms.

My father, Thomas Michael Shaw, and I are even less close. When I was growing up, he was rarely home. When he was, he was in meetings with colleagues, at the country club golfing, or sleeping with his mistress. Holidays and public appearances summed up our quality father-daughter time together. Once a week, I have my obligatory call with my mother so that she doesn't get mad and cut off my trust fund, or stop paying for college.

"Did the furniture arrive?" she asks, bored.

"It did. We're all set up and comfortable. Thank you for arranging it."

One of my mother's favorite ways to control me is with money. While I've earned enough to pay my expenses, she still holds college, and now our furniture, over my head.

Her lips press together. "I don't like that I haven't seen the apartment for myself."

I try not to roll my eyes—my mother hates it. "It's in a safe neighborhood. It's five minutes from campus and it's very clean and well-kept."

I leave out the part about Lincoln; she knows nothing about him anyway.

She falls quiet. "You said that about your place in London. I almost called the US embassy when I arrived and saw the horrible conditions you were living in.

Thank goodness we were able to find you a suitable flat. You have the worst judgment, I swear."

"It was a school-issued flat and it was fine," I sigh, ignoring her insult.

It was perfect. Just not up to my mother's standards. Nothing and no one ever is.

"Have it your way. Eventually your father and I will see for ourselves," she warns.

"Can't wait." I fake a smile, and she throws a displeased look at my sarcasm.

"That reminds me. What day do you want the maid to come?"

I squint my eyes. "We don't need a maid."

"Is it clean?"

"The apartment?"

"No, Emerson, your sink drains," she chastises. "Yes, the apartment. Is it clean?"

"Yes." I don't hide my annoyance. "Both the sink drains and apartment are clean."

"If I came in there wearing white gloves, what would I discover?"

"That you couldn't pull off being a mime?" I quip, causing her to sigh heavily.

Twenty long, painful minutes later, she's releasing me from listening to any more of her backhanded insults or incessant chatter about her so-called friends and the gossip she has on them and their children. In her high-society world, the sole reason children are conceived in the first place is to pass on family names, heirlooms, and fortunes.

It's a lovely little circle of fictional bliss she lives in.

With a growl, I shut my laptop and throw it to the side, where it lands on the fluffy couch cushion. Relieved our weekly call is done, I grab the remote to turn on some reality TV. A loud bang from outside my doorway pulls my focus. I stare at the back of the door for a moment when the sound of wood clanking and another loud sound has me up and walking over toward it.

"Fuck!" someone growls, and I yank the door open.

Standing in his doorway, in all his shirtless glory, is Lincoln.

When he turns and faces me, I see his that his features are pinched.

My eyes immediately roam over him, unable to help my appreciation of the way his gym shorts hang way low on his narrow hips, just below his ripped stomach muscles.

I try to force my gaze up to his, but I get distracted by tattoos on his chest and sides. They're new and I gape and grip the door knob until my knuckles start turning white as I realize how much he's changed physically. And how much I like it.

"Hey," Lincoln says, sounding strained.

I let go of the door and cross my arms over my chest.

"Are you okay? I heard a loud thud, followed by some choice words and growling. I thought that maybe you were being murdered. Or abducted by aliens."

Lincoln's brows lift. "Aliens?"

"It's possible. People go missing all the time." I stop, realizing how stupid I sound.

He lifts his swollen hand. It's wrapped in white gauze and a melted ice pack.

"What happened?" I step closer to get a better look.

When I do, he steps back a bit, letting me know not to get too close to him.

Hurt at the rejection, I stop and manage not to show him how much it stings.

"Baseball practice. It was stupid. I grabbed a fly ball without my glove. It's why my shirt is wrapped around my neck—it throbs when I lift it. I was trying to carry my gear and get my key out, but my attempt just"—he shrugs—"fell apart. I guess."

My eyes meet his. Part of me wants to leave him be. The other half wants to pull him in and heal him. Every part of him. Not just his hand. That part wins out. It always will.

I step closer and swallow. "Where's your key?"

He looks down into my eyes. "Front left pocket."

I inhale sharply and drop my gaze to his shorts before blinking. "May I?"

Frozen, Lincoln nods his head. With one step closer,

I slide my fingers into the pocket. Once my fingertips brush his key, I grab it and slowly slide it out, pulling my hand away.

Holy hell. I exhale the breath I was holding. It's been so long since I've touched him that even that small amount of contact has me reeling. My grip on his key tightens as I lift my gaze and meet his unfazed expression. I try to hide my disappointment because it feels like my fingertips are on fire, while he's casually standing there, clearly unaffected.

When Lincoln steps aside, I manage to move my feet forward toward his door and unlock it. Once it swings open, I take a few steps back, grasping at the much needed space.

"A-All set," I hand him his key, taking more steps back until I'm in my own doorway.

"Would you mind helping with my bag while I grab a new ice pack?" he asks.

"Um. Yeah, sure. Of course," I ramble as I unlock my door and close it.

"Thanks." He walks into his apartment, leaving the door open behind him.

With both hands, I pick up his heavy equipment and take a few steps into his apartment, dragging it. He points to a pile of baseball stuff and I drop the duffel bag next to it while he strolls into the kitchen. His apartment looks like ours, except flipped.

Standing close to the open front door, I look around and internally laugh at myself. I should have known better than to think his apartment would be warm and inviting. There is nothing in it. No decorations or color. No paintings on the blank white walls. No lamps to soften the bad apartment lighting. Lincoln doesn't even have a scented candle.

I take in the large TV on the wall and black leather furniture facing it.

Everything is sterile and cold.

"How long have you guys been here again?" I ask.

"A little over two years."

"Two years," I repeat in a whisper.

Kennison hasn't even moved in yet, and our place looks like we've been there for years.

"You can leave the door open," he says. "*Safety* first. Right, Em?"

I frown, recalling how I'd left the door open when we first met in his dorm room. Annoyed that he brought it up, I slam the door shut and walk into the kitchen just as he opens the freezer. He watches me as I step around him, grabbing a bag of frozen peas.

"I didn't expect you guys to have frozen veggies," I point out, turning toward him.

"We're ball players. They're for injuries. We don't actually eat them."

"What about the fruit?"

"We use it for protein shakes."

I smile and close the freezer. "Let me see your hand."

Lincoln shakes his head. "I can do it."

I look up at him, and he's watching me with those intense eyes of his.

"Sports medicine major, remember?" he rasps.

I gently move toward his hand. "It's easier if I do it, Lincoln."

We both stare at his hand before I clear my throat, trying to find my voice.

"It might hurt a bit," I warn.

Lincoln laughs as though he knows pain and this isn't it. He doesn't flinch, or even make a sound when the bag of peas touches his skin. I try to ignore him. Try to focus on his hand and getting the bag of peas settled onto the swollen parts without hurting him.

Our faces are so close. With each exhale, his breath tickles my cheek. He's so still. Our eyes lock a second longer and then I refocus on his hand, but he's not looking at it. He's staring at me, watching my movements, completely fascinated by each one.

"Doesn't that sting?" I whisper, pressing down on it.

"No."

"Why not?" His hand is huge; even the slightest pressure should hurt.

Lincoln swallows. "I'm numb to the pain."

His words slay me, because I was right.

He knows pain.

Real pain.

He leans against the counter, holding the frozen bag of peas to his hand gently while watching me do my best to ignore the fact that he's so close. I should go. I shouldn't be here. I've helped him and now . . . now I'm just looking directly at him as he stares at me.

"Who hurt you?" I ask in a small voice.

"Who hasn't?"

"Lincoln."

"What, Em?" he breathes out.

I step toward him and his breathing rate increases as I search his eyes. "Tell me."

Lincoln looks down at me as I take the last step into his space. He's working his jaw back and forth like he's fighting some internal battle with himself. I can see it on his face.

At some point, I can't take the hurt etched deep on his expression, and I reach up and cup his cheeks, shaking my head. "Forget it. I'm sorry I asked. I didn't mean to pry."

Lincoln's eyes slide closed, and with his non-injured hand, he finds my waist, pulling me to him as he drops his forehead onto mine. We stand like this for a long time.

He inhales as I exhale, stealing each one of my breaths in our familiar dance.

"I should go," I say.

"I know."

"I don't want to," I whisper.

"I know."

When his lids flutter open, we stare at each other. Unmoving. I lie to myself and remind myself that I can't be with him. That I don't feel that way about him anymore.

"Most recently, you," he rasps.

"What?" My brows pull together, confused.

"You asked who hurt me. The last person to do so was you."

My lips part and I stare at him, not knowing how to reply to his admission.

"Daniels?" Josh's voice breaks the spell. "Did you get home okay?"

With a shaky breath, I step away from him just as Josh enters the kitchen.

"Emerson?" Josh meets my eyes, surprised.

"Hey, Josh. It's good to see you," I manage.

"Yeah." He looks between us. "You too."

An awkward silence settles around the three of us as we stand in the small space.

I curl my fingers into my palms nervously. "I ah, live across the way."

"Lincoln mentioned." Josh smiles brightly. "It'll be just like old times."

My throat is suddenly very dry and scratchy. "Just like . . . old times."

"Has Kennison moved in yet?" he asks.

"Tomorrow."

"It will be fun to have you ladies so close again. Right, Daniels?"

I smile at Josh.

Silence from Lincoln.

All around us there's this uncomfortable awkwardness.

Lincoln clears his throat and for some reason that brings me back to my senses.

"I should . . . go." My eyes slide from Josh's to Lincoln's.

"Yeah, okay." Josh nods.

"Lincoln, hope your hand fe—"

"Thanks for your help, Emerson," Lincoln interrupts me with a biting tone.

My heart almost stops completely. He called me Emerson. Not Em. Got it.

I've officially been excused. From the apartment, and probably his life.

Josh tilts his head in confusion at us, watching the weirdness.

Lincoln looks at his hand, focused on it like it's going to explode or fall off if he looks away. I look away, pretending it doesn't bother me that he's dismissed me so abruptly.

"So . . . I guess I'll just head home then," I manage.

I chance a look at Lincoln. He's still looking at his hand, taking up all the space in the kitchen and making me feel all sorts of contradictory feelings. My focus slides to Josh. He offers me a sympathetic smirk as he steps back so I can slide out of the room and escape.

"See you later," Josh mutters as I step around him.

I rush to the door, pull it open and slam it shut behind me. Once I'm in the hallway, I'm finally able to breathe normally again. I stand here for a few moments, then race across the hall, open my door, and slip into my safe haven. Once the door is closed, I lean my back against it and slide down to the ground, dropping my head between my knees, and remind myself not to get sucked back into Lincoln or his world.

I can't. Not again.

CHAPTER 13

Narrowed brown eyes stare at me from across the couch. I shift uncomfortably and look at Kennison as her gaze searches my face. She takes another sip of wine before speaking.

"Lincoln Daniels lives across the hall?" She smirks. "From us. From *you*?"

"Yup."

"Holy shit! I knew about Josh, but I had no idea he lived with Lincoln."

"Really?" My lips draw into an awkward frown-smile-pout thing. "How is it that you've stalked Josh for two years and had no idea he was living with Lincoln?"

"I swear." She puts her glass of wine on the coffee table. "If I had, no matter what psycho stalking I'm doing with Josh, I'd never have asked you to move in here, Em."

I sigh and sink deeper into the cushions. "It's just weird."

"Josh and I never really spoke about Lincoln after you left."

"No?"

"Lincoln sort of disappeared for a bit."

"That's odd."

"Not really. If, or when, I brought him up, Josh said Lincoln was busy with school and baseball. That's it. He didn't give details or anything. He was pretty vague about him."

"Well, he's around now," I sigh.

"Maybe it's serendipity," she suggests.

"Serendipity?" I throw her a disbelieving look.

"Fate pulling you two together again."

My gaze slides behind her as I scan the living room, avoiding her dreamy look.

"It's not. Besides, getting close to Lincoln again is a horrible idea." My guard is up.

"And why is that?"

"Because. Either he'll fuck up, or I'll fuck up. Either way—"

"There's fucking." She smirks wickedly when my unamused gaze collides with hers.

I wrinkle my nose at her. Wherever she is going with this, I don't like it. "Can we just go back to talking about how annoyed I am at you? That was more fun for me," I pout.

She laughs and shakes her head. "Listen, Em, Lincoln has always been into you. I mean, you walk into a room and you're all he sees. He watches you with this expression, like you're something to appreciate. He listens to every word you say, even if you aren't speaking to him directly. If you're near him, he gets this rigid protective stance. He's fallen. Hard," she says. "And no matter how hard you try to hide it, you have too."

"He *used* to do those things," I correct. "I've been gone for two years."

"When you're in as deep as he is, time and distance . . . they don't matter."

I know she's right. Yesterday, I felt it all over again. Every time he looked at me.

"Regardless, he probably has a girlfriend or something," I reason.

"Subtle," she smirks. "What he has is a reputation for sleeping with a shitload of girls."

I frown. "Really?"

"You weren't here to see the shitstorm right after."

"What does that mean?"

"He was pissed off when he found out you left for London. I swear, I thought he was going to jump on a plane and follow you. Josh said over the summer, he started to unravel. That he was lost. It destroyed him. By the time sophomore year started, he'd disappeared."

"Then how do you know about all the girls?"

"I've heard the rumors and stories of his . . . activities. He's legendary."

"Why didn't you tell me any of this when you visited?"

"What good would it have done? You were living this amazing life. Dating cute guys. Studying. Working. You were *living*. Eventually, Lincoln began living his life too."

I nod. "I guess you're right. We've both moved on."

"Ah, no. Neither of you have actually *moved on*. And, now, you're both terrified of each other." She tilts her head. "Neither one of you knows how to deal with the other. He doesn't feel worthy of the kind of love you can give to him. And you—you're scared to death of how you feel when you're with him."

"I'm not scared," I lie.

"Yeah, Em, you are. Because he sees through your Little Miss Perfect façade."

"Little Miss Perfect?"

"Yes. And Lincoln sees through it."

"I don't want to talk about him anymore."

She sits forward and takes my hand. "You've been given a rare second chance with him. I think it'd be a mistake not to take it. Not to *try*. Mistakes can easily become regrets."

I drop my head on the back of the couch. "The idea of him and me together is insane."

A light chuckles falls out of her. "They say the best kind of love is the insane kind."

I breathe in deeply. "Maybe I do still have feelings for him."

"I'm glad you are finally being honest with me." She smiles brightly. "And yourself."

I roll my eyes. "That doesn't mean I'm thinking about exploring them."

"Maybe it's time for you to think about it," she encourages.

My gaze drops to the throw pillow I'm absentmindedly playing with the fringe on.

A knock at the door has her popping up off the couch. "Pizza's here."

I think about what Kennison said as I watch her grab the cash off the counter and reach for the door. At the same time she opens our door, Josh opens his, and she freezes.

Josh glances at the ground, then lifts his gaze to hers, and I sit up more to watch them.

He gives her a shy-guilty look from across the hallway. "Sorry. We thought he was here for us. We ordered like an hour ago," he explains. "It's taking forever tonight."

Kenz waves him off. "Do you want ours?" she offers.

I stand and rush over to the door. "Ah, no. We've been waiting for an hour and a half."

Josh laughs and shakes his head. "Nah." He holds her eyes. "We'll keep waiting."

As I look between the two of them, I can't help but think Josh is talking about more than just waiting for the pizza. The energy between them is palpable.

"You guys owe me $22.79," the pizza guy says.

After a moment, I grab the cash out of her hand and give it to the delivery guy while she takes the box and bag of appetizers before disappearing into our kitchen. I wave at Josh politely and just as he begins to close his door, Lincoln appears behind him. His eyes meet mine and just like that, I'm lost in him. Everything else fades away. All I see is him.

Once their door is closed, I shut ours. When I turn around, I notice Kenz has returned and is eyeing me closely. She gives me a thoughtful look from beneath her long lashes.

"I wish someone would look at me the way Lincoln looks at you."

CHAPTER 14

I'm organizing the stack of papers on my desk when someone slides into the empty seat next to me. I jerk my head up and twist when I see Lincoln. He settles in, twisting to look at me as he offers me a bright smile. His hair is messily wind-blown; his eyes are bright.

"Morning," he says in a deep voice.

"Morning?" It comes out more as a surprised question.

Lincoln chuckles and settles in, kicking his feet up on the seat in front of us.

My eyes glide around the lecture hall before returning to him. "What are you doing?"

He tilts his head back against the seat, his eyes on me. "Waiting for class to start."

"Class?" I whisper.

"Yup."

"This is Architecture 101."

"Then it would appear I'm in the right lecture hall."

"You're a senior," I point out, confused.

"So are you."

"This is a freshman-level class," I whisper-shout.

"It is," he confirms.

"Why are you in here?"

"Why are you in here?" he counters.

"I'm the TA. I hand out the syllabuses, take notes, help grade papers, etc."

"Looks like I made a good class choice, then."

"What?"

"Had I known the teaching assistants in architecture lectures were so cute, I might have taken this class earlier in my academic career." He winks and gifts me a sly smirk.

I blink. "Still not following."

Lincoln looks up through his long lashes and sighs. "I still haven't fulfilled my art science credit," he explains. "A long time ago, someone recommended I take this class. I believe she said, 'It's not an easy A, but it's stimulating.' And I like to be stimulated."

His words linger between the two of us, causing heat to rise to my cheeks.

I shake my head at his innuendo. "How did you know I'd be here?"

He sits up and forward, lowering his voice. "I didn't.

I need the credit to graduate. Your presence is just the icing on the cake. Plus, now I have my own built-in tutor."

Lincoln is the kind of guy who leaves you exhausted and exhilarated at the same time.

"I'm not tutoring you," I grumble.

A slight grin appears on his face as he twists a bit more in his seat, causing his knee to brush mine. Every single muscle in my body locks up and becomes painfully tense.

"Does it bother you that I'm in here, Em?"

"Should it?"

"Nope."

The door at the front of the lecture hall opens and Dr. Garcia walks in, ending our standoff. Dr. Garcia gives me a brief nod before taking his position at the lectern. Lincoln and I face forward, and after roll call, Dr. Garcia explains the ins and outs of the semester and expectations of his students. Shortly after pointing out who I am, he begins enthralling the class with his elegant Mediterranean accent. Halfway through class, I chance a look at Lincoln, but he's not paying attention to Dr. Garcia; he's watching me.

I flatten my lips, annoyed that he isn't taking the class seriously, and sift my fingers through my hair. Running from my car to class made it all messy and untamed. I twist a strand around my finger and nervously twirl it while trying to figure out why Lincoln waited until now to take this credit.

Our college has certain general requirements you are expected to complete before graduation, regardless of your major. Most students get them out of the way their first year, since more often than not, they come in undecided. Lincoln has always known his major, so it's strange that not only would he wait, but then use architecture as his credit.

All that said, he couldn't have known I was going to be the teaching assistant, because I just found out yesterday, after applying for the position more than two months ago.

The moment class is over, I stand and begin to pack up, Lincoln doing the same next to me. It feels weird to have him so close and yet, so far away. I quickly look at his hand, which is still bandaged, but his fingers look less swollen than they did before.

"Thank you, again." He lifts it a bit, and I dip my chin in acknowledgment.

"What class do you have next?" I ask.

"Cryotherapy." He chuckles at my surprised expression. "What about you?"

"Interior Drafting and Design."

"Sounds fun," he teases.

I tilt my head. "Why are you really taking this class?" I ask quickly. "I mean, I'm sure there's an art science class in your major that would fulfill the general requirement."

"I told you, you sold me on it that night in the laundry room," he charms.

I narrow my eyes at him as we start walking toward the exit. "Maybe I should go into sales, then, instead of design," I mutter under my breath, and storm toward the exit.

Just as I'm about to leave, Lincoln's gentle fingertips on my elbow stop me.

I turn and look up at him, melting at his soft expression.

"Truth?" he asks.

"That'd be nice, Lincoln."

"It's something you like. And——"

"And what?"

He shrugs. "I guess I just want to learn about the things you like."

His steely eyes practically hypnotize me as they bore into mine. Feelings of heartache and guilt suddenly run through me. I missed this. Whatever *this* is that we do. Or are. I missed it. Him. All of it. I hadn't even realized how much, until now.

"I'm sorry I left for London without telling you," I exhale.

A throaty moan drifts from his lips in response. "Don't apologize," he says gruffly.

I blink at him. "With all the tension and hurt between us—"

"I never meant to hurt you, Em," he whispers.

"It wasn't just on you."

"Your leaving didn't give me the chance to make it right. When you suddenly appeared in front of my door a few weeks ago . . ." he trails off. "I felt like maybe this was my chance to make things right between us. If you'll let me."

I sway a bit under his gaze and the weight of his words. "I'm sorry."

"So?"

"So, what?" I ask.

"Will you let me make things right?"

Unable to help myself, I smile and nod.

"Good," he exhales, smiling back. "Because—"

"Because what?" I interrupt.

"You're in my veins, and I just want to be in yours."

CHAPTER 15

My eyes slide closed and my head falls back against the door. It's been two hours and Kennison still hasn't answered any of my texts. Neither has anyone from the management office. I shift and shiver, which causes the loose knot on the top of my head, secured with a pin, to wobble a bit.

The elevator dings again and this time, I don't even bother to look to see if it's her.

My hopes of my roommate saving me died an hour and fifteen minutes ago.

A dark shadow passes over me, then stops and lingers. When my eyes pop open, I look up to see Lincoln staring down at me, grinning. His amused eyes fall to my bare legs and run over me, taking in the pajama shorts and light, fitted T-shirt I'm wearing.

"Cute jammies."

"Thanks," I mumble, ignoring the way his gaze is heating my skin.

"Are those"—he pauses, tilting his head—"skunks eating ice cream cones?"

"Honey badgers," I mutter.

Lincoln arches his eyebrow. "Honey badgers," he repeats.

I shrug. "Don't judge. They're fearless. And cute."

He nods as if he understands, but there is a wicked gleam in his eye that tells me he's simply amused with my absurd reasoning. "Why are you wearing them in the hallway?"

"I was wearing them while studying," I explain. "I opened the door to accept a flower delivery for Kennison from a guy in one of the fraternities on campus. He was asking her to one of their dances. Then, I got locked out when I ran after the guy to get his name."

"So, the flowers weren't for you then?" he inquires, trying to sound casual.

I shake my head. "I don't have anyone serious in my life who would send me flowers."

His brows furrow as a deep scowl slowly appears on his face. "You're locked out?"

"Yeah," I exhale. "Kennison isn't answering her phone. Neither is the office."

He holds my stare. "How did you manage to lock yourself out?"

"The bottom lock was pushed in," I mumble. "I forgot, and the door closed on its own."

Lincoln falls quiet for a few seconds while he thinks. "It's almost midnight. No one from management is going to be able to help you until the morning. Why don't you hang out with me until Kennison comes home?" he suggests, motioning to his door.

He's right.

And, he's my only option, especially if I want to pee.

"I have to pee," I say out loud, without meaning to.

"That settles it," he says, grabbing my hands in his, pulling me away from the doorway and to my feet. "Let's get you inside my apartment and warmed up."

With my heart rate beginning to speed up, I follow him into his place and with a nod of his head toward a closed door, I make my way into his bathroom. It's oddly clean. I figured between him and Josh, it would look like a tornado ran through it. But it's neat and tidy. After I wash my hands, I glance at myself in the mirror and wince at my state.

Squeezing some of their toothpaste on my finger, I faux brush my teeth and fix my hair before releasing a few controlled breaths in order to calm myself down enough to decide whether this is a good idea or not. I'm only on my second breath when I open the bathroom door and walk quietly into the living room to escape.

Just as I round the corner, I see Lincoln.

He's leaning against the door as if expecting me to bolt, like I was planning to.

"It's warmer in here than in the hallway." He pushes off the door and walks past me into the kitchen. "Have a seat. I'll grab a blanket and something for you to drink."

I watch him for a moment, soaking him up with my eyes before resolve hits me and I pad over to the couch and plop down on the black leather. Seconds later, he's leaning over the back with a sweatshirt and blanket. I take both gratefully. The moment my head slides through the neck of his sweatshirt, I'm engulfed in all that is Lincoln.

His scent.

His warmth.

Everything that makes him appealing is lingering in the cotton threads.

With a final shift, I wrap my legs up in the blanket as he reappears with a water.

"Are you hungry?" he asks.

"I'm good. Thanks."

"You sure?"

I nod as he hands the glass to me and then takes a seat at the end of the couch.

Nervous, I look down at the glass, then back to him. "Thanks."

He motions for the glass, which I hand to him. "I forgot you don't like to accept open glasses of liquid," he teases. "I'll drink from it first, so you'll see that it's safe," he offers.

I barely hear what he's saying because his voice is soft and warm, like a blanket.

With an absurd amount of interest, I watch as he brings it to his lips, takes a slow sip, and hands it back to me. All without ever breaking eye contact. How can he make something as mundane as drinking water look seductive and sensual?

Good god, I need to get a grip.

"See. Totally safe," he rasps, handing it back to me.

"Thanks," I manage, my voice embarrassingly weak.

It's suddenly too quiet. My anxiety levels kick up a notch, and I have to breathe deeply to ward off a panic attack. It's been two years since my last one. I know he's seen me have one before, but I don't want to show him another one. As if understanding what I need and why I'm doing it, Lincoln gives me the space I need to calm myself down.

Once I do, he lowers his voice. "Still having them sometimes?" he asks.

"They've plagued me all my life. It's not like something traumatic happened or anything, just growing up the way I did, with my parents, as ridiculous as it sounds, the pressure triggered them. I always felt trapped. The expectations, constant nagging, struggle to be perfect—it takes a toll. Trying to be someone you aren't is exhausting."

"I understand," he replies quietly.

When my gaze floats back to him, I notice he's wearing black dress pants and a white button-down shirt. He has the top button open and the sleeves rolled up to his elbows, showing off some of the beautiful ink designs that cover his golden-tanned skin.

"Were you on a date tonight?" I ask, because he looks so damn good.

His lips curl into a barely there smile but he doesn't answer.

He was.

It's obvious.

I blow out a controlled breath, because that kind of hurts a bit.

"It must not have gone well." I don't hide the annoyance in my voice.

"Why is that?"

"It's early for you." I don't care if he knows that I'm feeling all sorts of bothered.

"Are you keeping tabs on me?" he asks, seemingly amused.

"No. I just meant, if it went well, I'm sure you'd bring her back here," I clarify.

"I would have," he nods.

"Since she isn't here, I assumed it didn't go well," I whisper.

"Maybe she didn't like me," he throws out.

"Doubtful," I blurt out without thinking.

"What's that supposed to mean?" He chuckles lightly.

"It's just," I rush out, trying to explain. "You're a bit of a player. And women love players, especially dark, sexy, brooding ones. We're drawn to you, like moths to a flame."

"*Women* are drawn to players?" he asks, looking confused.

"We want to save you. Change you. Win your heart and stop your playboy ways," I exhale. "We want to be the one who makes you forget all the others. We want to be *it*."

I blush when I realize he's just staring at me, silently considering my words.

He looks at me like I've suddenly grown two heads. "I don't want to be *saved*, Em."

I clear my throat. "I know that."

"Do you?"

Looking down at the glass, I swallow and nod before I meet his gaze again.

He gives me a tight-lipped smile. "What makes you think I'm a player?"

Taking in a deep breath, I press my lips together. "I've just heard."

"You've just heard?" he repeats, his tone questioning. He shifts and looks at me with an intense expression. "The simple truth is, I don't play games. I'm very upfront about what I need and want out of someone. If that makes me a player, then so be it."

Flustered at his honesty, I grip the glass tighter, taking a sip slowly.

"What do you mean, you're upfront about what you want out of someone?"

"I prefer my relationships with women to be," he continues, "uncomplicated."

He's studying me, gauging my reaction to his blunt words. Even if I want to, I don't give him one. Despite what he's saying, things are always complicated between us, whether it's intentional on his part or not. At the realization, something in me changes. I don't know what, but the need to strip him of this armor he's hiding behind takes over.

"What about me?" I whisper.

"What about you, Em?"

"Things between us always feel"—I pause —"complicated."

He runs his hand through his hair, gripping the back of his neck. His eyes leisurely search mine and it takes everything I have in me to remain on my side of the couch. All I want to do is crawl over to him, straddle his lap, and devour his mouth with mine.

"I'm attracted to you," he says, his voice low. "I want you. I just . . ."

"You just what?" I urge him to finish.

"I don't want you to have expectations that it's going to lead to anything . . . more."

Biting my lip, I try to decide whether to be flattered or punch him in the face.

"I don't have it in me to be what you deserve, or need. I never have," he adds.

Flattered. I decide I'm flattered because holy shit—the way he is looking at me, a bit shy and nervous. I have no idea how to respond. Or what to say. His admission is beautiful.

And dark.

And desperately in need of more clarification.

"So, you want to have sex with me, but you don't want to date, or love me?"

He's watching my mouth like all my words burn. "I know it makes me sound like an asshole, but yes. I can't offer you more. It's that simple. I'm sorry if that seems harsh."

Sex with Lincoln is . . . amazing.

More sex with him would be convenient, given he's my neighbor.

We aren't really friends in the true sense, so honestly,

we don't have to worry about ruining a friendship. We'd just be two adults, consenting to occasionally getting whatever this is out of our systems. *Right?*

"Okay," I reply nonchalantly.

"Okay, what?" He looks at me with a challenging stare.

"Let's have meaningless, hot sex with one another. No expectations."

He chuckles. "You aren't serious?"

"I'm not seeing anyone at the moment," I point out. "Neither are you, right?"

"Nothing that's serious."

"Then, let's have casual sex without commitment." I exhale slowly.

Lincoln swallows as his expression turns slightly nervous. His jaw is working overtime as he considers my suggestion. I know he's hesitating because he doesn't want this to become more. I'm uneasy because I know this isn't meaningless. The way we're drawn to each other, there is no way in hell things between us are just going to be casual.

And yet, I don't care.

Because I want more. Of *him.*

I'll take anything he gives me, in whatever form it comes.

"That isn't what I meant, Em. I was answering your questions, not implying—"

"I know," I interrupt him.

"I don—" he begins to say no.

Before he can finish, I place the glass on the table next to us and move toward him slowly. I swear he stops breathing as he watches me, waiting for me to change my mind.

When I reach him, I place my hands on either side of his face and allow my fingertips to softly caress his cheeks. "It's been two years, Lincoln. I've missed your touch."

He takes in a shaky breath while looking at my mouth. "This isn't a go—"

"Are you afraid that you can't handle it?" I whisper across his mouth.

Without answering me, he closes the distance, bringing his lips over mine. My body liquefies against him as his tongue slides across my lips then dips inside my mouth, tasting me. I moan softly, because holy shit, he's so good at this. The sound causes him to place one hand on my waist and the other behind my head, pulling me closer. I've missed this.

My fingers splay across his cheeks, pressing down, forcing him closer as I try my best to crawl inside of him, making us one person. After what feels like an eternity, we both pull away the slightest bit to catch our breaths. Panting, I drop my forehead to his.

Lincoln exhales harshly. "You make it so damn hard to breathe sometimes."

I lean back and look into his eyes. "Are you saying I take your breath away?"

His gaze searches mine without humor as he studies me. My response was meant to be funny, but there is nothing funny about the way he's looking at me. Or holding me.

"What if I break your heart?" he asks quietly.

His eyes stay focused on mine for several seconds before I lean forward and place a light kiss on his forehead, ignoring the fear behind his gaze. I don't want to see it, because I'm afraid too. I'm afraid of how this is all going to end. Because it will end.

There are no what ifs.

Lincoln Daniels *will* break my heart.

And I am going to let him.

CHAPTER 16

I try not to fidget too much in the booth I'm sitting in at a popular bar in town, near the college. Kennison comes here regularly, but at the moment, she's left me alone and is flirting with the manager across the room, a few feet from the bar, trying to get hired.

Some random guy seated with his friends at a high-top table next to me has his eyes glued to my chest. Feeling a bit self-conscious, I wipe my sweaty palms on my jeans and readjust the off-the-shoulder T-shirt that I'm wearing. If Kennison weren't trying so desperately to get a job here, I'd put a heeled boot right into the creepy gawker's crotch.

He sips his beer, winking at me, and I try not to vomit before I've eaten.

Grabbing the menu, I lift it and pretend to be totally

engrossed by its contents.

"I got the job," Kennison squeals as she slides in across from me.

I tilt the menu down a bit and look at her over it. "Don't you have to interview?"

"Just did." She wiggles her eyebrows and fixes her shirt, which is hanging low.

I shake my head at her. "Well, your boobs are your best asset."

"Right?" She winks. "I'm so glad you came out with me tonight."

"Oh yeah? Why's that?"

Kennison's manicured fingers curl around the top of the menu, forcing it down further so I have to look at her. "I feel like you've been a million miles away since you got locked out of our place and I found you all snuggled in and cozy sleeping on Lincoln's couch."

"I told you, nothing happened," I reply.

After our conversation and kiss, Lincoln fell quiet for the rest of the night. We ended up watching a movie. I was so comfortable and warm that at some point I actually fell asleep. A few hours later, Kennison was spastically banging on the door, apologizing because her phone died earlier that night and she'd missed my panicked texts and calls.

"Liar," she counters, picking up her own menu and reading it over.

My eyes slide to the window and I watch as the rain falls angrily on the pavement. I don't want Kennison knowing about Lincoln's and my conversation. She'll just try to talk me out of it. If we even are going to do this. I haven't seen Lincoln since that night.

Typical—something real or uncomfortable happens between us, and he disappears. He wasn't in class this week, leaving me to wonder what his absence means. I fear he regrets our conversation—or kissing me. I'm sure he's going to just pretend like nothing happened. Or he'll keep ignoring me forever. Either way, I've mentally prepared myself.

"Em?" At the sound of Kennison's voice, I snap my attention back to her.

"What?"

"He asked you what you want. Do you know?" she asks with a concerned look.

My gaze slides over to the server and I realize they're both staring at me, waiting.

"Sorry." I quickly place my order.

When I'm done, I look over at my friend, who is watching me with furrowed brows.

I give her a smile and pretend like Lincoln isn't invading my every thought.

After a second, she starts chatting about how she and Josh went for coffee the other day. She's excited and hopeful that this means they're finally getting to a point where they can be friends and maybe spend more time together. I really want that for her, for them.

As soon as our food comes, we eat, drink, and laugh. Things have felt so intense lately—*normal* feels good. Over the course of the night, the bar gets busier and I decide to go grab our second round of drinks without waiting for the server to come back.

Just as I'm heading back to the table, I falter a bit because creepy boob-guy is sitting in our booth with one of his friends, who is shamelessly flirting with my roommate.

I groan and unhurriedly make my way back to the table.

Kennison beams at me as I approach and place our drinks on the table. "Emerson, this is Scott and Connor. Guys, this is Emerson. Be nice to her," she giggles. "She's my bestie."

"Hi." Connor slides over, making room for me with his eyes firmly on my chest again.

"Hey." I sit close to the edge in the event I need to make a quick escape.

Connor motions to my drink. "I would have ordered you ladies another round."

"Thanks, but I don't accept drinks from strangers."

A slight frown crosses his lips. "We're friends now, not strangers."

"Noted," I mumble under my breath.

"Do both of you go to school here?" Scott asks.

"We do," Kennison says, brightly.

"Us too," Scott smiles at her.

"What are you majoring in, Emerson?" Connor asks me.

I hate the way he says my name. It feels creepy and cold. Not velvety and sexy like when Lincoln says it. When he says it, it's like being wrapped in a cozy blanket of warmth.

"Teaching," I lie.

Kennison's eyes meet mine across the table and she frowns as I shake my head, letting her know that I am not interested in Connor knowing what my actual major is.

He nods, sipping his beer, and I try not to punch him for staring at my chest again. I think of Lincoln and how he always looks me in the eyes, sometimes so deeply that it heats my skin. It's amazing how he can do that—turn me into liquid with just one look.

"I'm pre-med," Connor says.

"Impressive," I feign interest.

"We both are," Scott interjects.

"Oh, sexy doctors," Kennison chimes in, flirting with Scott.

"You girls should come back to our place," Connor suggests.

"No." I snap out the word quickly.

Kennison nudges my leg under the table and gives me a questioning look.

"Thanks," I add, trying to sound polite.

"Why not? We could have some drinks . . . hang out." He slides closer to me.

"I can't, sorry. I have plans after this," I lie.

"You do?" Kennison asks. "What plans?"

Connor reaches for my hand. "Are you against having fun, Emerson?"

Annoyed that he's being so forward, and saying my name again, I pull my hand back and narrow my eyes. "I'm against drinking with strangers in non-public places."

Something off crosses his expression. "Ah. You're one of *those girls*."

I'm just about to tell him off when Kenz's eyes widen in surprise as she looks over my shoulder. Curious as to what she's looking at, I follow her sightline. When I do, my gaze tangles with Lincoln's. A flash of annoyance crosses his face as he gives Connor a quick menacing glance. Then his gaze returns to mine and a smirk crosses his lips.

"Nothing happened my ass," Kennison mutters.

I throw her a glance before looking back at Lincoln, who is now standing next to our table. He takes my face between his palms and then, without warning, his lips are on mine in a searing kiss. I'm so taken aback that I don't push him away. I just let him devour my mouth in front of everyone at the table. After making his point very clear, he leans back.

"Come with me," he whispers across my lips, ignoring the table.

Without hesitating, I let him help me out of the booth. I'll get an earful from Kennison later, but for now, I'm much more interested in spending time with Lincoln rather than sitting next to a guy who stares at my chest. Besides, Josh is making his way over to our table and I know he'll take care of and watch over my friend.

Lincoln drags me away, toward the hallway near the restrooms, and out the back door into a dark alley. I don't waver, even though I'm stepping into the unknown with zero idea of what he wants from me right now, or how he feels about me. I'm naïve as to how this works. Should I be acting disinterested instead of just easily doing what he's asking?

Once we're far enough from the door, he backs me up until I'm pressed against a wet brick wall. The rain is still falling hard all around us, soaking our clothes quickly.

"Who is the guy, Em?" he bites out.

"Nobody," I reply quickly. "Just some idiot that Kennison invited to our table."

He grabs my waist, arching my hips against his body as he leans down and presses his lips against my forehead, holding them there for a few moments like he's in pain.

"Besides, what do you care? You haven't been around lately."

"I'm sorry," he whispers.

"Why have you been avoiding me?"

"I was scared," he says with such sadness, I almost burst into tears.

"Of me?"

"You," he admits, his voice hoarse, "and other things."

He pulls away, just far enough to stare down into my eyes, but close enough that I can feel his breath against my skin. He kisses me softly, barely touching my lips.

His kiss is slow. And filled with fear.

It causes a deep ache to ignite and burn within me.

An ache filled with want and need for him.

I pull back a little to look him in the eyes. I want to tell him not to be scared. That I'm not. But it would all be a lie. I'm terrified. Instead, I take his face between my palms and kiss him. Hard. Frantic. Our kiss turns into a full-blown lip-biting, devouring one that leaves us both panting with need. Drops of water crawl over us, but do nothing to cool my heated skin as he kisses my mouth with an urgency that feels out of control.

His hands leave my waist and wrap around my wrists. As he brings my arms above my head, he links his fingers through mine, pressing my hands against the brick wall behind me. His mouth is still on mine, wet and hot. With each kiss, I tighten my grip on his fingers, afraid he'll slip away and fade into the night.

He steps between my legs, pressing me into the wall. There's not one hint of gentleness in his kiss. It's raw, rough, and demanding. When my lips part in an attempt to moan, his tongue invades my mouth as he continues his never-ending assault.

One of his hands untangles from mine and he edges it down the nape of my neck, over my bare rain-soaked shoulder, closing it gently around my throat. My back roughly slides over the wall and I can feel the bricks scratching my skin through my wet shirt. The pain mixed with his annihilation of my mouth sends waves of pleasure throughout my body.

He leans back, both of us panting as he stares down into my eyes. My pulse jumps wildly under his large palm covering my throat. Warmth floods between my thighs despite the chill in the rain-filled air. Closing his eyes, Lincoln lowers his head and slowly drags his nose across my cheek, licking the drops of water off the skin before meeting my mouth again and brushing his lips back and forth in a teasing manner over mine.

"You should tell me to stop, Em." His voice is deep and husky.

My heart is pounding in my chest. "Don't stop."

With a low rumble, he clenches my throat tighter, pulling me toward him.

I hold his stare. "I want to feel you in my veins again."

He silences my gasp when he fills my mouth with his tongue again. Trembling with a mix of desire and fear, I grip his shoulder with my free hand as he shoves his leg farther between mine, pushing my thighs apart. His wet jeans brush against my own, which feel too heavy on my body. I move my hand to his face, but he snatches it and in one move, turns me so I'm facing the wall as he pins my wrists above my head with his right hand.

Lincoln places his left hand lightly on my throat again and moves it down, over my chest, then my stomach. I arch back into him, dropping my head onto his shoulder, and he begins to unbutton my jeans. At his touch, my entire head spins in a desire-filled haze.

"Tell me to stop," he demands again.

"No," I moan out.

The moment his hand slides into my panties and I feel the pressure against my clit, I lose the ability to think or breathe. His fingers languidly glide back and forth, coaxing me, teasing me until he moves lower, sliding two fingers inside of me. My hands flex against the brick. At the same time, he presses his thumb against the sensitive spot he was just coaxing, tracing lazy, unrushed circles over it.

His lips hover over my ear and the sound of his ragged breaths, combined with the pouring rain, becomes an intoxicating, heady mixture that has me rocking into his touch.

"Keep your hands on the wall and don't move." His husky whisper fuels the fire.

The hand he was using to hold mine together disappears. I blink rapidly when his left hand disappears from inside my pants. Somewhere in the back of my mind, I realize he's sliding my wet jeans down my hips. Common sense and morals almost have me hesitating for a split second, but I'm on the edge and decide that his skilled fingers should finish what they've started. For once in my life, my safety rules go out the window.

Suddenly, my hair is tugged roughly to the side, forcing my head to snap to the left. Lincoln brings his mouth down on my bare shoulder, which is showing thanks to my off-the-shoulder shirt, as I feel him roll on a condom behind me. When he's done, he brings his hand up, caressing my shoulder, then slowly trails his touch down my arm, lacing our fingers together. He positions my palms against the wall, his covering mine as he bends me slightly and with one quick move, slides into me from behind, causing me to cry out.

Lincoln growls against my skin as he stills inside of me, giving me a moment to adjust to him before he bites into the flesh of my shoulder, his wet tongue following, soothing and sucking the spot savagely. Compared to two years ago, he's gotten more dominant, and I like it. Every touch and sensation feels primal, like he's branding me. My soul.

"I like fucking you in the rain, Em," his deep voice rumbles in my ear.

I push against the wall with my hands, trying to get him to move, and feel his lips curve into a grin against my shoulder. Letting go of my hair, he takes both my hands in his, bringing them behind me and locking them around his neck, pressing my front into the wall more. He snakes his arms around my waist, holding me up with one hand and zeroing in on my throbbing clit with the other. Lincoln fingers it in perfect time with his deep, long strokes as I quiver and clench around him. My cries morph into deep gasps as my cheek presses and rubs against the brick. It stings and at the same time, it feels so damn good. Damp strands of hair stick to my face as he leans the top of his forehead against the back of my head and my body pulses and spasms as he brings me to an orgasm.

My deep cries disappear into the darkness of the night, absorbed by the rain.

"Oh shit," I manage to groan.

"Fuck, Emerson," he rasps near my ear, as his fingers dig into the flesh of my waist.

The way he says my name has me high on him as he

slides into me a few more times.

"Em . . ." He breathes out my name like a prayer as he releases inside of me.

We stay like this for a moment, Lincoln inside me with my body pressed against the brick wall. We're both panting uncontrollably. His face is buried in the top of my head.

My body feels numb and on edge all at once.

After a while, Lincoln slowly pulls out of me and steps away. My body immediately mourns the loss. With his heat gone, I shiver in the cold. Without looking back at him, I push myself off the wall a bit, but keep my forehead pressed against it while I look down.

I try to focus in the dark, but everything is still hazy. Once I've fully caught my breath, I yank my soaked jeans and panties back up, fixing myself as best I can in the downpour.

Behind me, I hear Lincoln zippering himself back up. He doesn't look at me when I face him. The fact that he isn't looking me in the eyes tears up my insides and leaves me raw. Robotically, he disposes of the condom in the trash behind the bar.

When Lincoln finally steps back into the small amount of light shining from a street lamp, the silent war he's waging within himself plays out over his perfect face. My heart sinks. I can see that he's already regretting what we did. From here, I can almost smell his fear and remorse. A stinging sensation on my right cheek has me wincing.

Seeing my flinch, he takes three steps to me. His fingers curl under my chin and move my face to the side, so he can look at what I'm sure are ugly scratches from the bricks.

"Shit, Em," he blows out in a rough exhale. "I'm sorry."

"I'm fine," I assure him, and try to pull my face from his fingers unsuccessfully.

His breath hitches as my eyes meet his in the dark.

Ever so slowly, his other arm wraps lightly around me, his hand moving up and slipping beneath my damp hair. We stand here, in the rain, holding one another a while before he leans his chin on the top of my head and releases a content sigh. I try not to get wrapped up in how perfectly we fit together. Or how safe and warm his arms are.

With his other hand, he runs his fingers up and down my back, pressing me into him. Each time, his fingers go a bit lower, over the small of my back and the curve of my ass.

My breathing hitches with each touch.

My fingers curl into his wet shirt as I bury myself into him, never wanting to leave.

"I never should have——" he starts.

I lean back and look up at him. "You should have. I

wanted you to."

His mouth is a tight line. "Are you sure?"

I nod. "This was the agreement, right?"

"Right."

"Okay." I sigh and let go of him, stepping back. "I'm okay, Lincoln."

"You sure?"

"Yes."

He gives me a hesitant smile while straightening his shirt. He looks oddly shy.

I smile gently back. "I should go. Kennison is probably freaking out."

Lincoln pauses, as if he might say something, but he doesn't.

"I'll see you soon?" I ask, hopeful.

"See you soon, Em."

Relief floods through me as he steps aside, letting me pass. He watches as I get back into the restaurant safely. Once I'm inside, I slip into the ladies' room and exhale. Leaning over the porcelain sink, I grip the sides and squeeze my eyes closed, slowly counting to ten, attempting to reel myself in before opening them again and looking in the mirror.

The reflection nearly makes me regret all my life decisions. I blink at myself. I'm a mess. My cheeks are tinted pink and my eyes are glassy. My wet hair is stuck all over my face and the scratches on my right cheek, which I thought were small, are red, raw, and angry. If Kennison sees me like this, she'll kill me for sure. And then she'll kill Lincoln.

What the hell was I thinking?

I don't do stuff like this.

When I'm lost in Lincoln, my common sense and control disappear.

I'm not sure that's a healthy situation for either one of us. Using some of the paper towels, I run them under the water and try to fix the charcoal eyeliner and black mascara now smeared in streaks under my eyes and on my cheeks. Ignoring my red, swollen lips, I wipe off all the residual rain from my skin and use the hand dryer, trying to look less like a walking disaster. Once I'm semi-dry and a bit pulled back together, I stare at myself.

My gaze drifts to the blotchy red mark on my shoulder as memories of Lincoln's mouth biting and sucking me as he gripped me tightly sends a desire-filled wave through me. My favorite new thing about Lincoln is this raw power he's gained. I love the way he doesn't hold back. He wants me, and he wants me to know just how much he wants me.

Which makes me want him all the more.

Over and over, no matter how little sense it makes.

I meet my own eyes in the mirror once more.

Nothing about Lincoln is casual or uncomplicated.

Even so, I don't want this to end.

CHAPTER 17

I tap my pen in a steady angry beat on the stack of papers in front of me as I stare at Lincoln taking his final. As if sensing the weight of my stare, he looks up briefly, catching my gaze, and the whole world around me fades away. Even though the scratches on my face have disappeared, I still feel them. Feel *him*. I can smell the rain and taste his lips.

After our alley sex, I'd woken up the next morning with a dull ache on my cheek. When I opened my door to leave for class, there was a gift basket of medical supplies for my face and detailed instructions on how to care for the bruises and scratches. That's the last correspondence we've had with one another. Even in class, he sits in the back row, slipping in after class begins, and leaves a second before it ends.

It's frustrating and annoying.

And yet, I know it's what I signed up for with him.

Casual. Meaningless interactions. Sex. No relationship.

I sigh, not knowing how to feel about what I've gotten myself into with him. He didn't promise me anything more than what happened between us. I agreed to it. Willingly. But this new distance between us—it hurts. There's this tiny voice in the back of my head that keeps telling me to walk away from this before it becomes too complicated.

Then the voice reminds me that it's already too complicated.

Lincoln looks straight at me for a moment, as if he can read my thoughts, before he returns his attention to the test booklet he's writing in. I glance at the clock and frown when I realize I have another hour of this torture. Sitting here in silence. Watching him from a healthy distance. I need to get a grip. All I can think about is how his hands felt on me as they burned my skin wherever they touched. I've become obsessed with the way he feels inside of me. I'm pretty sure I am not going to survive whatever this is we're doing.

Twenty minutes later, Lincoln slides out of his seat and places the test booklet in front of me. I lift my gaze and we lock eyes. He lingers for a second and I hold my breath. *God,* I just want to breathe again. Ever since he stepped into my world, I haven't been able to breathe like a normal person. He's branded my soul and there is no escape from him.

"You okay?" he asks quietly.

I nod, trying to act nonchalant. "Why do you ask?"

"You're pale," he sighs. "And you look like you're about to have a panic attack."

The accusation pisses me off. I have no idea why. It's not like he's wrong. Maybe it's the direct way he's using a weakness of mine against me. That has to be the reason.

"I'm fine," I clip out.

The lecture hall doors open and Dr. Garcia steps in, checking up on the exam. He looks around before stepping back out, closing the doors quietly behind him.

Annoyed that Lincoln's lingering, I sigh.

"If you've finished, Mr. Daniels, you may leave." My voice echoes in the room.

"Come over tonight?" he whispers.

"What?" I practically shout, because this isn't the time or place.

Students who are still taking the exam shift their focus to us. Lincoln looks over his shoulder at them, then back at me with a flatness to his lips. Once people stop watching us, I clear my throat and look at him again, this time with a challenging arch of my brow.

"Tonight. My place. Seven p.m.," he states, and walks away before I can say no.

This isn't a date. Just two people hanging out. No big deal. Nothing to freak out about. I frown at myself in the mirror and continue to attempt to coax my hair into a manageable style. I'm completely overreacting. I showered, twice. Shaved. Waxed. And went through six outfits before deciding that I need to look like I am not trying so hard.

After an hour, I finally settled on jeans and a black sweater. I brush my teeth for the tenth time before applying lip gloss, then immediately scrubbing it off like a crazy person.

Kennison appears in the doorway. Catching my eyes in the mirror with hers, she crosses her arms. "I thought you said nothing was going on between you and Lincoln?"

"Nothing is." I grab the mouthwash and rinse.

"This is a whole lot of effort for . . . *nothing*," she challenges.

After gurgling, I spit, then turn and face her. "We're just friends."

"Friends who have sex?"

I roll my eyes at her crassness. "So?"

"So," she draws out, tilting her head. "I don't want to see you get hurt, Em. This isn't exactly what I meant when I said you should think about a second chance with him."

Waving her off, I slide past her toward the kitchen, but she just follows me. "What makes you think I'll get hurt?" I ask, putting on my boots with her gaze still hard on me.

"He fucked you in an alley, then ignored you, and ever since, you've been moping."

"I'm fine with this situation, Kennison."

"When it comes to guys like Lincoln, and this situation, it's inevitable," she replies.

I look at her and tilt my head in confusion. "What's inevitable?"

"Hurt. You aren't built for a nonemotional sexual relationship," she explains.

"How do you know that?"

"Are you falling for him, Em?"

I shake my head. "No," I clip out. "It's not like that."

"What is it like, then?"

Quickly, I look away, because I don't even know.

"See?" she sighs.

"I can handle it."

"What if you can't?"

"What if I can?"

"This back and forth has been going on since freshman year between you two. Even when you were in London, you never dated anyone seriously. Do you realize not one of the guys you dated over there ever made it to a third date with you?" she poses.

"What's your point, Kennison?"

"My point is . . . it's always been Lincoln for you. But has it always been you for him?"

We're both quiet for a moment while I process what she's saying.

After a moment, she walks over to me and fluffs my hair, offering me a small smile.

"I'm fine," I assure her. "I can handle this."

"Okay. But if, and when, you can't"—she pauses —"I'm here."

She heads into the bathroom to get ready for her date and I go over to Lincoln's. I should have given myself ten minutes to get my head on straight after my chat with Kennison, but I didn't. Now my mind is filled with everything that she pointed out.

Like a poison, her words run through me. *You aren't built for a nonemotional sexual relationship.* My emotions are erratic and heightened. She's right. What if I can't handle this? I knock and fidget for a second before Lincoln opens the door, dressed casually in jeans and a dark blue thermal. The dark color makes his eyes look even more gray tonight.

Yup. I totally can't handle this.

He smiles down at me. "How do you feel about burgers?"

I pause, taken aback by his question. "I, ah, like them?"

"Good. I'm craving a burger. Want to come?" He slides on his leather coat.

"Um." I frown. "You want to go for burgers? Where?"

Lincoln brushes his hair off his forehead and steps forward. "I know a place."

I nod slowly, trying to be casual. "I need to grab a jacket."

"I'll wait." He closes the door behind him and I stare at him for a minute.

"You'll wait?" I repeat.

"Right here." He points to the ground.

"And then, we'll go out. For burgers?"

"Yes. Burgers."

I just stare at him for a moment, confused by what's happening. *Is this a date?*

"Em?" he prompts.

"Right," I exhale, and run into my apartment, grabbing my coat and purse.

When I reappear in the hallway, Lincoln has his keys out and motions toward the elevator with his head. "Ready?"

No. Absolutely not. "Sure."

As we step on the elevator, we stand on opposite sides, staring at the doors. I don't want to chance looking at him, because if I do, the desire for him to reach out and touch me will be overwhelming. Other than the brief exchange in class this afternoon, we haven't spoken or touched since the night in the rain. And I ache for both.

"What's your favorite burger topping?" he asks.

"Bacon. And cheese." My eyes slide to his. "Yours?"

"Same."

The elevator reaches the first floor and opens. When his hand connects with the small of my back, jolts of electricity burst through me. Every one of his touches, even the simplest one, seems to set my body off. It responds to him in a way it never has with anyone. I both suspect and fear that it never will with anyone else.

As soon as we step off the elevator, I expect his hand to disappear, but it doesn't as he guides me through the parking lot over to the passenger side of a black Range Rover.

"This is your car?" I ask, surprised.

"Yeah. It was a sign-on gift for coming here to play baseball freshman year."

"Isn't that against the rules?"

"Not if it's a *gift* and not a payment or a bonus." He holds the door open for me.

I smile and slide onto the soft leather seat. Once he shuts the door, I inhale the newish car smell mixed with

Lincoln's scent, and admire how clean his car is for a college guy.

As he slides into the driver's seat, he throws me a quick smile and starts the SUV, pulling out of the spot and onto the main street. We're quiet for most of the way, which I'm fine with, because small talk with Lincoln isn't something I could handle right now.

Pearl Jam's "Black" comes on the radio and we both reach for the volume to turn it up. His fingers brush mine and linger before he unexpectedly places his hand over mine and laces our fingers together, bringing our combined hands to rest on the gear shift.

Tensing, I swallow, trying not to freak the fuck out that he's holding my hand.

This is so a date. Holy shit.

"Is this okay?" He squeezes my fingers for a second.

I simply nod, because my throat is dry and the words are all stuck inside.

"You like Pearl Jam?" he asks.

"This is actually one of my favorite songs."

I realize I'm staring at the side of his face when he steals a glance in my direction before turning his eyes back to the road. I turn to look out the passenger window, not recognizing any of the streets he's taking. After about an hour or so, he pulls into the parking lot of a restaurant I don't recognize. I look up at the sign through the windshield.

Lincoln's hand disappears from mine as he shuts the car off and gets out. I'm still staring at the restaurant when my door opens and he holds his hand out for me to take.

Unbuckling, I slide my hand into his and he grips me tighter as he helps me out and shuts my door. He never releases my hand as he guides me to the front of the restaurant.

"Where are we?" I ask, pausing in front of the glass doors.

"Chucks. It has the best burgers you will ever taste," he replies.

Lincoln steps in front of me, placing one hand on the small of my back while he opens the door and lets me walk in first. The hostess makes her way to greet us and once we're seated in the booth, I take off my jacket and Lincoln slides his off at the same time.

I look around, curious as to why he picked this diner, an hour away in some random run-down-looking small town. "There wasn't a good burger place closer to campus?"

"I didn't want to be seen near campus tonight." He picks up the menu, looking at it.

My heart sinks at his admission. I can't help but think he doesn't want to be seen with me, around people we know. The server comes over and takes our drink orders as we sit in silence contemplating what we want to order. I look over the menu. The tension between us kicks up my anxiety and I shift, trying not to have a full-blown panic attack.

"Em?" Lincoln's voice is soft as he speaks.

I refuse to look at him, because if I do, I'm afraid he'll see my disappointment. I don't think that being disappointed on a faux date is really part of what we agreed to do.

"Emerson," he says more forcefully.

"What?" I practically growl between deep breaths.

I meet his gaze. He's looking at me with a serious look that makes me feel even more uncomfortable and nervous. When his hands reach for me again, my pulse jumps under my skin. He holds my wrists, his thumb caressing the skin over my pulse, calming the storm inside of me, sending my panic attack away.

"We're in Trenton . . ." He trails off for a second.

A long silence passes between us as I try to decipher the meaning behind this. We're both still quiet when the server returns to take our orders. Each of stares at the older woman's retreating form as she walks to the kitchen, before I cut my eyes back to him.

"This is the town where you're from?"

He gives me a slight nod but no smile. "I was born and raised here."

I want to ask a million questions. Like, why did he bring me here at night when I can't see much, or why just this one place? What does it mean that he's sharing this with me?

But I don't.

Instead, I ask, "What's your favorite movie?"

Relief crosses his expression. "Not *The Notebook*."

I roll my eyes. Typical guy answer. "Let me guess, something with blood and guns?"

Lincoln shakes his head. "*Caddyshack*."

My brows lift in surprise. "Really?"

He laughs. "Is my movie pick really that hard to believe?"

I shrug. "I guess things are always so intense between us. Fun seems . . ."

Lincoln stares at me blankly. "What's wrong with fun?"

"Nothing. It's just rare that I see you having any," I point out. "With me, anyway."

The blank expression slips away and his face softens. "I have fun with you, Em."

The waitress brings our burgers over, which are huge. When we both reach for the ketchup, I let out this awkward bark-laugh, because everything just feels weird tonight.

"This is weird," I exhale.

"What's weird?" he asks. "The burgers or pretending like I haven't been inside you?"

My eyes snap up to his at the forwardness of

his words.

He laughs at my reaction.

"Both," I say steadily, cutting my burger in half so I can pick it up.

He pops a french fry into his mouth. "What's your favorite movie?

"*The Princess Bride*. Hands down." I motion to the ketchup. "May I?"

"As you wish," he says as he hands it to me, quoting the movie.

I shake my head and smile. "Well played, Daniels."

He returns my smile and takes a huge bite of his burger, and I do the same. I try not to roll my eyes in the back of my head, because holy shit, he's right. This might be the best burger I've ever eaten. Even the bacon and cheese on it tastes better than normal.

I chew and moan at the same time, before I bring my wrist up to my mouth and lick off some of the ketchup that slid out between the buns because I need both hands to hold it. After a minute, I look up and notice Lincoln's burger is frozen in front of his mouth as he watches me with hooded eyes.

"What?" I ask.

"I'm not going to lie to you, Em. Watching you eat that is fucking hot."

Blushing, I shake my head and smile at him. The rest of the meal is much more relaxed. We talk about *safe* topics and embarrassingly enough, I finish everything on my plate, as does he. Several times I had to keep reminding myself that this wasn't a date, even though it sure as hell feels like one. Especially when Lincoln picks up the check after asking if I want dessert, which I decline for fear of exploding from being too full.

Just as we take a step outside, a light snow begins to fall, and I curl into my coat.

"Can I take you somewhere?" His voice is at my ear as he leans over my shoulder.

I look up at him. "Sure."

We get back in the SUV and a short ride later, he pulls up next to what looks like it used to be a play-ground. There are old swings that are rusted and broken, and a sandbox that looks like it's seen much better days. Everything just looks sad and forgotten.

Taking my mitten-covered hand in his, he pulls me over to what's left of a rotting picnic bench. After he tests its sturdiness, we sit on it, quietly watching the snow fall.

"You warm enough?" he whispers.

I nod, even though I'm freezing. For some reason, I don't want him to know I'm cold.

He leans into me so our shoulders are touching. "My best friend, Sean, and I used to come here when we were kids. We met in the third grade. We were both nine, trying to escape shitty parents and even shittier home lives."

"Has it always look this run-down and sad?"

"Trenton isn't exactly a town filled with old money," he says, not looking at me.

Unsure if that was a dig at my upbringing or not, I ignore the comment.

"What school is Sean attending?" I ask.

"None. As we got older, we got into things that made our lives a complicated and fucked up mess. I had one thing he didn't, though," he exhales.

I watch the cloud of steam that escapes his mouth disappear into the cold night air.

"What was that?"

"Baseball. A coach. A team. Something to focus my energy on."

"He didn't play?"

"No." His voice is thoughtful. "Sean didn't play."

"Where is he now?"

"Dead. A year ago today."

I peer over at him. He's looking up at the sky. "I'm sorry, Lincoln."

"Don't be. He died in prison. Hung himself."

"That's awful," I whisper.

"It was his only way out of this shitty life. Just like baseball was mine."

Something in my heart cracks, and I start to worry that there is even more darkness to Lincoln than I initially thought. My eyes are suddenly glued to him, waiting for more.

He gives his head a slight shake, clearing his throat. "I don't know why I brought you here. Maybe it's because all my memories of this park are shrouded in pain. Selfishly, I think I just wanted one memory of this place that was good. Does that make sense?"

He's still looking up at the sky and I have the sudden desire to ask him a million questions. About his parents, his childhood, his first love, his first kiss. I want to know more about his friend and why he has so many tattoos on his arm. I just want to drown in everything that is Lincoln. Each question lingers in my mouth, begging to be asked.

"Thank you. For inviting me into your life."

"We should go; the snow is picking up," is all he says.

I look up at the tiny flakes that have begun to fall faster. Neither of us moves as large snowflakes land on my cheeks, in my hair and on my clothes. I close my eyes and inhale.

When I reopen them, I look over to see Lincoln doing the same.

I slide off the table and step between his legs, taking off my mittens and placing them in the pockets of my jacket. My warm hands meet his cold cheeks and as they do, he opens his eyes and tilts his head down so he's looking at me.

Leaning in, I gently brush my lips over his. His are cold but soft, and with one gentle caress of his warm tongue against mine, everything inside me heats with a slow burn as I leisurely kiss him, trying to take away the bad memories, leaving only this one, of us.

His hands rest against my lower back, pressing me closer. I slide mine down and fist his coat, trying to meld even more with him. When we do finally pull away for air, he buries his face in the side of my neck and holds me tightly to him, as if I'm his lifeline.

"You have no idea what you mean to me, Em," he whispers against my neck.

"Tell me." My voice is shaky.

He falls silent, holding me for a few moments before he speaks again.

"Let's go," he says, and pulls away from me. "You're cold."

I take my mittens out and put them on. Lincoln slides off the picnic table and puts his arm around my shoulders, keeping me tucked into his side as we walk back to his car.

When we finally reach his car, he opens the passenger door and helps me in before closing the door and running around to the driver's side. Quickly, he turns the car on and blasts the heat. We both sit in silence, staring out the window watching the snow while the car warms up. When it's finally a pleasant temperature, Lincoln starts driving.

I drop my head back. "Thank you. For the burger. I had no idea I needed one so badly."

A slow grin spreads across his face. "Thank you for joining me."

An hour later, we're standing at my door. "Are you going home for Christmas?"

Lincoln nods, but it's forced. "It's been a while since I've seen my Mom, so yeah. You?"

I quickly nod too. "It will be my first one back in two years. My parents throw this ridiculous party at the club every year with friends and family. It's—" I stop, after what he shared with me tonight, I realize I need to learn to control what I say around him.

When I look up, he's watching me, looking at me as if I'm the most interesting person in the world. It's so odd how he can't seem to keep his eyes off me whenever I'm near him.

"Go on," he encourages.

"Lame," I finish.

"Come here." His hand reaches down and he pulls me to him.

"What are you doing?" I ask him.

"Wishing you an early Merry Christmas," he whispers.

His lips touch mine. His kiss is slow and gentle. He

explores my mouth as if it's an art form. One hand slips into my hair, holding the back of my head, and the other tightens around my waist. I melt at the softness in his kiss. It's raw and perfect. I never want it to end. But it does. He stops kissing me and takes my face with both his hands, holding me still as he looks into my eyes, seeking out something I don't understand.

When he finds whatever it is, his thumbs brush my cheeks and he closes his eyes, dropping his lips to my forehead. "Merry Christmas, Em," he whispers.

Feeling his internal struggle, I wrap my fingers around his wrists, silently pleading with him not to leave. I want more time with him. "Stay with me tonight?" I suggest.

He shakes his head. "I just wanted to see you, without expectations."

Disappointment fills me. "I thought *without expectations* is what we are doing?"

He forces a smile and kisses me once more with finality. "Good night, Em."

CHAPTER 18

Attending my parents' parties has always felt like a chore, and tonight's holiday auction is no exception. I scan the room, taking in all the wealthy people in their circle of "friends." Everyone is mingling and politely chatting with one another while sipping overpriced champagne. It's all so fake and formal. Tomorrow, they'll all be gossiping behind one another's backs. I should have stayed home, but I knew they'd never let me live it down.

As I look around, none of this feels right. I feel like a fraud standing in this room.

This life—it isn't who I am. Or want to be.

I miss Lincoln.

For something that is supposed to be casual, it certainly doesn't feel like it is.

"Emerson, stand straight," my mother's cultured, clipped, impersonal tone snaps.

"I am."

She rolls her eyes. "This is what you chose to wear?"

"No, Mother. This is my *arrival* outfit. I'll change into my *party* outfit later."

"Honestly," she sighs. "Your sarcastic quips are unwelcome this evening."

"It's a simple black dress. I don't have the fake cleavage and large diamonds to pull off platinum blond hair and slutty red dresses like the other ladies in the room."

"That is a very flattering portrait of my friends you're painting."

"I wasn't talking about your friends."

My mother arches a perfectly manicured eyebrow at me. "No?"

"I was talking about the other ladies in the room."

Her lips flatten at my snarky remarks. "You could at least try to act like you're having a good time. I mean, for god's sake, after the money we dumped into perfecting your smile, would showing it off kill you? Not to mention, frowning gives you wrinkles."

"Frowning is why the plastic surgeons in here tonight make generous donations."

Her eyes narrow. "The event is very important, Emerson. All the proceeds from the holiday auction go to the children's hospital. Your frowning is scaring away bidders."

I throw her a forced, tight smile. "School is an hour away. I can leave."

He shoulders sag. "Never mind." Her tone is full of defeat. "Frown away."

"Emily." One of her high-society friends strolls over, taking my mother's hands and kissing both her cheeks. "How lovely to see you. This event, as always, is such a treat."

"Thank you, Victoria." She peps up. "My daughter, Emerson."

"Nice to meet you," I say politely.

"Well, aren't you lovely." Victoria smiles at me with her collagen-filled lips.

"And wrinkle free," I quip, and my mother rolls her eyes.

"Your mother is just the best. Her events get bigger and better every year."

"Oh, Victoria, you're embarrassing me." My mother acts like she's embarrassed, but she's actually beaming, soaking up the compliments, which are empty, by the way.

Victoria flips her platinum extensions over her slender shoulder. "You must just love having Emily as a mother, Emerson. So much. She is everything I strive to be."

"She'd shame me into it if I didn't," I reply, but it goes over the social climber's head.

"How much have you raised for children's causes now, Emily?" Victoria asks insincerely. "Oh, who can keep track with all the parties you so skillfully throw?"

"Oh, now, stop it." Mom pets Victoria's arm as if she's ill at ease, which she isn't.

"Emerson, you must meet my son. He's pre-med. I do believe you both attend the same school," Victoria points out. "He's at the bar with some of his fraternity brothers."

My eyes follow hers and I freeze when I see that the boob-ogler from the bar, Connor, is her son. When I look back at Victoria, I can't help but notice the voluptuous size of her chest. I snicker. Now I see where Connor gets his fascination with boobs from.

"Oh, how lovely." Mom's eyes sparkle. "Emerson, be sure to stop over and say hello."

I feign excitement. "I'd be happy to say something to Connor before I leave."

"Wonderful. I think you two will get along swimmingly," Victoria winks.

My mother ushers her friend away, giving me a pointed glare that says *behave*.

Looking around the room one final time, I grab a cream puff off a silver tray and decide to give it ten more minutes before I slip out through the kitchen without being noticed.

An hour and ten minutes later, I'm back home, changing into a pair of sweats and a tank top, brushing my teeth, and getting ready for bed. Kenz went home for the holidays, so the apartment is quiet. And as much as I hate silence, tonight, I welcome it.

It feels good not to have to fake conversations, interest, and smiles. I head back to the living room to turn out the lights, leaving the white lights of the Christmas tree on for their warm, cozy glow, before making my way into the kitchen to grab a water.

I am sure that my mother will call me tomorrow, disappointed and angry that I slipped out of her event early and annoyed that I'll have to drive back for Christmas Day.

Taking a sip of water, I shake my head. I'll deal with her wrath tomorrow. Tonight, all I want is to watch cheesy Hallmark movies in bed and bask in some much needed alone time before I deal with round two of her holiday soirées and fake friends.

A sudden high-pitched giggle outside my door draws my attention, followed by the deep sound of Lincoln's voice telling the giggler to keep it down. I cap my water and put the bottle down on the counter before tip-toeing closer to the door, so I can eavesdrop.

"I'm glad we ran into each other tonight, Lincoln," the giggler says, slightly muffled.

"Me too, Jessica," Lincoln replies, and I hear his keys jingle.

"I just—" Jessica pauses. "I didn't want to be alone tonight."

"Me neither," Lincoln says, with nothing but sincerity in his voice.

Envy pours through me. I realize we have a *casual* thing going on, but it never even crossed my mind that we'd see other people while we were doing whatever it is we are doing. Pushing up on my toes, I look through my peephole and take in the leggy redhead wearing tight leather pants and fuck-me heels. Her red nails are nestled on his arm.

I can't see her face, but Lincoln's comes into view and I watch as he smiles down at her and opens his door. With a wink, he motions for her to step in. As she disappears into his apartment, my heart sinks and my breath catches with hurt. Before he follows Jessica in, he stops and looks over his shoulder at my door, staring at it for a long moment.

I jump back like a total idiot, afraid he can see me, which he can't. As soon as I hear his door shut, I take one more look, but they're gone. Seeing him with another girl hurts.

Numb, I grab my water bottle and all but run into

my bedroom, climbing into bed and turning on the TV. The longer I lie awake, staring at the ceiling, the more angry and frustrated I become. I try not to imagine all the things they're doing across the hall, but it's almost impossible. With a growl, I scold myself for even caring. It's not like we're dating. Or exclusive. My mind drifts to what it would be like to actually *date* him. Would we go to the movies? Or dinner, like we did the other night?

For some reason, it's hard to picture Lincoln taking girls out on *normal* dates. I chastise myself. If any other guy treated me the way Lincoln does, it would be over. And yet, I find myself constantly making excuses for him, justifying his actions. Why is that?

Eventually, I fall asleep with the TV on, watching a movie where the girl gets the guy in the end, and I dream of an ending like that with Lincoln, even though, for some reason, deep down, I feel like our story won't ever have a happily-ever-after, fairytale ending.

CHAPTER 19

Winter storm clouds line the sky this morning, threatening to dump snow. Before I head out to grab coffee, I grab my mittens and hat. I slip out of my apartment and turn to lock my door. Just before I finish and head to the elevator, Lincoln's apartment door flies open behind me. Looking over my shoulder, I watch Jessica stumble out. Her hair is all messy and her eyeliner is smeared under her eyes and I can't help but stare at her angrily.

Lincoln appears behind her, pulling a shirt down over his head, covering his bare chest, and my heart sinks a little further. Pissed and jealous, I'm glued to the floor, unable to move. The moment our eyes meet, confusion flickers across his tan face.

"Morning," I manage.

"Hi." Jessica smiles warmly at me and I want to rip her face off.

Lincoln just stares at me and suddenly I feel very small in their presence. I should go and let them have some privacy, but something in Lincoln's expression is holding me still.

Jessica's gaze slides between us before she places a palm on Lincoln's chest. "Hey," she grabs his attention. "I'm going to go." He looks down at her and nods. "Thanks again for last night, Linc. I really needed your company. I'll call you later."

"You want me to walk you to your car?" he asks her, and I die inside.

"I can manage." She smiles up at him, cupping one of his cheeks with her palm.

"Later, Jess."

I try not to flinch when she throws me a polite smile and skirts past me toward the elevators. We both watch in silence as the elevator doors slide shut and she disappears.

Swallowing, I make myself look him in the eye.

When I do, a wave of irritation passes over me.

Lincoln's gaze locks onto mine as soon as I look up, and I want to crawl inside my apartment and disappear. "I was just"—I clear my throat—"grabbing some coffee."

"Em?" he says calmly, stepping into the hallway,

keeping several feet away.

"Don't." The word comes out harsher than I actually meant it to.

"I thought you were going home for Christmas?" he asks.

That's why he brought Jessica home—he thought I wasn't going to be around.

"I attended my family's holiday auction last night. I'm driving back tomorrow."

He nods as if understanding that I couldn't stomach staying over.

"You said you were going home too." I snap out the accusation.

"I did. Then I came back," he answers quietly.

"Not alone," I add, then immediately feel stupid for saying it.

He never promised anything to me other than casual sex, and that is exactly what he gave me. I agreed to the terms. There are no rules about dating other people. I have no right to be hurt, or angry, but I am. I'm so pissed off and hurt. Kennison was right—I am not made for an unemotional, casual sexual relationship. Not with Lincoln, anyway.

I try to read the expression in his eyes, but I can't. My gaze falls and locks onto my feet. He takes another step toward me, closing the distance between us, but neither of us speaks. I can feel him assessing me, studying me, but I don't look at him. I can't.

"You're mad?" His voice is quiet, but sincere.

"I couldn't care less who you sleep with." My voice is tight. "It's none of my business."

"Em," he whispers. "Jess is just—"

My gaze snaps onto his chest and my jaw tenses, steeling myself for whatever is about to come out of his mouth. I fear that whatever he says is about to crush me.

"She's just what, Lincoln?" I blow out.

"A friend. But it's clear from your reaction that you think it's more. That *she's* more."

"She stumbled out of your apartment looking like she's more," I point out.

Lincoln takes another step, and I have to press my back against my closed door. He isn't touching me, but he's all around me, invading my space. I tense when he lifts his palms and presses them against my door on either side of my head and leans into me until our chests are touching. I'm not sure why, but suddenly I feel like bailing.

"Jessica is Sean's girlfriend." He winces as if in pain. "We ran into each other when I was home last night. We both"—he drops his gaze to mine—"needed to talk. To cry. To remember. That's it. She spent the night because neither of us wanted to be alone."

The explanation makes me want to wrap my arms around him and hold him.

I don't. I clench my teeth, pushing away the desire.

"I wanted to be there for her, as a *friend*," he adds. "That's it. Nothing happened."

All I can do is stand motionless under his gaze. I'm not sure what to say. I'm mad at myself for jumping to conclusions. I'm mortified that I'm feeling jealousy and anger.

I can't get a solid hold on my feelings for him.

Just the fact that I have *feelings* is bad.

"It doesn't matter. We aren't dating; I have no right . . ." I trail off.

Lincoln inhales. "You're right. We aren't dating."

"It's my own fault, really," I ramble.

"Em—" he tries, but I shake my head, stopping him.

"I knew you would ruin me." It just slips out.

Stormy gray eyes search mine and understanding crosses behind his gaze. He sighs, as if my words cause him physical pain. "I'm sorry," he says again, but this time, it feels like he's saying sorry for *everything*. "You don't deserve to feel this way."

I quickly look away. "No. I don't."

After this, things aren't ever going to be the same between us. I can feel it shifting.

"This thing we're doing," he says. "I wanted it to be uncomplicated. I didn't want— I mean, I never meant for either one of us to get hurt. If we keep doing this . . ."

"Do you want to stop?" I interrupt him.

"If we don't, it'll just get worse the more time passes."

I nod, feeling like he's saying we're done in more ways than one.

"We should call it off, then. Before either one of us gets in too much deeper."

Holding my breath, I wait for his answer. I don't want to call it off. I'm already in too deep with him. I want to immerse myself in his life. Find out more. Become more to him.

Lincoln narrows his eyes at me, then grabs my face, forcing me to look up at him.

"Problem is, I don't know how to stop wanting you," he says, his voice hoarse.

"Then don't."

Our lips touch and our breaths collide, but there isn't a kiss as he presses me back against the door, staring down into my eyes. We're panting, staring at each other without kissing, because what's happening between us is so much more than a simple kiss could encompass. It's raw and vulnerable. A confrontation. A dare for the other to end this.

Lincoln stares down at me, pressing his body into mine in an intimate way, and a strange feeling washes through me. It's as if something permanently ties me to him.

Something about the feel of his body against mine and the intensity of his gaze snaps my brain off. All thoughts dissolve, leaving this intense, burning need to be Lincoln's.

All his.

CHAPTER 20

L incoln sifts his fingers through my hair as we lie in my bed, staring at each other. I never got my coffee this morning. And we didn't end things. Instead, I pulled him into my apartment, and then into my bedroom, and kept him there until we both became too sore and too tired to do much more than curl into each other and pass out.

Now we're lying face to face as he twists a strand of my hair around his finger and his eyes hold mine with an intense look. I asked him about his past, and he's trying to tell me.

I want to know everything there is to know about him.

"Once you know the truth about me, it will haunt you, the way it does me," he says.

I lift my fingers and drag them down one side of his face. "Tell me."

"I didn't have the same upbringing as you. The same affluence and status."

"I was raised by a nanny," I sigh. "My upbringing was empty, hollow."

"At least you had a nanny who loved and protected you," he exhales.

"It's not the same as the love of a parent," I counter.

"Maybe not," he shrugs. "But you had someone who loved you, Em."

"Someone who eventually left," I argue. "I grew up in a world where nothing was authentic. It's about status, not friendship, or love. How I grew up, nothing was real."

He untwirls the strand of hair and twists it again. "Sean and I both learned quickly that life was too real. Hard. So we had to be harder in order to survive."

Lincoln releases my hair and rolls onto his back, placing his right arm under his head as he stares up at the ceiling. I curl into his side, gently placing my cheek over his heart, listening to it softly beat. The fingers on his left hand spread over the back of my head.

"Sean started popping pills as a way to escape the darkness that seemed to always find us. Then he moved on to the harder stuff and started dealing. He introduced me to marijuana—that's all I ever did—but it became a habit. I hid it better than he did, because I had to take random drug tests in order to play baseball. I dunno," he exhales. "We were young and both lost, searching for something to save us from the reality of our lives. That's not an excuse, just a symptomatic reason for the bad choices we both made."

I remain silent, taking in his words.

"Feeling alone when you're a kid is a shitty place to be in, but to actually be abandoned is worse. Especially when you feel like no one cares about you." He exhales.

Sitting up, I look down into his eyes. "Sounds like you both cared for each other."

"Like brothers. I stopped using senior year. My coach caught me smoking a joint after practice and threatened to pull the scout meetings he had set up for me. Those meetings were my ticket out. My freedom. And nothing was going to stop me from being free."

"Sean didn't want freedom too?"

"He kept dealing and using."

"Is that how he ended up in prison?"

"Yeah. I was in the car with him, heading to a graduation party, when we got pulled over. Sean had over four ounces of cocaine in the car. I learned later that he was planning to sell it at the party. Even though I had a clean record, I was still arrested and charged with possession and intent to distribute. Somehow, by the grace of god, the coach here, the prosecutor, and the judge agreed to let me off with no time served. I was placed on a five-year, zero-tolerance probation. Meaning if I so much as jaywalk, I can be arrested. Sean got fifteen years in federal prison. After serving three years, he killed himself."

With my index finger, I trace the curve of his jawline. "You only have a year left?"

He nods. "I have to meet with a parole officer every so often. Sometimes at the drop of a hat for random drug testing. That's why I tend to disappear occasionally."

My brows pull together and realization dawns on me. "That night in the laundry room, freshman year, you got a text and said you had to meet someone. Was that him?"

He dips his chin.

"Why didn't you tell me all this before, Lincoln?"

"I didn't want to drag you into my mess. My reality. You're too good for all that."

"Stop saying that. I'm not. Not really . . ." I trail off. "Anyway, you're lucky you got off with a slap on the wrist. You could have done some hard time."

"I know. One more year, and everything falls off my record. It all goes away as if it never happened. Except Sean's death. That will always be a dark stain on my soul."

I run my finger over his bottom lip. "Sean's death is on him. Not you."

"It's partly my fault," he mutters.

"No. It's not. The only thing you did wrong was get into a car with someone you knew was using and dealing drugs. You lost someone you cared about. And have spent the last four years making up for it. You made a poor choice, but that isn't a lifetime sentence."

"You make it sound so cut and dried."

"It is. You made a mistake, and you're paying the price."

"I never wanted to unload my secret on you, Em."

"Your secret is safe with me."

He blinks up at me and exhales a long, hard breath. "Even though I'm a different person than I was in high school—a better person—my past, it will always haunt me."

"Only if you let it." Our eyes lock for a few seconds.

"Tell me a secret," he whispers.

"For the first time in my life, I feel like I have something real. Something that no one can take away. Or control. Especially my parents."

"What's that?"

"You. Us. This." I motion between us. "Whatever it is, it's my decision, my choice."

With a slight frown, he brushes the tips of his fingers over my neck before trailing them up my jaw and then my cheek. I straddle him, my hair falling into his face. His hands begin to slide up my back, around my hips and then my waist as he pulls me closer, pressing his forehead against mine.

"I should never have kissed you," he sighs.

"I should never have let you."

"I'm serious. I don't deserve you."

"You do."

"I have demons."

"I'm not scared of your demons," I whisper across his lips.

"You should be. This has gone way past simple."

"Simple or not, being with you, like this, makes me happy."

Lincoln rolls us over so that I'm underneath him, bracing himself on his forearms above me so he won't crush me as he stares down into my eyes. His tight expression is guarded and yet, at the same time, dominant as he searches my gaze and licks his lips.

"I was so worried about protecting your heart, I didn't realize mine was in danger."

CHAPTER 21

I've stopped trying to figure out what Lincoln and I are. The little bit of information he shared with me a few weeks ago soothed the desire to know more about him, and things are no longer always so tense between us. We're finally having fun. Every once in a while, we even go out in between doing exactly what we agreed to do in the beginning of all this—have sex. Lots and lots of sex. Exclusively—a new rule we agreed to.

For now, we're both just taking what we can get and giving only what we want to.

No consequences.

Or talk of the future.

We're in his bed tonight. Just lying with one another, asking each other personal questions, and I love it so much. More so than any other day we've ever spent together.

My gaze falls onto his arm. Even though we're trying to keep things casual, Lincoln insisted on getting a tattoo. Something to remember our time together, he said. No matter how many times I tried to talk him out of it, he's got my name etched in an infinity design.

That way, we'll always be connected.

It's cheesy.

And so damn beautiful.

"How was practice today?" I ask.

Lincoln's baseball coach lined up an assistant athletic training job for him after graduation, which is only a month away, with a major league baseball team. It's an impressive three-year contract. They overlooked the fact that he has six months left of his probation when they met him and learned he was graduating with honors and more than the required training hours. Ever since, he's been a lot more relaxed and easygoing.

"Insane. I can't believe how much of a learning curve there is. But I love it. Plus, I get to travel all over and still be part of the game I love. So there's that," he replies.

He looks up at me with a peaceful expression as his eyes roam over my face.

"Any word from any of the design firms you applied to?"

"Not yet," I lie, as his fingers slide across my lips, trailing down my neck.

His eyes follow his fingers as they toy with the collar on my T-shirt, teasing me in a playful, relaxed manner. "Have you and Kennison decided to renew your lease?"

I gasp a little when his finger caresses the skin on my neck. "Not yet."

"I'm going to miss you living across the hall from where I live," he whispers.

The team is putting him up in an apartment in the city, closer to the ball field and a hospital where he's going to have to continue to work on his first aid and medical training.

I try to contain it, but his words cause me to frown. In just a few weeks, this will be all over and we'll disappear from each other's lives. He notices the change in me.

I hold my breath. I know he's going to remind me that this was all we were meant to be. That we can't be more than this. But I don't want him to. Not tonight. Tonight, I want more. Of him. Of us. His eyes dart to my mouth, then back up to my eyes again.

I see the flash of fear behind the gray.

The uncertainty.

His fingers have stilled on my collar.

Lincoln sits up on his knees and I do the same. He

slides his palms over my cheeks, cupping my face at the same moment his lips connect with mine in a deep kiss.

It's dominating. Full of something that's never been there before, something *more*.

I grab his shirt and pull him to me, closer, knowing something between us has changed. I want all of him, everywhere. There's not a part of me that I don't want him to own. I get lost in our consuming kiss that blurs the lines of where I end and he begins.

Warm fingers dig into the flesh of my waist under the cotton material of my shirt. I want him to throw me down on the bed and brand every inch of my body, making me his.

Unhurried, he leans away, putting a sliver of space between us. Painfully slowly, he pulls my shirt over my head, his gaze following the material with appreciation. Tossing it aside, his warm hands return to my body, his palms curling over my hips, sliding up my sides and my lower back. They keep moving up, edging to the clasp of my bra. In one quick flick, he undoes the clasp and slides the straps over my shoulders and down my arms with a sigh.

"You're so fucking beautiful, Em." His voice sounds pained.

With his right hand, he reaches behind his neck and yanks off his shirt.

I stroke his stubbled jaw. "So are you."

His lips touch mine again, soft and pleading, and his fingers undo the button of my jeans as I unbutton his. His mouth slips down across my throat, and his teeth nip a trail before kissing each quick bite. After a second, he pushes me gently onto my back and makes quick work of removing the rest of our clothes and rolling on a condom.

As soon as he's back over me, he pushes inside me without giving me a second to prepare. He stills, hovering above me with his hair falling into his eyes, staring at me.

Our lips don't touch as our breaths mingle and our eyes hold each other's. My hands cup his face as he slowly moves in me, never fully pulling out. With every thrust, his eyes stay on mine. My heart beats in perfect time with his as we get lost in each other.

This feels so different than all the other times we've done this—more intense.

"I like you, Em," he whispers hoarsely.

"I like you too, Lincoln," I breathe.

Faint sighs and throaty moans drift from my lips in response to his rhythm. I want to give him everything. To take everything. To stay in this moment forever. He lowers his hand between us, placing pressure against me in a way that has me almost blacking out, while at the same time he shifts angles, entering me deeper, slower with each thrust, taking his time.

"Oh, my *god*," I moan.

As I begin to shudder, he kisses me deeply as he thrusts and stills deep inside of me, holding me firmly against the bed with his weight. My body clenches around the length of him as above me, tremors rack his body, and we both fall into pure ecstasy, together.

CHAPTER 22

Lincoln kisses me harder as I try to get the door open. I've been trying to leave since last night, with no success. We spent the entire night lost in our own world. Turns out, we're good at making our level of crazy make sense when sex is involved.

"I have to go," I whisper against his mouth, trying to pull away.

"Come over later?" He finally releases me.

"I nod and bite my bottom lip, smiling up at him. "Just for a little while."

We're still staring at each other like giddy teenagers when he opens the door and I slip out, across the hallway and back into my apartment. It only takes a quick second before I realize I'd been so distracted by his lips, I left my phone in his kitchen.

"Damn it." I head back over, because I need it for the day.

I knock, but no one answers. I test the door knob and realize it's not locked, so I open it, slip inside, and quickly head into the kitchen. I make quick work of grabbing my phone and turn to slip out undetected, but I hear Josh and Lincoln arguing in another room.

Hearing my name, I decide to stay and listen, even though I shouldn't.

"How much longer are you going to let this go on with Emerson?" Josh asks.

"I don't know," Lincoln growls.

"Graduation is in a few weeks."

"I know."

"Are you planning to continue seeing her after?"

"Since when is any of this your business, Josh?"

"She's a nice girl, Daniels."

"And?"

"And she deserves more than what you are doing with her."

"Emerson is a grown woman. She can make her own decisions," Lincoln says.

"Do you even love her?" Josh asks point blank.

Silence.

Slowly I back away toward the door. Lincoln and I had been in such a good place this morning, and this conversation is wrecking it. I shouldn't have listened. I need to leave and pretend this never happened. We're doing fine. I don't want anything to change that.

"No," Lincoln states after a long pause, and I stop moving.

No.

I should have expected his answer. Still, hearing him say it out loud hurts.

"You're an asshole," Josh bites out.

"I never claimed to be anything but," Lincoln snaps out.

A second later, Lincoln steps into the living room. Every instinct in me suggests I duck and run for cover. I don't. Instead, I look into his terrified gaze. His eyes widen in surprise before turning apologetic and filling with regret. My heart pounds in my ears.

I hold up my phone in an explanation of why I am standing in his apartment without an invite. "I left it here. I knocked; you didn't answer," I say flatly.

Lincoln stares at me like I am foreign to him; reality and sadness crash down on me.

"I'm sorry, Em." Lincoln takes a step toward me, but I hold my hand up, stopping him.

"For what, exactly?"

"For what I'm sure you overheard."

"Did you mean it?"

"He had no right to ask me. I didn't want to lie to him."

I blink rapidly, fighting back tears of anger and hurt. "You've been nothing but honest about what you wanted from the start." My tone is low. "Haven't you?" I challenge.

"I just—"

"Don't," I exhale. "You didn't want to lie to Josh, so don't do it to me."

I back away toward the door, holding his gaze. This was all a mistake.

He stares at me. "Em." He swallows, his eyes darkening. "Wait a second."

"I can't."

"Em—"

"I can't do this anymore. We need to stop."

"No, we don't."

"I can't pretend I don't have feelings for you," I blurt out.

That stops him. His entire body becomes rigid and his expression tight.

"Fair enough," he replies coolly.

I nod and leave.

Lincoln doesn't stop me.

He lets me go.

———

I cross my arms, staring out the glass doors of my building, mentally bracing myself for the rain. I have to get to the campus center in order to grab my graduation cap and gown for this weekend. The minute I step into the heavy rain, I regret not having grabbed my umbrella. In a hurry, I take a few steps through the empty parking lot and get soaked.

I'm halfway to my car, considering going back and just doing this tomorrow instead, when I see Lincoln, leaning against the my driver's side door. What the hell is he doing here? After finals, he started traveling with his new job. I can't say it was unexpected. The distance it offered came as a relief. I'd finally managed to breathe again. Until tonight.

I stare straight at him. Droplets of rain run down my face and his. The parking lot's dim lights cast him in a soft glow. I notice his white T-shirt is soaked through, as are his jeans and heavy black boots. Clenching my teeth, I study the expression on his face.

Dark circles are etched under his eyes, as if he hasn't slept in days. Every sharp line of his face seems wired, on edge. His eyes meet mine, and suddenly, I feel vulnerable and weak. I squeeze my eyes tightly and take in a deep breath to calm myself and get control of my emotions. When I slide them open, Lincoln is watching me, eerily calm.

I take my time approaching him. Something feels off. Different.

The rain falls around us in a merciless assault as I stop in front of him.

"Why are you here, Lincoln?"

"I don't know." The uncertainty in his voice cuts through me like a knife.

I sigh. One of has to be the stronger person here. Guess it's me.

"Just let me go." My voice is flat.

Fury flashes in his eyes. "I can't. I tried."

Numb, I just stand in the rain, letting it soak me, chill me to my bones.

"We both knew this was always meant to end. So let it," I plead.

"You don't just fall out of lo—" he starts, then stops.

My stomach twists. "Fall out of what?"

Something changes in his expression. The look on his face is one I've never seen before. Like he's about to tell me something I don't want to hear. Something that will hurt me. In one move, he lunges for me, cupping my face in his hands and looks deep into my eyes, as if he's trying to brace me for something.

Dread grips me as I stare at him.

"On the flight home, I got to thinking," he whispers.

"About?"

"You."

I remain silent, terrified of his words. I used to live and breathe for his words. Now, they cause a deep fear within me. As if each one is a tiny bomb, ready to blow up my world.

"I kept thinking, what if, this thing between us turned into more?"

The word *more* slays me, because I know it doesn't mean love. It just means he's afraid of losing me. It's as if everything he's made me feel all this time hits me all at once and ignites an angry fire within me. The sincerity in his voice is too much for me to handle.

I pull my face away and shake my head no. "I can't do this anymore."

I try to step around him, but he grips my upper arms and twists us, pushing me back against the wet car. I still under his hold as the rain jumps off the metal roof behind me.

"Don't walk away, please." His voice is timid.

His fingers tighten around my arm—so much so, I can feel the hurt in his heart.

We stand quietly in the rain. After a second, Lincoln takes a step away from me.

"This was supposed to be uncomplicated," I remind him.

"We were never *not* complicated, Em." His tone sounds bitter. "Since the moment we met, everything about us has been nothing but fucking complicated."

His words bring more tears to my eyes, because I know they're true. They mix in with the rain, washing away as Lincoln releases me and take a few steps, giving me space.

"What do you want from me, Lincoln?" I whisper.

"Honestly, I don't know," he says flatly, barely catching his breath.

I exhale at his indecisiveness.

"What if—"

I shake my head, cutting him off. "I can't live in our world of *ifs* anymore."

The rain is coming down in sheets now. Holding my eyes, he walks backwards, taking a few steps away from me, and even as close as he is, I can barely make out his silhouette.

Watching him disappear in the rain breaks something inside me, and I panic. I take a step toward him. He clenches his jaw and shakes his head no, taking another step away.

Emotions flood through me—hate, guilt, grief . . . love.

My heart aches with so many emotions, I can barely keep track of all of them.

Everything we've ever been through replays in my mind and at the end of it, the last memory is of him kissing me. I don't want to be done. I want him to know that I love him.

With one final sad smile, he turns.

Just before he disappears in the rain completely, I rush after him.

"Wait," I shout.

Lincoln stops and faces me.

I take a step toward him, holding his gaze. "I lo—"

A sharp white light from the side blinds me, interrupting me.

It takes me a second to realize what it is and when I do, I panic and fly at him, shoving him out of the way. Tires screech loudly at the same time sharp pains rack my body.

Everything suddenly falls silent around me, except for the lulling sound of the rain and Lincoln screaming out my name, just before everything goes black.

CHAPTER 23

The hospital bed creaks and moans underneath me as I shift. An ache in my left side quickly makes itself known, stealing the breath from my lungs. I wince as a sharp pain shoots down my body. A second later, relief rushes through my veins, ending the pain.

"There," the nurse says. "The morphine should help take the edge off."

"Thanks," I manage, and look around the stark hospital room.

"Where is she?" Kennison's demanding, high-pitched voice shrieks outside the door before she storms in and makes a beeline straight for me. "Holy shit, Em. Are you okay? Lincoln left me a message that you were . . . hit. By. A. Car," she emphasizes each word.

I rub at my head. "Who are you?"

"OH MY GOD!" She pins the nurse with a hard glare. "She has no memory?"

The nurse frowns and shakes her head at me. "She's fine. Just a bruised rib, a few scratches, and a sprained wrist. We're only keeping her for another hour for observation."

Kennison's narrow stare meets mine. "Who am I?" Her tone is annoyed.

"Hi Kenz," I smile up at her.

"You're lucky you almost died. I swear to *god*, Em."

Once the nurse finishes checking my vitals, she slides out the room.

Kennison sits on the bed beside me. "Seriously, are you okay?"

"I'm fine. Sore, but the drugs are helping."

"When I got Lincoln's message, my heart stopped."

"Where is he?"

"The ER. They're putting stiches on a gash above his eye. Josh is with him."

"But he's okay?"

"He's fine. He was giving his statement to the police officer when they finally told me what room you were in and how to get up here so that I could see you."

My eyes widen. "Police officer?"

"The guy who hit you had been drinking. With the rain, he didn't see you guys standing there. You're lucky. When you pushed Lincoln, he rolled you under him, protecting you. Then he managed to get you guys out of the way before he ran over you."

"Really?" I frown.

"If he hadn't reacted so quickly, I hate to think about what would have happened."

"Damn. I thought I saved him," I pout.

She rolls her eyes. "It's not a competition. What the hell were you two doing in a dark parking lot in the rain anyway? I thought you were getting your cap and gown?"

"He was waiting for me at my car, and we started talking."

A quiet knock at the door has both of us looking up to see Lincoln walk in with Josh.

Lincoln throws Kenz and me a tight smile.

My eyes immediately go to the bandage over his right eye.

"You okay, Emerson?" Josh asks quietly, and I nod.

"She's good," Kennison replies for me. "We have an hour before they release her."

Josh inclines his head toward the door. "Let's get some coffee then."

Her lips pucker in a small frown as she looks me over. "Will you be okay if I leave?"

I hum my agreement and wave her off. "Bring me back a cheeseburger."

She rolls her eyes and slides out of the room with Josh, leaving me alone with Lincoln.

He steps closer to the bed, sliding his hands into the front pockets of his jeans. His eyes look up and down the length of me, taking me in, before he gives me a pensive look.

"What you did was . . ." he begins.

"Heroic?"

"Stupid."

"I thought I was saving your life," I mutter.

"Why?"

"Why?" I pin him with a hard look. "Because you're worth saving, Lincoln."

"I don't need you to save me, Em."

At his words, something happens to me. I don't know what, but it's as if he's stabbed me in the heart. I want to scream at him. I'm tired of him thinking that he's not worthy of love. Of something good in his life. Of me. I'm done pretending I don't love him.

"Well, you did tonight," I counter.

"Do not ever put yourself in a dangerous situation again because of me."

"For the record, this is the worst thank you I have ever received."

"This isn't funny," he snaps.

"I know." I look him directly in the eyes. "Nothing about *us* is funny."

He cocks his head to the side and narrows his eyes as he considers me intently.

"You could have died tonight."

"So could you."

He looks at me, seeming calm, but I see his jaw clench.

I notice that everything about him has changed since yesterday.

A part of me has been holding on to the hope that he'll eventually overcome whatever it is that is holding him back and tell me how he really feels. Earlier, in the rain, I thought I saw a glimpse of it. Now, it's gone. Disappearing, along with my hope.

I've lost it.

Lost him.

But you can't lose what you never had.

Watching Kennison wash dishes is like watching an elephant take a bath. There is water everywhere, and she used way too much dish soap. Bubbles are literally flying all over the kitchen. I shift on the counter and continue to pick the M&Ms out of the trail mix.

"Are you ready for tomorrow?" she asks, her back turned to me.

"Which part—graduation, or my parents?" I groan.

She throws a knowing smile over her shoulder. "Both."

"Graduation? Yes." I pause, fingering the contents of the bowl, pushing away all the gross raisins and sad nuts. "Can one ever truly be ready for Emily and Thomas Shaw?"

Finished, she turns to face me, wiping her wet fingers on the towel.

"What?" I ask, because she's giving me that look.

"Have you told Lincoln yet?" she asks.

I put the bowl of trail mix down. "Told him what?"

"That you got a job? That you're moving?"

I shake my head. "That would involve calling or texting. Or speaking."

"So?" she laughs.

"So, we don't do those things anymore."

"Ah." A sympathetic smile spreads on her lips.

A quick knock on the door has us both glancing over at it, neither of us moving.

"He's your boyfriend," I sigh, referring to Josh. "You have door duty."

Kennison rolls her eyes at my response and walks over to it, opening it.

"Hey, thanks for coming over," she says to whoever is at the door.

Lincoln comes into the kitchen and Kennison smiles at me from behind him.

I narrow my eyes at the traitor before she winks and motions to the door. "I'm going to go across the hall and see if Josh needs help packing. Be back later." She leaves us alone.

Lincoln leans against the wall and folds his arms across his chest, his eyes roaming over me. We stare at one another for a few silent seconds. What's left to say?

"What do you want?" I clip out.

His eyes are everywhere now but on my face.

"Kennison asked me to check on your injuries," he admits softly.

Ugh. The sneaky, conniving brat. "Did she?"

He dips his chin in confirmation. "How are you feeling?"

"My wrist is fine. My rib is still a little tender," I mumble.

He looks me over, not believing my quick response.

"Mind if I take a look?" He motions to my wrist.

I chew on the inside of my cheek. After a second, I hold out my wrist to him.

He pushes off the wall and strides over to me, taking my wrist in his hand. Carefully, he pushes up my sleeve and inspects it. He makes quick work of removing the bandage the hospital put on it for support. Once it's off, he looks at the bruises and applies a gentle pressure on it. It hurts, but I don't let it show. After a moment, he grabs the bandage and rewraps it a bit tighter, which actually feels much better.

The pain subsides with the added pressure.

When he's done, our eyes lock, and I exhale the breath I was holding.

"That should feel better now," he smiles.

"How did you know it hurt?"

"I know you, Em."

He does know me. Part of me hates that he does. And part of me loves it.

He stares at me, and I do my best to ignore the way he's breathing.

"Can I look at your rib?"

"Yeah," I say in a quiet whisper, wondering where the rest of my voice went.

Stepping between my legs, he holds my gaze while gently lifting up the side of my shirt. I should be focusing on how my rib aches, but instead, I get lost in the feel of his warm fingertips as they brush against my skin. He grazes my rib and goose bumps form across my body. Definitely *not* the way the doctor did this at the hospital.

His hand slowly begins to slide around my waist to my back. Swallowing, he removes his hand and drops the material of my shirt. It feels like his hand left marks everywhere he touched. His breath fans my face and all I want is to be swallowed up by him.

"Is there still an ache there?" he asks quietly.

I inhale through my nose, feeling like his words have a double meaning.

"A little," I barely say.

Slowly he begins to lift his fingers to my face, placing them under my jaw as his thumbs tilt my head up. His eyes roam over the scratches that have almost disappeared.

"Any headaches?"

I shake my head no.

When he's done, he holds my face in place and looks into my eyes. For a moment, we just stare at one another, lost in our own thoughts. He swallows and his lips part.

"Seeing you in the hospital," his voice shakes. "It made me realize something."

"What?"

"I don't want to pretend I don't have feelings for you anymore," he whispers. "You could have died, Em. The fact that you pushed me out of the way—" He pauses. "You risked your life for mine," he growls. "Seeing you lying on the ground, hurt, in the rain . . ."

"Hey," I tilt my head. "I'm fine. I'm here."

Lincoln's jaw tenses. "I still don't think I'm good enough for you. I've had a fucked up life and made a ton of mistakes, most of which I'm still paying for. I mean, my issues have issues." His voice has taken on a heartbreaking tone. "But, if you're willing try, so am I."

That familiar lump in the bottom of my throat suddenly makes a comeback.

"Are you saying this because you're afraid of losing me?" I ask.

I squeeze my eyes tightly, bracing for whatever words he is about to say; I somehow know they will slay me. He blows out a steady, controlled breath while he looks at me.

"Partly. I can't imagine a world where you don't exist," he replies.

My lips part and it seems like it's taking forever for me to catch my breath.

"In fact, I don't want to live in a world where you don't exist. Do you understand?"

Silent tears run down my face, and he becomes impatient with my lack of response.

"Fuck it," he says, taking my face in his hands and kissing me, hard, catching me completely off guard.

My heart beats wildly as he moves his thumbs lazily over my cheeks. I can feel him thinking. I break away from his lips, gasping for breath as I study his expression.

"And partly because," he whispers, "I might be in love with you."

His voice is soft and deep in the quietness of the room.

"Might be?" I blink.

A shaky breath escapes him. "Am. I am in love with you."

My lips part in shock. He's in love with me? Oh, god.

I've waited for this moment for four fucking years.

And now, I have to go and completely ruin it.

I *have* to tell him.

"I'm moving to California," I blurt.

He stares at me with a torn look on his face. "What?"

"The design firm I interned at in London has a Los Angeles office. They offered me a job and are willing to relocate me." I swallow hard over the dread in my throat.

Squinting, he rubs his fingertips across his forehead and then down his face. He's quiet for a long time as he stares at me, considering what I've said.

I'm almost afraid to move.

Afraid of his response.

When his lips part to finally speak, I still. "What if . . . maybe we find a way to make it work? We could still see each other when I'm traveling to LA with the team."

Hope fills me. "That's true."

"We can call. Text. FaceTime. We can work around it. If you want to."

"Really?" I ask. "Calling and texting is . . . new for us."

"I think we can handle it," he smiles.

"We're really going to do this?"

"We'll take it day by day. No pressure."

"Uncomplicated?" I smile back at him.

He laughs, stepping toward me again. "I think we're way past uncomplicated."

CHAPTER 24

L incoln is watching me. I can feel his eyes on me from the other side of the tent. I bite my lip, wishing we weren't surrounded by every last member of the graduating class and their friends and families. Because he looks amazing in his black dress pants and dress shirt. The sleeves on it are rolled up to his elbows, showing off his tattoos.

He still hasn't shared what each one means to him. Only the reason for the one with my name subtly designed into the infinity sign. There are still so many things left unknown between us, but we still have plenty of time to learn them.

My mother texts me for the hundredth time, asking me to come outside the tent for our photos because she wants the sunshine and greenery in the background.

When I meet Lincoln's gaze, I give him a smile and

incline my head toward the door, letting him know where I'll be. He lifts his chin in response but keeps talking with Tyler and Josh. They are going out to celebrate, so I won't see him until later anyway.

As I round the corner, my pretentious mother's form comes into sight. When I approach, she doesn't say anything at first, just looks at me. Her gaze focuses on the bandage on my wrist. Both my parents were unhappy when I called them to explain what happened. Meaning well, Kennison had made the mistake of letting them know I was in the hospital. This led to excessive phone calls, plastic surgeon FaceTimes—in the event my face was forever scarred by the tiny scratches—and my mother reminding me of how I never seem to be able to make good decisions about my life. The accident included.

"There you are," my mother finally sighs.

"Here I am," I push out.

"Wrinkles are forming on my face as I wait for you in the sun," she huffs.

"That's what they have Photoshop for, Mother," I retort.

"Emerson, please try to curb your witty remarks today."

We take the obligatory graduation mantel photos and my father slips away as my mother and I mingle with my friends. My father is an alumnus here, so he is circulating, talking to his fraternity brothers and other alumni, making a sizable donation.

An hour later, my parents and I are sitting in the private room at my father's favorite restaurant, celebrating my graduation and discussing my upcoming move to California.

"What are Kennison's plans now that she has graduated?" My mother sips her wine, eyeing me over the rim of her glass. "She does have plans, Emerson, doesn't she?"

I shift under her gaze, uneasy. "Of course she has plans."

Normally when my mother looks at me over her wine glass, she is setting me up for something. Nine times out of ten, it's a lecture from my father.

"Well?" my mother prompts. "What are they?"

"She got a teaching job near campus. Third graders."

"How charming," Mom uses her fake-excited tone. "Where will she live?"

"Josh is going to move into our apartment, since his roommate, Lincoln, is leaving."

My mother lowers her glass, holding it with two hands as her lips flatten at the mention of Lincoln. For whatever reason, they were less than pleased that he was involved in the accident. And even less pleased that he lives across from me.

"Emerson," my father's deep voice fills the empty room. "Your mother and I wish to have a word with you about the accident you were recently involved in with Mr. Daniels."

I take in his speculative look and sit back in my chair. "What about it?"

"Mr. Daniels is not someone whose company we want you keeping," he states.

I look between the two of them, confused. "You don't even know him."

My mother glances at my father quickly, then down at the table.

"I know Mr. Daniels quite well." He sits back in his chair, eyeing me.

"How? Did you hire a private investigator?" It wouldn't be the first time. Or the last.

My father has a habit of wanting to know everything there is to know about everyone.

"No."

"Then how do you know Lincoln?"

"Your father was the judge who tried his case, Emerson," my mother interjects.

My lips part and I laugh incredulously. "You can't be serious."

"I assure you, your mother is very serious." His voice booms around the room.

"I don't understand."

"It's simple. Coach Dawson asked me to oversee Mr. Daniels's case. As a financial contributor and alumnus of your school, I agreed. Aside from owing the coach a personal favor, financial endowments are easier to obtain when your sports teams win playoffs. A Division I school needs the best players to make those wins possible. Like Mr. Daniels."

I'm floored, my gaze sliding between the two of them. Given their history, it shouldn't surprise me that not only was my father the judge on Lincoln's case, but that later, he threw money around to control the situation and leverage his position of power.

We're all just puppets in my father's financially focused world.

"Does he know I'm your daughter?" I grit out through clenched teeth.

"Not that I'm aware of," he says, looking anything but happy.

My heart suddenly free-falls, and I have to turn away from him.

The one thing I thought my parents could never control, or be part of, was Lincoln.

I was wrong. My father is the judge that oversees his parole.

He controls Lincoln's future.

And in turn, mine.

"Oh, god," I whisper.

I shake my head, but the tears won't stop threatening to fall. Somewhere deep inside, I know my father is about to take him away. Take away the one real thing I've ever had.

"From Kennison, it has come to our attention that your relationship with Mr. Daniels is"—he searches for the right words—"personal in nature. Even inappropriate at times."

I stare at my father's tight expression and I realize in this moment, this is it.

Lincoln's past will be the reason we can't ever have a future.

There is no way in hell my father will allow it.

"There is nothing *inappropriate* about it. I love him," I whisper.

My father looks me over, appalled at my outburst. "No. You don't."

"It's a really long story, but I do." My voice is small, childlike.

"Good god, Emerson, you have absolutely no common sense when it comes to choosing men," my mother hisses, placing her crystal glass on the white linen.

"It's an unacceptable match," Judge Shaw says plainly. "We don't approve."

My father's words cut through my soul. "He's not the person he once was."

"Emerson," my father deepens his tone. "Since it's apparent he's made this known to you, I feel the need to reiterate that Mr. Daniels was almost sent to prison for possession and dealing. He's lucky Coach Dawson was in his life and put his name and career on the line for him. Otherwise things could have ended differently for him. He. Is. Not. Suitable."

"Has he ever once missed a parole meeting? Or failed a single drug test?" I challenge.

"You know I am not at liberty to answer either of those questions."

"He hasn't. I know he hasn't. That isn't who he is. Jesus, he just graduated cum laude. With a sports medicine degree and a job with a major league baseball team," I argue, almost hysterically.

"Regardless. I won't allow it. You are the daughter of a federal judge for god's sake, one that oversaw his federal drug trial. I sign off on all his parole meetings, Emerson."

"You can't take him away. I'm an adult now."

"That is quite enough," my mother scolds, and I snap my gaze to hers. "Your father's decision on the matter is final. You are no longer to see this young man. Adult or not."

I sit back in my chair and exhale. My gaze slides between the two of them, because no matter how much

I argue or fight for Lincoln, their decision isn't going to change.

Politely, I fold my napkin and place it on the bone china in front of me.

I push out my chair and stand, lifting my chin and straightening my spine.

"Sit down," my father orders.

I ignore his demand. "Thank you for dinner. I am going to call an Uber, go home, and finish packing for the movers. They're coming tomorrow to take my stuff to LA."

I turn and walk to the door, stopping when my father's cold voice booms after me.

"Emerson," he clips out.

I don't face him. I already know what Judge Shaw is going to say.

"Mr. Daniels has a few months left on his zero-tolerance probation. It would be a shame if something occurred where he violated the terms set forth by me, including visiting certain people or places that may potentially jeopardize his parole. Or even committing other crimes or offenses, such as being involved in motor vehicle violations."

My jaw clenches as I reach for the doorknob. "He wasn't driving the car."

"Mr. Daniels's limitations are clearly defined in my order. If I feel certain individuals in his life are hindering his rehabilitation, I can, and will, step in to remove his rights to see or communicate with those individuals. Including you," he warns.

I swallow the tears, knowing his threats aren't empty. "Are you saying, if I don't walk away from him, you'll put him in jail for violating his probation?"

"Mr. Daniels has a bright future ahead of him. As do you. It would be a terrible tragedy for either of those futures to be ruined by a case of infatuation." His tone is sharp.

And there it is. I have no choice.

If I don't end things with Lincoln, his future will be ruined.

Resigned, I wipe away the lone tear that has fallen down my cheek.

"I'll end things with Lincoln," I say flatly, meeting my father's pleased look with anger. "But I won't do it for you." My eyes slide to my mother. "Or you." I inhale through my nose, pulling the door open. "I'll do it for him. And only him. We're done here."

I turn my back on them, leaving my parents in the past.

Lincoln will be the last piece of my life they will ever control.

CHAPTER 25

I 'm staring at the door across the hall. I haven't yet found the courage to knock. I have no idea what to say, or how to end this. Maybe saying nothing at all is better than saying everything. I told Kenz I was coming over here to say goodbye, but that's a lie. I'm here because I just want one more minute with him before I break his heart and mine.

I love him, which is why I will do what my father has asked.

I've loved him from the first moment he stepped into my world.

Even though he warned me not to.

Lifting my hand, I knock on his door. It opens instantly and my eyes fall to his feet, because if we lock gazes, he'll see desperation and fear, not courage. Because Lincoln sees me, not the façade I always wear.

There's no immediate reaction from him. He senses my apprehension. He knows me. I hold my breath, my gaze finally making the journey up to his. A torn look crosses his expression as he pulls me into his chest in a tight embrace. He doesn't say anything. I wrap my arms around him, burying my nose in his chest and, for just a moment, I let myself pretend that my father didn't threaten to take away his future.

Lincoln closes the door and pulls back a little. Lifting a hand, he brushes away a teardrop on one side of my cheek, then the other; I hadn't even realized I was crying.

Frowning, he cups my face, stroking my cheeks with his thumbs. The gesture is so heartbreakingly tender that I have to close my eyes as more tears fall. Then I feel them. His lips softly brush mine, causing a quiet sob to escape from the back of my throat.

I kiss him back. His thumbs continue to stroke my cheeks, taking away the tears as he kisses me in a way he hasn't before. It's soft, tender, and full of promises to take away whatever is hurting me. Sighing, he pulls away, moving his right hand from my cheek, his fingers running through my hair and down my back, resting on my lower back.

With his other hand, he cups my face, dropping his forehead to mine.

"I don't want to talk tonight." My voice is strained and thin.

Lincoln looks at me with a mixture of desire and resignation. As if he knows this moment is all we have. Without a word, he holds his hand out, waiting for me to take it.

I take a deep breath and slide my palm over his. He squeezes my hand and guides me into his bedroom, shutting the door behind us. Cocooning us in our own private world.

With our fingers interlaced, he tugs me toward the bed. Sitting down, he brings me forward so I'm standing between his legs as he releases my hand. His fingers wrap around my waist and he leans his forehead on my stomach. I shiver and lift my hands, sliding my fingers into the soft strands of hair on the top of his head. We stay like this for a moment.

Lincoln's hands slide off my waist and over my ass before he runs his fingertips up and down over the backs of my bare legs, just below the hem of my skirt.

I shiver at his touch, trying not to think about how cold and empty I will feel without him. Chasing my goose bumps, his fingers move up my leg, under my skirt, until they reach the bottom curve of my ass.

Slowly, he traces the seam of my panties with his fingers, making my blood heat and my skin tingle. When his hands slide under the material, squeezing my ass, I grip his hair tighter. His fingers twist in my panties. He takes his time pulling them down as he slides off the bed, lowering himself onto his knees in front of me. At the same time, his hands drift over the back of my legs—slowly taking the thin material with them—behind my knees, ending at my ankles. Letting the garment fall, his hands return to the back of my calves.

As I step out of my panties, kicking them to the side, his hands slide back up until they reach my ass again. Lincoln grins up at me before his head disappears under my skirt, the material covering him so I can't see what he's doing. But I can feel it. Every touch. I gasp as his fingers find my damp center, already heated and aching for his touch. My legs shake as he slips his fingers inside of me and flicks them back and forth. My eyes become heavy with his assault and I squeeze them shut when his tongue finds my clit, circling it with languid strokes that match the rhythm of his fingers. Mine dig into the tops of his shoulders, partly for support, and partly from pleasure. He takes his time, savoring me.

I bite my bottom lip and cry out when his teeth nip at the sensitive spot he was circling with his tongue. Of their own accord, my hips buck forward as he picks up the pace, licking and sucking me with his tongue, stroking with his fingers. I make a guttural moan as my body pulses around him. My thighs shake and I push up on my toes. Lincoln growls against me, sinking his fingers more deeply into me. I moan in response, and whisper his name.

He pushes on my clit a little harder and with one last long lick, I cry out, yanking on a handful of his hair. His fingers and mouth disappear before he squeezes my ass and leans back, his head emerging from under my skirt. In one smooth move, he stands.

Gripping my ass tighter, he lifts me, turns us and gently tosses me onto the bed. Before I have time to catch my breath, he pulls a condom out of his night-stand, undoes his pants, and removes them quickly, along with his boxers and shirt. After kicking his clothes away with his foot, he rolls the condom down his shaft and then he's over me. In one, long, smooth stroke he slides inside of me and my entire body clamps down on his.

Lincoln breathes into my neck, burying his nose in the curve of my shoulder. He rocks his hips into me and grunts as I lift mine slightly. We barely move against one another. His thrusts are steady, unhurried. With each one, he goes deeper and deeper. Taking as I give him everything.

His face appears above me and leans down, his mouth a millimeter from mine as he grinds into me slowly. Intense eyes hold mine. Our lips never meet; they just hover there, almost touching. Both of us holding our breaths the entire time. It's sensual and carnal.

This is something better and more gratifying than sex.

It's a deep connection. One that we'll only have with each other.

I whisper his name as I come apart.

When he follows me over the edge, he grinds out my name before dropping a searing kiss on my lips, lowering his weight onto me, pressing me into the mattress, fitting perfectly against me. It's a shame nothing else in our lives fits this way. So completely.

A strong hand presses hard on my lower back, pressing me more firmly against a muscular back. My right cheek nestles into the cool sheet covering the soft mattress.

The movement causes the tip of my nose to brush against the smooth skin on Lincoln's back. The curve of his tight, bare ass presses against my stomach as we lay sleeping on our sides, both of us in an odd position, facing his tufted gray headboard.

I curl into the warmth of his body and his left hand drapes over my left hip, over the light fabric of the white sheet. We haven't left his room the entire night. Nor had we spoken, other than crying out each other's names in quiet whispers and deep moans.

My eyes flutter open, and I stare at the middle of his perfect back.

Exhaling a shaky breath, I realize just how much I'm going to miss him.

Saying goodbye to him is going to leave a scar on my heart.

CHAPTER 26

I feel the tears burning at the back of my eyes. I thought loving Lincoln Daniels was overwhelming. Love had nothing on missing him. I sink into the chair at the terminal. The weight of what I've done, what I've *had to do*, consumes me. It will for a long time.

I'm running away.

Running away from what I'm feeling.

Running away from my father's control.

Running away from Lincoln's past and our future.

I look at my phone, sighing. Kennison drove me to the airport this afternoon with tears in both our eyes. I'm going to miss her. I take a deep breath, reminding myself that she'll be visiting in February, during her teaching break. After the movers showed up this morning, and there was nothing left to distract me, I booked an earlier flight to California.

I handed the key over to Kennison to give to Josh, scanned the apartment one last time to make sure I packed everything, and bolted. I know it was selfish, but I just couldn't face Lincoln again and hurt him. So I took the coward's way out and ran away.

Numb, I stare out the window, watching the planes take off and land as I recall our last moments together this morning.

"Hey," Lincoln rasps through his morning grog. "Where are you going so early?"

"Go back to sleep," I smile sadly at him, getting dressed. "I have to go."

"Come back to bed." He shifts onto his side, looking at me from his pillow.

"The movers will be here soon. I have to go make sure every-thing is pulled together."

Lincoln frowns, watching me slip my skirt on. "What time will they be done?"

I shrug, averting my gaze. "Not sure."

"I have to head into the city for a team meeting. I should be done in time to take you to dinner tonight. You up for a night out, followed by a night in?" he asks, watching my every move.

Nodding, I tuck a piece of my hair behind my ear and cut him a look out of the corner of my eye. "Sounds great." I try to make my voice sound light, but it comes off as shaky and timid.

"Em," Lincoln's tone is deep and dominating. "Look at me."

Swallowing, I meet his gaze.

"We're going to make this work." I wish his words were true.
I just stare at him. Not wanting to let go. But I have to.
"I love you," I whisper. "Always remember that."
Something crosses his eyes as he stares at me. "I love you, too."

My phone beeps with a text message. I look down and see it's from Lincoln.

Lincoln: Look behind you

I stare at the three words before squeezing my eyes closed, exhaling heavily. I know he's standing behind me. Even before the text came in, I knew he was there. I felt his presence. I stand and turn slowly, my gaze colliding with his stormy one. He's leaning against the check-in desk, holding his phone. Unshaved. In jeans and a T-shirt.

He's staring at me with a mixture of longing and pissed off contemplation.

I didn't want to see him.

I didn't want a confrontation.

I didn't want to say goodbye, not like this.

I just wanted to disappear.

I just wanted this to be easy.

I just wanted . . . uncomplicated.

Lincoln narrows his eyes and takes three large steps

toward me. I back up, keeping a healthy amount of space between us. As I do, he stops advancing. The expression on his face is hard. Furious. And full of disbelief that I have the gall to back away from him.

We stare silently at one another for a long time, until he rubs his hands over his face.

"Fucking say something here, Em." His voice is low and deep, gutting me.

A few of the other passengers seated near us share quick glances.

"I thought they only allowed ticketed passengers at the gate."

"I bought a ticket. Fucking say something else," he snaps.

"How did you know I'd be here?"

"Josh called. After Kennison told him that she dropped you off."

Exhaling slowly, I nod my understanding. "Those two can't keep a secret. I swear."

He watches me with a torn look on his face. "What's going on here, Em?"

Exhaling slowly, my eyes dart around the airport before landing on him again.

"You were right all along. We have to end this, Lincoln."

"I thought we had this all figured?" he points out calmly.

"We did. But—"

"But what?"

"Things have changed."

"What things?"

My hands are trembling. I become so wrapped up in my own head and my own spiral of emotional nonsense that I don't pay attention to the fact that he's taken a step toward me.

"What things, Em?" he snarls.

"My father." The words fall out before I realize what I've said.

His eyes narrow. "What the hell does your father have to do with any of this?"

I look over at an older woman watching us with bated breath.

"I can't do this here."

Lincoln scoffs, holding his arms out to his sides. "This is where you chose to have this conversation when you left this afternoon without saying a fucking word to me. I mean, what were you even planning on doing, Em? Moving to California and blowing me off?"

The moment I fall silent, understanding crosses his face.

"Holy shit. You were?" He pins me with a hard stare.

"Yes," I admit quietly.

"Why? Why the fuck would you do this to me? To us?"

"My father is Judge Shaw," I answer flatly.

His face falls and he takes in a sharp breath. "What?"

I nod and watch a thousand emotions cross over his face as realization sinks in.

"He informed me during my graduation dinner that he—" I pause, looking around again at the passengers watching and listening. Annoyed, I walk over to Lincoln, grab his wrist, and pull him into a private corner near the gate's door so we can speak more privately.

Angry, he yanks his wrist out of my hold. "Don't touch me. Not now."

I lift my chin, trying not to appear hurt. "My father told me that he was the judge who oversaw your case. That he signs off on your parole officer's reports."

Lincoln's jaw clenches. "Yes. A Judge Shaw is in charge of my case."

"Did you know I was his daughter?"

"No, Em. I had no friggin' idea that Judge Shaw was your father."

I search his eyes, the truth as clear as day behind the angry storm brewing in them.

"I would never have put you in that position if I had known," he adds.

"I know you wouldn't," I reply blankly.

My shoulders sag from the weight of everything lingering between us.

Taking advantage of the fact that my guard is down for the briefest moment, Lincoln steps into my space, not giving me time to retreat. I tilt my head back to meet his gaze.

"That's the reason that you're running from this?" He motions between us.

Blinking, I chew on the inside of my cheek. I don't want him knowing my father threatened his future. He doesn't need to know. It's better if he thinks it's something else.

"My father is the judge in charge of your parole," I state. "Our relationship could put his job at risk. Besides," I pause, swallowing. "How do you think it's going to look if a judge's daughter is dating a parolee?" The words taste like poison coming out.

He goes unfocused for a moment; he's lost in thought.

"If I didn't know any better, I'd think you were shoving my past in my face."

I stand my ground, staring straight into his eyes.

I have to do this. I have no choice. I have to be strong.

"Your past is the reason we can never have a future."

He closes his eyes, trying to compose himself, and I glance around, seeing that we're making a scene. People are walking by slowly, staring, and whispering to each other. Heat spreads across my cheeks, triggering my eyes to water. I need him to just . . . leave.

"I know what you're trying to do." He opens them again, pinning me with a look.

"I'm trying to say goodbye."

He shakes his head, cupping my face. "Don't," he whispers hoarsely, dipping his head so our noses are almost touching. "Don't do this. Whatever shit you're spinning in that beautiful head of yours, stop. I need you. We said we'd try. We can face whatever it is."

"I don't want you," I barely push out.

Hurt flickers across his face. "I don't want anyone else but you."

His words are like a punch to the gut. I flinch, unsure if I can do this.

I remind myself I have to.

"It was only sex, Lincoln. Nothing more," I lie. "We can . . . still be friends."

Abruptly, he lets go of me. "You want to be just friends. Fine, we're friends. But you and I both know that what's between us isn't just sex. It's more. So much more."

The intercom comes on, and the agent invites first class passengers to board.

"They're boarding. I have to go," I say quietly.

He steps back. "Don't do something here you will regret for the rest of your life. You can stand here and pretend not to give a shit about me all you want, but I know that you're lying. I've seen how you look at me. I know that you love me. I see you, Em."

I swallow back the tears, pressing my back against the wall.

"Do you hear me?" he hisses. "I know it's easier to pretend that I mean nothing to you, rather than to bear the thought of leaving. But I deserve better than that. And so do you."

"I'm sorry. I don't love you," I lie, just needing him to stop.

"Fine. You don't love me. All this was just about sex. Guess what? I don't love you."

I physically flinch at his words—my body jerks back, and my knees almost give out.

I close my eyes in pain, hating that he caused so much hurt so deep inside of me.

Tears threaten, stinging my eyes. "I'm sorry, Lincoln. For all of it."

I storm past him and exhale the breath I was holding. An escaping tear falls down my cheek and I quickly wipe it away, not looking back at him. I don't want him to see my pain.

My heart aches with so many emotions, I can't keep track of them all.

I guess that happens when you lose everything.

CHAPTER 27

F rozen, I stare at Lincoln. We tried. We tried so damn hard, frantically and desperately holding on to each other. I know this, because I was the cause of our destruction.

In the end, letting go was the only option.

With Lincoln, there is no future—only the ifs that linger.

Cocking his head, he does that thing he always does when he stares at me. He looks directly at me. Not through me. Not around me. But *at* me. To the point that I become the sole focus of his attention, pulling me in and making everything around us fall away.

It's addicting. Even more so because this look is only mine.

He never does it with anyone else.

Like a familiar dance, everything around me in the

church fades away as my feet automatically walk to him. I don't think, or care, about anyone else in this moment.

And that's the problem—when it comes to Lincoln, nothing else matters.

There is only him and me in our world.

He pushes his tall frame off the pew he was leaning on and stalks toward me without releasing my gaze. I become light-headed because I still haven't taken a breath. Lincoln always did take up all the air in the room, making something as simple as breathing become a chore.

When only a sliver of space separates us, he wraps his arms around my waist, pulling me into him, and buries his face in the curve of my neck, inhaling as his lips brush my skin, sending shivers throughout my body. My eyes slide closed and I bask in his familiar scent—a heady combination of cigarette smoke and freshly cut grass. It's all Lincoln.

Clean and dirty at the same time.

"Em," he rumbles into my neck.

His voice gives me goose bumps. He sounds as if he is in pain. I both hate and love it.

Being this close to him again, seeing and touching him . . . it's soul-crushing.

I loosen my grip on him and force myself to step away just as Jake approaches us.

Jake's hand flattens on my lower back, bringing me

back to reality, providing me with support whether he knows it or not. With that one touch, I inhale and compose myself.

Jake is my present.

Lincoln is my past.

Jake is easy.

Lincoln is complicated.

Jake is whole.

Lincoln is broken.

I step closer to Jake to ground myself and keep my thoughts clear. When I do, Lincoln's sandy brows turn into a deep V. The corner of his mouth turns down angrily.

"Who the hell are you?" he asks Jake.

"Lincoln, this is Jake Irons," I introduce them. "Jake, Lincoln Daniels. Lincoln and I went to college with Josh and Kennison," I explain, as if we're simply acquaintances.

"It's nice to meet you, Lincoln." Like the gentleman he is, Jake gives Lincoln his hand.

Lincoln looks at it and scoffs. Instead of shaking hands, he lifts his chin at Jake in slight acknowledgment before turning his darkened gaze back to me.

Words aren't needed. Everything unsaid is in his eyes.

"Jake is my—" I start, but get cut off by the approach of a pretty brunette.

"Hey Linc, I think you're starting," she says as she steps up beside him.

I watch as she slides her left hand into Lincoln's right one. A glint of light bounces off an engagement band and my heart crumbles. *She's his fiancée? He's getting married?*

Forcing a smile, I study his face. Lincoln's expression seems sad and lost.

"Hi. I'm Tricia." She clings to Lincoln's arm, as if she knows.

Of course she does. Any woman within a five-foot radius can sense the threat—me.

Jake, however, is oblivious and politely introduces us to Tricia, because that's how he is. Respectful. Kind. Mannered. In my peripheral vision, I notice Kennison as she walks out of a back room in the church with someone who looks like she's the wedding planner.

My best friend's soft brown eyes meet mine and widen when she takes in the scene.

I fake a reassuring smile and wave her off. It's her special weekend and I don't want this to be about Lincoln and me. I want this weekend to be all about her and Josh.

And their wedding.

As we discussed a thousand times on the phone, I am okay. Or at least, I will be. We have a plan. I am in control of the situation. I inhale deeply at the ten thousandth lie I've told myself since my plane landed earlier today. It's obvious that the truth and I are going to be frenemies this weekend. Then again, when it comes to Lincoln, honesty and I were never really friends. More like acquaintances who ignored one another.

Leeza, the wedding coordinator, makes a brief welcome speech and explains how the rehearsal is going to work. Those who aren't in the wedding party are asked to take a seat, while those of us who are get ushered into another room. The coordinator yells out directions to the large group, trying to control the excited chatter and lack of attention.

I attempt to relax and appear unfazed. But it's almost impossible to ignore Lincoln's presence, because he knows how to command a room. I chat with the bride's cousin, and attempt to ignore him, but I can't. He's everywhere. In every thought and every corner of the space.

When my name is called out, I look up to see him stalking toward me.

Confused, I look around and realize everyone is being paired up.

Which means . . . Oh. Hell. No.

Peeling my eyes away from him, I step closer to the wedding planner. "Excuse me, Leeza," I say. "I'm supposed to be paired up with Tyler Hamilton." I explain in a polite whisper, so as not to cause a scene and alert Kennison to the fact that our well-designed plan is starting to collapse already. This has to be a record for us.

Panicked, I watch as Leeza frowns. "Tyler isn't here yet; he won't be here until the ceremony tomorrow. For tonight, you and Lincoln are together," she says, preoccupied.

Shit! Tyler is always ruining my life.

Kennison and I established this beforehand.

I was not, under any circumstances, to walk down the aisle, at a wedding, in a church, with Lincoln Daniels.

Lincoln steps into my space, looking down into my eyes. I hold my breath again, because touching him is bad. It's like an alcoholic taking one sip after years of sobriety. If we have any more contact, there will be no putting me back together. I will break all over again.

He leans in, his lips brushing over my cheek and his breath at my ear, warm and damp against my skin. "I always hoped someday I'd walk you down the aisle."

"I thought you never wanted to get married," I challenge him, my voice only a whisper.

He stands up and looks me in the eye. "That was before you."

His words hurt.

They weren't meant to. They were meant to ease the tension.

Instead, they open a wound I've spent the last year trying to heal.

Feeling breathless and overwhelmed, I step back. He holds out his palm, waiting for me to slide mine across it. When my hand lifts, I notice it's shaky. He does too. With a heavy sigh, he folds his hand over mine and pulls me closer so our chests are touching.

"I have you, Em. I'll always have you," he whispers in my ear.

I shake in his arms.

Lincoln calls me Em.

Jake prefers my full name, Emerson.

The huskiness of Lincoln's velvety voice takes me back to when we first met five years ago. Before we allowed the darkness to pull us both under, leaving me to drown in it.

Unable to speak, I simply nod.

Lincoln slides in next to me, placing my hand into the crook of his elbow. Just as we're about to take our practice run down the aisle, my eyes seek out Jake, needing him to help me breathe again so I can focus. He smiles warmly at me from his seat and I calm a bit.

Sensing the change in my demeanor, Lincoln grips me to him tighter before leaning into my ear and growling, "He isn't the right guy for you."

The fiery heat of anger inside me roars to life, covering up the smoldering of something else that only

Lincoln causes beneath the surface of my skin. Something that makes me feel alive.

"You don't even know him," I grind out.

"How long have you two been together?" he asks as we start to walk.

"A year."

"And no ring?"

"Not everyone finds salvation by running off and getting married to someone else."

My dig shuts him up until we are ready to part at the front of the aisle.

Releasing me, he barely says, "Some souls were never meant to be saved, Em."

CHAPTER 28

I thought the wedding day would be better. Leeza has me walk down the aisle with the right usher, Tyler, this time. But it isn't better. It's far worse, because at the front of the aisle, looking amazing in his tux, Lincoln is watching me, fixated on my every move.

A sad, distant expression mars his face as I approach the front of the church.

The future we should have had, but don't, flashes before my eyes.

The reminder that we were not meant to be hurts.

It hurts so badly that I have to put a hand to the center of my chest and push against the pain to try to ease it. Because when something is broken, shattered to the point of no return, you can fix the pieces, but you'll always see the cracks that were left behind.

The ifs.

Holding my breath, I manage to remain standing during the ceremony, even though my knees are trembling under my gown. It wasn't until we moved into the candlelit grand ballroom that I felt the full force of Lincoln's overwhelming presence again.

Smiling, I walk through the sea of guests as they dance and mingle. Jake left my side to grab some drinks for us at the bar and I curbed the desire to cling to him.

Instead, I'm standing next to the dance floor listening to one of Josh's uncles talk about his latest hunting expedition. Years of my mother's country club gatherings have conditioned me for proper etiquette, so I'm smiling politely and nodding as if I'm engrossed and fascinated that this man and his friends love to hunt and kill Bambi.

Looks like my mother's etiquette rules are finally useful. A ping of sadness falls over me thinking about her. I haven't spoken to either of my parents since I walked out of that dinner. It's been over a year. These days, our only contact is through financial planners and lawyers, now that I'm of age to access my trust fund, much to my mother's dismay.

I understand that she is more upset about the fact that she can no longer control me through money than she is about me not calling, or visiting, her for an entire year.

The band on the stage switches songs from something upbeat and light to something soft and moody, and a warm hand lands on my lower back, searing me through the satin.

I don't need to turn to see who it is; from my reaction to the touch, I know it's Lincoln.

He leans over my shoulder and whispers in my ear. "Dance with me?"

His tone is suggestive and smooth; a tone you can't say no to. Politely excusing myself from the Bambi-killing conversation, I turn and lean back, meeting his eyes.

That intense gaze of his holds mine without wavering, and a familiar feeling washes over me. A feeling that used to live and breathe inside of me—panic. His presence is causing my heart to beat erratically. I inhale, not wanting to have an attack here.

Sadly, my deep breaths do nothing to calm the chaos his closeness is causing.

Leaning in, he interlaces his fingers with mine, and his mouth is back at my ear. "Please?"

I nod, allowing him to lead us onto the dance floor, where he stops just at the edge.

I squeeze my eyes closed for a second before opening them, because that's exactly how this feels, like we're at the edge. My heart pounds hard when he pulls me into his arms and our chests touch. Looking down at me, he raises my left hand, placing it behind his neck before his own hand wraps around my waist in a light hold.

The gentleness of his movements cause an ache within me.

"You look beautiful, Em."

"Thank you," I whisper shakily.

He stares at me. "Where is Jake?" He exaggerates the *k* sound.

"At the bar, grabbing our drinks."

We dance in silence for what feels like an eternity as he looks around the room.

"I saw him, you know." His eyes travel back to mine.

"Who? Jake?"

"The team was in Los Angeles for a game about a week after you left. I'd finally convinced Kennison to give me your address. I went to your place, but you weren't there. Your neighbor, the older lady, told me where I could find you when I said I was your brother." My brow arches. He keeps rambling, nervous. "You were having dinner with him. At some restaurant on Vine. You had the salmon. And you wore a black dress."

My heart plummets. *He came looking for me?*

"That was our first date. Jake's and mine," I explain.

His gaze bores into mine. All his thoughts and emotions swirl in his eyes like they've always done. With me, Lincoln was never able to hide his feelings. I saw them.

All of them. Swirling in the storminess of his eyes. His eyes make me ache.

Lincoln nods absentmindedly. I watch him, wondering what he wants. Answers? Closure? Whatever it is, I need it over quickly, because I need all the space I can get.

"I've thought about this," he tells me.

"About dancing with me at Kennison's wedding?"

"About seeing you again." He drinks me in, like he's been wandering, lost and thirsty.

I grip his neck tighter. "Yeah?"

"Every time I have to go to LA. I replay all the things I want to say to you over and over again in my head while I'm on the plane." He smiles, but it's not the same. This one is guarded.

Tucking a piece of hair behind my ear, I shift under his gaze, heated by his look.

His eyes roam over the blush I know is on my cheeks.

"Do you love him, Em?" he asks.

"Yes." My answer comes out way too fast and shaky.

"Like you love me?" His voice is bitter and jealous as he stares at me.

"No." I blink up at him rapidly, trying to remember how to breathe.

He pulls me in, closer to him. I feel the tension in his body. It radiates off him.

It's completely gut-wrenching.

It hurts to look at him.

Even more, it hurts to still love him.

"Then what the fuck are you doing with him?" he asks hoarsely.

His voice is a plea for me not to be with Jake. To pick him. I ignore the question.

"Do you love her?" I counter, referring to his fiancée.

He grips my waist tighter. "Who, Em?"

"Your fiancée," I remind him.

"My . . ." He trails off before a chuckle falls out of him.

"What's so funny?" I bristle.

"Tricia is not my fiancée."

"She had a huge ring on her finger, Lincoln."

"She's a friend. The fiancée of the pitcher on the team I work for."

"Oh." My shoulders fall.

"She came with me to the wedding as a personal favor," he adds.

I pause, needing a moment to process, because I wish she were.

It would make all this so much easier if he had moved on.

"I'm sorry." I shake my head. "I had no right to pry."

"You have every right," he replies firmly.

Something in the fierceness of his look has me on edge.

"No. I don't. We should stop dancing." I try to pull away, but he won't let me.

"Why?"

"Jake will be back soon."

"No, why don't you think you have a right to ask me about Tricia?"

"Because you're not mine!" I snap out in a low, quiet voice.

The silence between us becomes deafening.

"Yes, I am. That's the whole fucking point."

I snap my mouth shut and clench my jaw.

"I have always been, and will always be, yours, Em."

"Linc—"

"I've missed you," he whispers. "Say you've missed me too."

My breath catches at his admission. I do miss him. For the first few months, all I did was grieve the loss of him. Even while trying to start something up with Jake. Every second I spent alone, I was drowning without him. But then, little by little, Jake slowly eased the pain. Before this weekend, I went an entire month without hurting.

Now, the wounds have opened again.

They're too fresh and raw.

Too real.

"Can we go somewhere and talk?" He shifts with uncertainty.

Apprehensive, I look around the room. "I don't—"

"It can be somewhere public, if you don't want to be alone with me. I just—" He pauses.

"What?"

"I need to talk before you leave for LA again."

"We're talking here. Now."

"I don't want to talk in a room where I am about to release you into the arms of another man."

Every muscle in my body tenses at his words. "Okay."

"Okay," he dips his chin. "I'll text you tomorrow with a place and time."

I nod and the song ends. Slowly he leans in and places a light kiss on my cheek. My skin burns under his lips as I stand motionless. Lincoln smiles and winks at me, backing up.

"Wait." I clear my throat. "D-do you need my number?"

"No, Em. I've always had your number."

CHAPTER 29

I stare at Jake across the hotel room. Part of me feels like the world's suckiest girlfriend. I haven't been listening to a word he's said all night. Instead, I've been playing my conversation with Lincoln from the dance we shared over and over again in my head.

Seeing him again has stirred something deep within me. Something I can't explain. It's like he switched a light back on that I had shut off over a year ago. And no matter how hard I try, I can't get it to turn back off.

"So? What do you think?" Jake says.

"About what?"

"Moving in with me when we get back to LA?"

I get a text and I offer Jake an apologetic smile before reading it.

It's from Lincoln. There is only an address, tomorrow's date, and a time on it.

I don't reply. I don't know if I should. I have no idea what the hell I'm doing.

"Work?" Jake asks innocently.

"An old friend."

Jake just watches me for a moment. "Emerson?"

"Hm?"

"I asked if you wanted to move in with me," he reminds me.

"I know. I just—"

He shifts on the bed, fixing the pillows behind his back so he can sit in a more comfortable position as he prepares to read before bed—his nightly ritual.

Once comfortable, Jake sighs. "Look, I know you don't like it when I push, so I try hard not to. I just thought that maybe coming home for your best friend's wedding would open you up to the idea of taking another step in *our* relationship."

"Another step?"

"We've been seeing each another for almost a year. I haven't met your parents. I haven't actually met anyone in your life that is important to you. You didn't even let me near Kennison and Josh until a month ago, when they surprised you with a visit and I happened to be there. It took three months for you to share where you worked with me," he points out. "I'm all about taking this slow, but I'd like to think we're going . . . somewhere."

"Somewhere?" I repeat.

"Moving in. Marriage. A family someday," he ticks off.

As I watch him speak, something dark and heavy grows in the pit of my stomach. I don't want marriage or children, not with him. I should. He's perfect. But I don't.

His forehead bunches up, watching me freak out in my head.

"I-I can't, Jake." I blurt out.

Hurt falls across his expression and I wince, knowing I caused it.

"I'm sorry. I just . . . can't."

"I don't understand. I thought you wanted all those things?"

"You want them. I don't even know what I want for breakfast."

"I didn't mean tomorrow," he points out.

"I know. I just . . ." I exhale. "It's too soon. Too much."

Frustration fills his voice. "It's been a year."

"Do you love me?" I whisper.

"Are you serious?" he questions. "I just asked you to move in with me. Told you I wanted a future with you, a family—to which you said flat out no. What do you think?"

"It's a simple question, Jake. Do you love me?"

He blinks at me, seemingly confused.

"Or do you just love the idea of me?"

"Of course I love you."

"No." I stand, walk over to the bed, and sit next to him.

"No?"

"Do you *love* me?" I ask again.

"I don't understand what you're asking."

I'm asking if this is real. If his love is real. If he's going to fight for us. Stand by us. Always be there for me and never leave. Because in my life, only one person has —Lincoln.

"I want to know if it's hard for you to breathe when I'm not around? If you'd be willing to give up everything in your life, including your future, for just a second with me? No matter how many times I'd pushed you away, would you find a way to come back?"

Jake's eyes search mine. "Is this about that Lincoln guy? You know, you've been off ever since you saw him. And let's be honest here, I know something happened between the two of you. I spent the entire reception watching you stare at him and his fiancée."

"She isn't his fiancée," I counter. "She's just a friend."

"How do you know that?"

"I asked him," I reply. "When we were dancing."

"I see."

"Answer my question, Jake. Do you love me in that all-consuming way?"

"I love you, Emerson. Isn't that enough?"

It should be.

But it's not.

CHAPTER 30

I close the door to the Uber and look around the neighborhood; the address Lincoln texted me is located in Boston proper. As soon as I step onto the sidewalk, I see Lincoln leaning on a motorcycle, parked in front of a brownstone. He has on jeans and a white T-shirt, looking as amazing as he always does, and my heart does this fluttery thing.

"Aren't you cold?" I ask, curling into my leather coat.

"Nope. You look pretty. Hot date tonight?"

"Nope."

"Where's Jake tonight?" he asks, again emphasizing the *k*.

"On a plane back to LA."

"When do you go back?"

"Tomorrow night."

"Where did you tell him you'd be tonight?" I don't miss the bite in his tone.

I step closer to him, shifting my voice into a playful, teasing one. "I told him I'd be having hot sex with an old friend." I smile at his surprised reaction. "On a motorcycle."

"Oh yeah?" He plays along. "And how did he take that?"

The humor on my face slips. "Fine. We broke up."

He stares at me, all playfulness gone. "I told you he wasn't the right guy for you."

"I really don't want to talk about Jake tonight," I exhale.

Nodding, he pats the seat on the motorcycle. "Want me to take you for a ride?"

Shaking my head, I can't help but smile, knowing he means something different.

He inclines his head to the bike. "Let's clear our heads and get some fresh air."

I walk over to him and he hands me a helmet.

"Safety first, right?" he says, securing it to my head.

"I've always been safe with you." I reply, and his fingers still.

He closes his eyes. He's so still that for a second, I start to worry that something is really wrong. When his lids reopen, the gray shines so bright, it takes my breath away.

"Lincoln?" I prompt.

"We need to get out of here. Before I do something stupid like kiss you," he mutters.

He straddles his bike, sliding on first, and I climb on behind him, slipping my arms around him. With one of his hands he repositions mine, folding them across his chest. Once he's satisfied I'm holding him tightly enough, he pulls back the throttle on the bike, and the engine roars to life before he takes off, racing down the road.

I rest my cheek against his back, closing my eyes, breathing in his scent mixed in with the cool night air. The city blurs past us, the wind whipping across my face. I stop paying attention to where we're going and just focus on being present with him in the now.

Maybe that's what I should have been doing all along. Focusing on the present and not worrying so much about the future. Right now, the only thing I care about is the feel of his warm body pressed against mine. There is no destination or time limit. We just drive down the streets, long after they become abandoned by everyone but us.

After a while, he circles back onto the street he asked me to meet him on. An underground garage opens up in front of one of the brownstones, and he pulls into it and parks. Ungracefully, I climb off the bike and wobble a bit, as the vibration from the bike ride has my legs feeling tingly and a bit numb. I shake them out, taking off the helmet and handing it back to Lincoln. He puts it away and watches me rake my fingers through the tangles in my hair. Annoyed with its crazy, I tip it upside down, shake it out, and stand upright again. Snapping my head back, I meet his amused expression and smile.

"What?"

"That was . . ."

"What?"

"Fucking hot to watch, Em."

I roll my eyes at him and look around. "Is this your building?"

He nods. "Want me to take you back to the hotel?"

I press my lips together. "No. Show me your place."

Lincoln takes a deep breath and nods.

We head over to an elevator and take it up to the top floor, three stories up. The doors open onto a long hall-way. It's bright and has an old-Bostonian feel to it, with brick walls, parquet floors, and detailed moldings. There are only two apartments on this floor, according to Lincoln. The building is historic and full of East Coast charm, unlike my place in LA, which is Spanish in décor and architecture, and has an open outdoor courtyard in the middle of it with a water fountain and tall palm trees.

I watch as he pulls out his keys, avoiding his eyes, because even though this is a different building and another time, it feels familiar. Like we've done this a hundred times.

He opens the door and waits for me to enter. "Welcome home."

I try not be so emotional about the fact that he called it *home*, as if I belong here.

I step into his world and it looks just as empty and flat as all the other places he's lived in. Void of anything personal or decorative. This time, though, there is a scented candle.

"You should hire an interior designer," I tease.

"You up for the task?" He winks.

"Maybe."

"How's work?" he asks, like he's nervous.

"Good. It's the same company I worked for in London. The LA office is newer, so that means I'm more hands-on for projects that I normally wouldn't be, given my experience."

"Sounds like a nice setup for you."

"How about with you?"

"I was promoted to trainer, no more assistant. We just finished up the season and we have a few more months before we head down to Florida for spring training. I'm thinking of opening up my own practice to run during the off-season," he explains shyly.

"That's . . . amazing." I smile at him and blow out a tension-filled breath, making a strand of my hair jump off my face. This is weird. Normal. Not us at all. I hate it.

"Want something to drink?" He breaks through my thoughts.

"Water, if you have it."

"I do. Capped and bottled, at that."

When he steps into the kitchen, I take off my coat and throw it on his couch, taking in his place. After circling the room and appreciating the brick and moldings, I see it.

On the fireplace mantel, in a plain black frame.

My lips part as I walk over to the photo and pick it up, staring at it.

Lincoln walks back into the living room and freezes.

"I-is," I stumble. "Is this me?"

"Yes," he replies, barely.

"Y-you have a photo. Of me. In your home?" I meet his gaze.

All I can do is stare in awe at him, because he once told me that he doesn't need photos or objects to remind him of people. He looks to the ground with his eyebrows pulled together, then back up at me. My lungs stop working as he watches me nervously.

"I thought you were against reminders?"

"I'm against trinkets and dust collectors. That's why I have my tattoos—they're my reminders of people or places. My tattoos are my photos and memories, Em.

The only pieces of the past that I keep close to remind me of those who are important," he explains.

"And this?" I hold up the photo.

"I needed a visual reminder that you were —are—real."

I walk slowly toward him, not sure of what to do. "How long have you had this?"

"Kennison gave it to me right after you moved to LA."

Trying to gather my thoughts, I suddenly can't look away from him. Not a day has gone by that I haven't worried about him. Haven't missed him. Haven't grieved him. Every minute we spent apart, every second, I spent drowning in loneliness and regret.

Stepping closer, I touch his cheek. Something feels different about him tonight. His eyes aren't stormy. They're peaceful and calm, like the sea after a storm has passed.

He looks so different than he did yesterday that I can't reconcile it.

"You were always so lost in the dark," I whisper. "And now, you aren't."

"You found the light in me that I couldn't find in myself."

He leans into me, bending and placing the water bottles on the coffee table.

"I miss you," I whisper.

His eyes close. "Say it again, Em."

"I miss you. So much. I've missed you every single day we weren't together. Since the moment we met. All I've done is miss you," I say quietly, and his eyes flutter open.

How much he wants to love me is radiating off him —and my heart squeezes.

"Why didn't you call? Or reach out? You knew how to get in touch with me."

"I couldn't. I wanted to, more than anything. I just— couldn't."

"Why the hell not? I mean, when you left, Em, I fucking lost it."

Hurt fills me. "I didn't want you to give up your life —your future—for me."

He shakes his head. "My future? What are you talking about?"

Slowly, I release a breath, knowing I have to tell him. If I don't, it will shatter the paper-thin composure I am barely holding on to right now, standing in front of him.

"I left the way I did because my father threatened me with your parole."

His jaw clenches, but he remains silent, staring at me, hanging on to every word.

"He said if I kept seeing you, he'd mark that as a violation against you. I didn't want to be the reason that you didn't have a future. So I let you go. Made you think—"

Everything in him tenses and becomes rigid and hard. "He threatened you?"

I nod. "I tried. Tried to let you go. Tried to forget you. Tried to move on with Jake. But every day . . . I was just going through the motions. I couldn't breathe without you."

Lincoln studies my face for a second while he tries to figure out how much truth is in my statement. "I should have never dragged you into my world, Em."

"You didn't drag me. I stepped willingly into it, because I wanted to."

"I've spent every fucking night of this past year going over and over the last few hours we spent together. I knew you were lying to me and yourself at the airport."

"You knew I was lying?"

"There's no way I can be this much in love with you, and not know when you're lying."

"You're in love with me? Still?"

"Still. Always." A small smile plays on his lips. "My record is clean."

Those four words have more meaning and weight than anything else he's ever said to me. I nod, under-standing what he's saying. My father is no longer a threat.

He can't prevent us from being together.

Not ever again.

"I'm sorry it took me so long to tell you," I say remorsefully. "I'm sorry I lied to you that day and got on a plane with you thinking I didn't love you. Because I did. I do. With ever fiber that I have in me. I love you. The part of you that's in me will never die."

Tears cascade down my cheeks and he wipes them away. Then, he's kissing me.

With each stroke I'm more able to finally breathe again, after holding my breath for a year.

Lincoln pulls away first, but just barely. "Your parents are assholes."

"I know."

"I hate that they threatened you. Even more so, I hate that they've made you think love is conditional on doing the right thing all the time and being perfect. It's not."

Nodding, my eyes bore into his, telling him I get it—I understand.

"Real love is unconditional. Beautiful. Broken. Like us."

CHAPTER 31

Over the years, Lincoln and I have had moments so perfect, so poignant, they're etched into my memory. Tonight is one of those moments. We're sitting on his couch, eating pizza and laughing. He's relaxed and happier than I've ever seen him. We both are.

Suddenly, I'm suffocating in the rightness of it all.

I never want to be without this again.

I never want to be without him again.

"Want to talk about what happened with Jake?" he asks.

"Nothing major. I asked him questions that he couldn't answer."

"I'm sorry to hear that."

"No. You aren't." I laugh and roll my eyes.

"You're right. I'm not. He wasn't the right guy

for you."

"If not Jake, then who is, Lincoln?" I wrinkle my nose at him.

"Me."

"Oh yeah?" I sit up and move closer.

"You fit into my life. The idea of you not being here tomorrow, of this"—he motions between us—"going away again, it terrifies like me nothing I've ever felt before, Em."

"What are you saying?"

"I like having you in my house and in my life. I want you to stay in both."

The quiet settles between us, making me feel like I want to jump out of my skin.

"I can't move back. Not now, anyway."

"I know. I didn't ask. I just want you to think about us. About trying again."

Us. I try to shake off the panic, because the doubt and fear linger. I'm not used to easy or simple with Lincoln. It's always complicated. The idea of simple freaks me out.

I clear my throat. "I'll think about it."

"It scares me too, Em." He moves closer. "A simple life, with you."

"How do you always know what I'm thinking?" I whisper.

"I know you. There is no pressure here, just,

306

what if."

I lean forward and press my lips to his. I've spent so much time without him that the idea of being without him any more burns through my blood, alongside my want and desire. Lincoln is mine and I am going to do whatever it takes to keep it that way.

I devour his mouth, letting him feel all the things I can't say. Lincoln grabs me and pulls me over his lap so I can straddle him. His hands tangle roughly in my hair. There is no gentleness in our kiss or in his grip on me. All that we care about is feeling good.

What exists between us, in this moment, is a blinding need to release some of the want and need, the tension that has been between us over the past few days, and the anger that I know still lingers between us from being apart this past year.

I suck in a tense breath as we rush to get naked. Somewhere in my head I know I need to slow down, need to get back in control. Lincoln whispers my name, trying to get me to slow down, but I don't. I am ready for him to be inside me, to bury all the fear and uncertainty that burns in me. I'm operating from a place that I know I'll regret in the morning. But right now, I need him to help me out of the dark. To be the light.

By the time we're naked and positioned, I'm wound too tight, ready to break. He thrusts into me and my eyes squeeze as I wrap my arms around his neck and he buries his face into my neck. We fit together so perfectly, it's as if we were made for this sole purpose. Lincoln holds me to him tightly, guiding me as I rock over him. I'm breathing hard and my knees suddenly feel like they aren't going to hold me up anymore.

When his mouth finds mine, our tongues meld together as he teases me through our kiss. His mouth leaves mine long enough to taste my jaw, my neck, my shoulder. With every spot his lips touch, I become completely consumed by him again. He owns me.

Lincoln's grip tightens around my waist.

"I love you," I whisper, between faltering and shallow breaths.

"I love you too, Em," he says with a smug grin, and then takes us both over the edge.

When I wake up, I'm disoriented for a few seconds. Blinking, I look around at the unfamiliar bedroom. Then the memories of yesterday seep back in, and I turn to see Lincoln, sleeping on his stomach with his head turned toward me. Smiling down at him, I brush a few strands of hair out of his eyes before slipping out of bed to use the restroom.

I wash my hands and try to freshen up as best I can without any of my products before making my way into his kitchen and figuring out the coffee maker. It takes me twenty minutes, but I finally get it to produce caffeine. With a contented sigh, I head over to the window and look at the park across the street from his place. It's such a pretty view.

Nothing beats fall in New England, not even the sunshine and warm weather of California. All the trees' branches are covered in warm auburn and deep crimson colors.

I'm staring out the window when two large arms wrap around my middle; Lincoln's warmth drifts into my back as he presses his chest against it. He kisses the side of my neck, nipping and licking before he brings his mouth to my ear.

"What are you thinking about?"

"I feel like I'm in a dream. Like tomorrow I'll wake up and you'll disappear."

"A dream, huh?" He takes my coffee mug from me with one hand.

"A really, really good dream." I turn and face him as he brings my mug to his lips.

Releasing my waist, his left hand is soft and warm as he intertwines my fingers with his. I don't pull away. I bask in the simplicity of holding his hand. Being so close to him feels both strange and exhilarating. I have to remind myself that it's real.

His face softens as he watches me with those intense

eyes.

"What time do you have to be at the airport?"

"My flight leaves around five."

"I'll drive you back to the hotel and then to the airport."

Despair settles into me. I have to leave him, again. I blink back tears, resigning myself to that reality. Sensing the change, Lincoln closes in on me and pulls me into a desperate embrace, and we cling to each other for a long time, neither of us ready to let go. I wish things were different. All I want is to finally start over with this man I love so much.

We're so close to getting there. So. Damn. Close.

"This isn't the end of us, Em. It's just the beginning."

Placing the mug on the counter, he cups my face and gently caresses my cheeks with his thumbs before he takes my lips. I pull him tightly against me and kiss him hard. I kiss him in every way I possibly can kiss him, because I plan on loving him in every way that I can. This kiss, right here, it's worth all the tears and heartache, all the pain and struggles. He kisses me so soft and deep that I swear he's trying to steal my heart.

What he doesn't realize is, he already owns it.

I gave it to him a long time ago.

And never truly got it back.

And I never truly will.

CHAPTER 32

I shouldn't be this nervous. It's ridiculous that I am, because it's only Lincoln. I open the door to my apartment and drink in the sight of him. I'm just staring. I guess I expected him to look different after we'd spent a month apart. But he doesn't. He looks the same.

He looks amazing and sexy and *calm*.

Having him standing here strips me of my ability to breathe.

An amused smile crosses his lips where he's still standing outside the door, and it sends my pulse into a frenzy. I can't decide if the sight of him has me wanting to jump into his arms or crumble into a pile of tears. I've missed him so much. For years I've loved and hated him and everything in between. I truly never expected us to have this ending.

"Hi." My voice is a shy whisper.

The last time I felt this nervous around him was before everything went to hell for us. It's been four life-changing weeks since we've kissed or touched. Other than a few phone calls, texts, and video messages, we haven't seen each other. A few days ago, he called saying he'd be in town for work and asked if we could spend the weekend together.

"Hey." He slowly steps closer to me, his smoldering eyes focused on mine.

My heart flutters as he backs me into my apartment, grabs my face in his hands, and slams his lips against mine. My legs buck as he steals my breath away. He sweeps his tongue over my lips and into my mouth and a faint whimper escapes me. I reach up and position my arms around his neck, pulling him into me as he slams my door closed behind us with his foot. He moves his hands to my waist and lifts me up, and I wrap my legs around him. He spins us and uses his body to pin me against the door as he kisses me.

I pour all the emotion and passion that's been bottled up inside me for weeks into our kiss. This wasn't how I planned on greeting him. But it's without a doubt what I need and want. Him. This. Nothing has ever compared to the feel and taste of him. Nothing ever will.

He pulls back and we stare at each other breathlessly.

He strokes my cheek. "I miss you."

I lean into his touch. "I miss you too."

His thumb moves across my bottom lip and I pull his lips back to mine. He devours me as I grip his shoulders and tighten my thighs around him. His lips move to my neck, his teeth biting and nipping the flesh, his tongue following, soothing each spot. His fingertips dig into my waist; as he shifts, the desire burns between us.

Everything about us just makes more sense when we're together. He makes me feel beautiful. Revered. Loved. I just feel *more* of everything when I am with him.

He lifts his head away from my lips but keeps our faces close enough that our noses brush when his forehead meets mine. The way he's looking at me, as if I'm the only thing that matters in his world, makes everything around us fade away. It's just him and me.

Lifting my skirt, he slides his hand beneath my panties, his fingers slipping inside the edge of them, causing my muscles to clench beneath his touch. When his fingers glide over me, finding me wet and ready for him, he groans deeply in his throat.

With a smug grin, he begins to run his fingers slowly up and down me, circling at the top before descending and starting the torture all over again. I arch my back against the door, pushing against his touch. I cry out, gripping him tighter when his fingers enter me.

I'm completely consumed by him. Before I met him, I had no idea I could feel this much, this deeply with another person. I had no idea I was capable of sharing this kind of connection.

Lincoln frowns when a tear falls from one of my eyes. He lifts one hand and wipes it away, then dips his head and kisses me, gentle and soft, coaxing even more tears out of me. I know he knows what I'm feeling. The raw emotions that he conjures within me.

He leans into my ear. "Want me to stop?"

I quickly shake my head no.

Skilled hands slide up and down and over me. Every touch sends waves of heat coursing through me. His lips brush across my mouth and I shiver under his touch.

"Are you nervous?" he asks.

I nod, and his eyes soften with understanding.

"Me too."

I can feel my entire body relax at his admission, and when his mouth takes mine again, I lose all control. Reaching between us, he pushes his jeans and boxers down, and slides my panties to the side just enough to slowly slide himself fully into me, knowing that this is what I need more than anything. To feel him inside of me. For us to be one.

He pulls in and out of me in a slow rhythm. My need for him grows instead of diminishing as he gives me what I need. The more my desire builds, the more impatient I become. Sensing this, he pushes inside me, making me his completely. We kiss wildly and ferociously as he thrusts in and out of me, harder and faster. Finally, we both find our release, and a sense of peace washes over us. Cupping his cheek, I draw his mouth to mine and kiss him.

"I can't believe this is real. That I actually have you," I exhale.

"You have me," he groans. "You so fucking have me."

I love this man, with everything I am.

I'm sitting in the chair and fidgeting nervously. Touching everything in sight that isn't a needle or wrapped in plastic. The tattoo shop is near my apartment. Lincoln's friend from high school, Tommy, owns it. We bumped into him the other night at a restaurant. The two of them got to talking and after a few drinks and easy conversation, it was agreed that this is where I would come to get my first tattoo done.

"Are you sure you want to do this?" Lincoln watches me fidget.

"I'm sure."

"You look like you're ready to run away. Or throw up."

"I do?" I meet his gaze.

"Yeah, Em. You do."

"It's not going to hurt, right?" I swallow.

"Only for a minute. I trust Tommy," he assures me.

I try to give him a calm smile, but I can see he's not buying it.

Tommy opens the door and walks in with a little metal tray in his hands. Everything on it looks sterilized and smells like hospital antiseptic. I resist the desire to bolt.

"You ready, Emerson?" Tommy asks in a deep, friendly voice.

I nod and place my left wrist on the small table, under the light, trying to control my rapid breathing. Lincoln sits on a stool to my right, takes my hand in his, and interlaces our fingers. He brings them up to his lips and gently brushes his lips across my fingertips.

"I've got you, Em," he whispers, and I relax.

"I'm fast. And it's only two letters, so it'll be over quick," Tommy says.

He sits down, turns the light on, and prepares the table next to him by removing the needles and ink. When he's ready, he winks at me and presses the stencil to my wrist.

After I agree to the placement he turns on the tattoo gun and presses it to my skin.

I tense at the sound of the buzzing, but focus on Lincoln.

"Take really deep breaths and let them out slowly and evenly," he says.

I nod as the needles slide over my skin.

"Keep your eyes on me," Lincoln orders.

I do. For the longest time I just look deeply into his stare, getting lost in the storm.

It's not long before Tommy pats my arm, letting me know it's done. "All set."

Smiling, I watch as he spreads a clear ointment across the ink and places a protective plastic wrapping on it. "Plastic on for a day, and while showering. Ointment for three."

"Got it." My gaze drops to my wrist and I smile.

I'd always wanted to get a tattoo; I just never knew what of.

Until today.

I look at the two tiny lowercase letters now adorning my wrist in black ink: *if*.

Just like Lincoln's tattoos, they will serve as my daily reminder.

It doesn't matter if he breaks my heart . . .

It doesn't matter if it's not meant to be . . .

The ifs will always linger, but so will my love for him.

EPILOGUE

LINCOLN

Six months later . . .

I watch her sleep. The sun's rays beam through the window in our bedroom, caressing her face. Em doesn't know this, but it's something I do every morning—when I'm home and not traveling with the team. A few months ago, I accepted a job as an athletic trainer for one of the major league baseball teams here in California. Best decision I've made, aside from Em.

I smile down at her. She always looks so peaceful and untroubled when she sleeps. Sometimes I have to remind myself that she's real. And mine. I went so long refusing to allow myself to feel anything for anyone. Convinced that I was unworthy of love. I thought I didn't deserve something good and decent in my life. That I was unworthy.

Until her.

I love her.

I love everything about her.

I love that she's never judged me. That she understands me. Despite everything we've put each other through, we made it.

I lift my fingers and brush them across her cheeks. A hint of a smile plays on her lips as she rubs her cheek on my fingers and curls into me. I moved in a month ago, and when I did, I promised myself when I wasn't on the road for work, I would be the first thing she saw each morning. I shift and wrap myself around her.

My fingers run over the tattoo on her wrist.

I can't help but think:

What if she never came to that party freshman year?

What if she never stepped into my room?

What if she never went to London?

What if she never returned?

What if she never let me touch her? Kiss her? Love her?

What if she died that night in the parking lot?

What if she hadn't listened to her father?

What if she never got on that plane?

What if we never made up?

In the end, the ifs don't matter anymore.

She loved them all away.

THE END

REVELATION

THE REVELATION SERIES

I'm running, and not very well, might I add. My lungs burn and my shallow breathing erratically bounces off the slick stone walls. I keep moving forward, forcing myself farther and farther into the dark underground passage. It's cold, damp, and smells like musk.

"What the hell is following me?" I ask myself, as confusion sets in. The only thing I'm certain of is that I'm bone-chillingly terrified, down to the core of my very soul. I'm frightened that whatever is chasing me will catch me, because when it does, there's no doubt it will kill me. Its hatred and anger rolls off it in waves, crashing through me like a sharp gust of wind, suffocating me. I'm positive it's pure evil.

Just as I reach the end of the tunnel, I hit a solid wall, ceasing my progress and ending my futile efforts at escape. "Shit," I whisper out loud, while I strike my palms against the water-slicked stones. Feeling defeated, I place my forehead to the damp wall and release a soft whimper.

I need to figure out my options, quickly. I sense its presence closing in, dropping the tunnel's temperature from cool and damp to downright frigid, the glacial air settling around the passageway. My breath comes out in a cloud in front of me. My heart rate increases as I stifle the gag reflex being challenged by the rancid smell of sulfur and sour milk.

"Eeeve," it hisses, mocking me. Sensing my deepest fears, it begins to play with me by using those emotions against me. "Oh God," I exhale, as I close my eyes and rub my temples, trying to ease the dread rising in my throat.

Panicked, I start talking to myself. "Think, Eve." I turn around, allowing my eyes to scan over the dark enclosed area. All I can see in front of me is black. Blowing out a harsh breath, I begin to pray for a miracle as I wait for it to manifest.

"Nope, nothing," I say dejectedly to no one.

I twist back to the wall. In a frantic state, I push and pound on the large, dark gray stones, trying anything. I'm desperate, and there's an off-chance that located somewhere is a hidden opening that could grant me freedom.

Then I hear it. The thing I fear most. I spin and freeze, fixed in my spot at the hissing sound of slithering snakes. Oh shit, now I'm really afraid. My heartbeat echoes in my ears as a severe chill runs down the length of my spine. My lips force air out sharply in a frenzied state, causing strands of fallen hair to jump away from my face with each irregular breath.

Without warning, the tunnel goes silent. The only sound rico-

cheting off the wet stones is my strained breath being forced into the dark abyss. I remind myself to inhale before I suffer from a full-blown panic attack. With great slowness, I rotate to face my attacker.

No one is there.

As I swallow hard, my eyes shift down to the floor and take in the dark tendrils of smoke that crawl around my ankles, rooting me to the ground. What the hell? My eyes dart around wildly, searching for the point of origin of the wisp, but there isn't one.

With my back pressed flat against the cold concrete wall and the dampness seeping into my shirt, I've resigned myself to the fact that this is how I'm going to die. I close my eyes in acceptance and attempt to steady my breathing, listening to the droplets of water hitting the ground.

Drip.

Drip.

Drip.

I try to convince myself it will be okay as the dark cloud works its way up my body, wrapping forcefully around my neck and cutting off the oxygen supply sustaining me.

Black spots form behind my closed eyelids as I become light-headed and dizzy. The lack of oxygen begins to take hold of my body, and I start to lose consciousness. Crap.

"Dimittet eam, Nero," I hear a strong male voice order, in a calm yet deadly tone.

I can't see my savior. Everything is shrouded in darkness.

Maybe he isn't even here, and I'm hallucinating in my final moments of life.

The black mist loosens its choke hold on my neck while hissing angrily. *"Deus tuus, ibi est filia eius."*

A putrid gust of air blankets my face with each seething mock. Changing its mind, the evil smoke cackles, wrapping around my throat again and gripping firmly, causing me to wheeze. *What the fuck?*

"Dixit mittam tibi pergat ad profundum inferni, sive," my liberator says heatedly in Latin.

Nero releases me, then turns to my rescuer, morphing into the outline of a man. At the discharge of its hold, my body slides down the slick wall, landing harshly on the glacial, water-soaked stone floor. I begin coughing and gasping for air as I place my head between my legs, willing air into my lungs.

"Et subdit quod me putesssss?" Nero hisses.

"Yes, you repulsive excuse of an existence, I do think I can send you back to the depths of Hell," my protector replies calmly, yet cockily.

"Et veniunt ad me ut, gurgulio," Nero states, in a final slithery tone. At that command, my savior pulls out a long, black, granite sword that reflects the water cascading down the passage walls.

"Delectabiliter," the dark knight replies coldly, before he attacks.

Even wrapped in blackness, I can sense he's a trained warrior. His body moves with ease and agility as he engages Nero. I hear *each whoosh the sword makes as it slices effortlessly through the air, making contact with each thrust.*

I can't make out any of the warrior's facial features, but I know he's large and moves fast and efficiently. I close my eyes for a brief second, only to throw them open in alarm at the high-pitched shriek coming from the thing called Nero, as it bursts into blue flames and vanishes.

That's when I officially lose control over my emotions and begin to shake uncontrollably, with tears flowing down my pale cheeks. The blackness engulfs me, choking me. I shut my eyes, wishing that everything would just stop, and that I was anywhere else.

All of a sudden, I feel warmth and calm flow through my veins, as my guardian kneels down next to me and pulls me into his safe embrace with gentleness. He strokes my hair, trying to pacify me as I cling to him for life.

The masculine scent of smoky wood and leather fills my nose, as his deep voice whispers in my ear.

"Hush. It's all right. You're safe. No harm will come to you. I've got you." His tone is slow and soft, as if speaking to a wounded animal, lulling me into a state of calmness.

With great tenderness, his large, warm hands cup my cheeks and lift my face to meet his, wiping the tears away with his thumbs —a pointless effort, since the flow increases with the kind gesture.

My gaze lifts and connects with a pair of glowing indigo eyes. They're staring at me with such intensity and affection that his look creates an ache deep within my chest, as my body draws itself to his of its own accord, like it knows him.

The voice belonging to those eyes speaks with a firm vow. "I will protect you . . . always."

Gasping for air, I abruptly sit up in bed and swallow down a scream. My fists clutch my blanket in a severe death grip, as pieces of my light brown hair fall from my ponytail and stick to the sweat on my face and neck.

I drop my head into my waiting hands and realize my cheeks are wet, most likely from the tears that escaped my hazel eyes during my nightmare.

The dampness causes my long, dark lashes to stick to one another while I rub them. The lids open, then close again, and I order myself to take even breaths to calm my erratic heartbeat. As I slowly open them for the final time, my heart rate picks up once more, at the realization of what's coming next.

I turn to my left and steel myself.

"What. The. Hell. Eve!" Aria, my roommate and self-appointed best friend, screeches, and I wince from the high-pitched octave. *Crap.* I woke her up, again.

She's sitting on her bed, looking like a pissed-off fairy. Her normally cute pink, pixie-cut hair is suffering a major case of bed head, sticking up in all directions.

"Are you okay?" Aria asks, with an irritated yet concern-laced voice, and her petite hands on her curvy hips. She's staring at me, waiting for an explanation as I open and close my mouth like a gaping fish, trying to form intelligent words.

"Sorry, I um, bad dream," I mutter inarticulately.

"No shit," she says, with sarcasm dripping from her lips. "Same one?" The question is thrown out along with some serious stink eye radiating from her round chocolate orbs.

Arianna "Aria" Donovan dislikes being woken up in the middle of the night. I know this because we've been college roommates for all of one month now. Which means I've woken her up more times than I care to count.

We met over the summer during freshman orientation, and according to Aria, it was "friendship at first sight." As new students, we were placed into groups of ten and forced to play this ridiculous get-to-know-you game where each person had a photo of a particular cartoon character taped to their back. The goal was to ask the group questions in an attempt to gain enough information to guess who your character was, so you could partner up with your match for the rest of orientation.

Aria was *Bert* and I was *Ernie*. We've been inseparable ever since, even requesting to room together this semester. Well, in truth, Aria demanded we room together, and since I'm pretty easygoing, I didn't put up a fight, figuring it would be nice to know someone.

At the moment, I'm thinking she's second-guessing her choice in roommates.

She sighs and prowls to the minifridge, grabbing a bottle of water and shoving it in my hand before turning on the crystal-embellished lamp on the pink thrift-store-revived table between our beds.

Our dorm room is a decent size. We got lucky in the housing lottery and managed to snag a suite. Unfortunately, that means we share it with two other roommates.

The space consists of two shared bedrooms, a common lounge area, and an attached bathroom. Overall, it's your typical college dorm room, amped up with Aria's thrift store finds reincarnated into amazing pieces of art, because she is an eternal optimist and believes everything can be redeemed.

Her décor style matches her schizophrenic personality to perfection—Barbie meets Marilyn Manson. She's the only person I know who can pull off pink combat boots, black nail polish, and dark black smoky eyeliner with a pink sundress, and have it look adorably sexy.

I like her one-of-a-kind style. It offsets my average, girl-next-door fashion sense, which usually consists of skinny jeans, knee-high boots, and a cotton long-sleeved shirt. I suppose it's what originally drew me to her—

opposites attract. I also presume that's what makes our friendship fun.

The cousins, our other two suitemates, are a different story. Speaking of which, I need to take cover as the door to our room crashes open in dramatic fashion and both Abby and McKenna enter the room like a Victoria's Secret pajama commercial.

Abby, the younger of the two cousins by only a few months, smiles with her delicate arms folded, allowing her long red hair to cascade over her refined shoulders.

"You okay, Eve?" she asks with concern.

Even at three in the morning, Abigail "Abby" Connor is ethereal looking. She's wearing her black flannel pajama bottoms and a cute green T-shirt that says, *Kiss Me, I'm Irish.* The green brings out the flecks of shimmer in her crystal-blue eyes.

I force a casual shrug. "Yeah. Just another bad dream. Sorry to wake you guys up again."

She responds with a warm smile.

On the other hand, McKenna just grunts. I've deduced it's simply because she hates talking to people.

Now that I think about it, McKenna "Kenna" McIntyre just dislikes people in general. She's always ranting about the "human race" being inferior. Inferior to whom, she's never clarified. Most of the time, her offhanded comments go in one ear and out the other, because they're so frequent.

I exhale and take a sip of water, the cool liquid hydrating my dry throat.

McKenna narrows her sapphire eyes, outlined with lush black lashes, at me. "Seriously, Eve. I'm tired of waking up to your fucking screaming every night," she comments in a harsh tone.

I grimace. "Was I screaming? Sorry, I had no idea," I offer. Of course I was screaming. I was being choked to death, for God's sake. The shrieking might also be why my throat feels like sandpaper, making it painful to swallow or talk.

Turning like a graceful but angry swan, McKenna heads toward the doorway, stopping just before making her dramatic exit. "You look like shit, by the way," she snarls, and flicks her long, platinum-blonde hair over her shoulder to enhance her point. With that, she storms out, fuzzy slippers and all.

Most of the student body on campus is terrified of McKenna. It would be wishful thinking to assume they're put off by her "sass" and "straight shooting" attitude.

I think she just gets off on intimidating people. She also has no filter, a vocabulary rivaling any truck driver, and can make even the strongest person fold into her- or himself with her malevolent stare.

Needless to say, the jury is still out on our friendship. It's only been four weeks. Abby, on the other hand, is extremely likable, and is becoming a good friend.

"Sorry," I mutter, for the fourth time this week.

The nightmares began on my eighteenth birthday. Each time, I wake up in a cold sweat, gasping for air, crying and screaming from being terrified and tortured in the outlandish dream. It's been rough, to say the least.

Lying back on my pillow, I put my arm over my eyes, willing my body to calm itself down, as the adrenaline still pumps wildly through my veins. I try using the breathing techniques I've learned through years of studying yoga. It's not working.

Abby fidgets with unease. "Kenna doesn't mean to be bitchy. She's just tired," she excuses the poor behavior, a maternal habit of hers.

With poise, she sits on my bed, removing my arm from my hidden face. "Do you want to talk about it?" She offers a small smile. "It might help make it less scary and real if you say it out loud." Abby pauses before continuing. "You'd be surprised at my level of understanding when it comes to fear-provoking things," she says at almost an inaudible level.

"No. Thanks, Abby. I'm good. Just a bad dream," I say as persuasively as I can, for both our sakes, because if she knew what lurked in the darkness of the dreams, she'd have me committed.

Abby studies my face for a moment, searching for a

hint of deceit. When she's convinced I'm all right, she stands to go back to her own room. "Okay, but if you change your mind, come and get me. I'm happy to listen, Eve. Night, girls," she utters in a sweet voice before leaving.

McKenna and Abby are both tall and built like dancers. While Abby exudes grace and regality, McKenna radiates fierce warrior princess. When they're together, it's intimidating.

Aria just stands there, staring at me, taking this all in while wearing her favorite pink T-shirt and matching boy shorts. All five feet of her looks both adorable and annoyed.

"Fine," she huffs, and relinquishes the idea that I want to elaborate on my nightmare-induced state. She crawls back into bed, pulls up her ruffled pink blanket, and turns off the light.

We sit in silence, the moonlight shining through the window, bathing the room in a blue glow and twisting the shadows on the walls. I turn my eyes upwards to the ceiling, focusing on it with immense concentration, wishing the terrifying dreams would stop so I could have a normal night's sleep.

After a few moments, Aria rolls over to face me as the night's silver light bounces off her features, masked in sympathetic concern. She goes to speak, but I cut her off.

"Please don't, Aria. I just don't have it in me tonight," I whisper, pleading for her to back off.

"Okay, but at some point we need to figure this out, Eve. I'm worried about you." She sighs, turns over, and goes to sleep.

I'm left to contemplate my dreams and their meaning while, once again, staring into the abyss of darkness.

VERNAL

THE ROYAL PROTECTOR ACADEMY SERIES

My eyelids slide closed as the tiny drops of water cascade from the darkened sky. The warm beads hit my face, trickling effortlessly across my cool skin. The sensation of being alive wraps around me, as my spirit connects to the energy the weather bestows. Strength bleeds into my body, penetrating each layer until the energy drifts throughout my veins.

I ignore the dull ache making its way into my neck, a result of tilting of my face skyward. Instead, I lift my arms and, without thought, twirl and embrace each tiny droplet of water as the rain soaks the crenulated coastline around me in a fierce assault.

The elements heighten my supernatural powers, causing my core to hum with vitality. My lips form a small smile as I pirouette my way through the mist-shrouded, endless emerald hills. Each rise is crisscrossed by tumbledown ancient stone walls. My laughter floats in the wind. It's the only other sound encircling me, aside from the rainfall.

I loved doing this as a child. Spinning so fast I'd become dizzy and disoriented, until the earth around my feet would simply slip away, and breathlessly I would collapse onto the blades of grass. I miss the carefree days of my youth. There's something freeing—liberating—about standing in an open field, with your arms extended, allowing the rain to wash away your inhibitions. Not that I have many hang-ups, but the ones I do —they wrap around my heart like chains, squeezing until the simple act of breathing becomes almost impossible.

Another childish laugh escapes me as my body tumbles and collapses onto the soaked ground. I stretch my lean limbs and sink into the sponge-like soil, becoming one with the aged earth below my undressed body. My wet, auburn hair falls messily around my face and some of the long pieces stick to my dampened skin.

I don't care.

For the first time in days, I feel alive again.

Lying on the ground, I simply stare at the dark sky above, as the world spins around me. For a fleeting minute, the dizziness offers a brief reprieve from the musings that constantly cloud my head.

My free-spirited revel ends abruptly at the sound of a

throat being cleared. I release a half moan, half sigh, knowing my moment of serenity has come to an end.

Rather than sitting up to face Rulf, the royal guard assigned to protect me, I pout like a child. My unhappiness overtakes the bliss I was feeling seconds ago.

It's not that I don't enjoy Rulf's company. It's just that his presence reminds me of my royal bloodline, my duties, and my obligations.

Knowing the gargoyle's temperament, he's probably standing with his arms crossed, aggravated by my lack of acknowledgment while he continues to get wet.

"Go away, Rulf."

"You're naked."

The statement comes from an unfamiliar, seductive, masculine voice, filled with an inherent confidence.

Definitely. Not. Rulf.

Unaware of who this stranger is, I remain still and strategize a plan of attack, should I need one. Though I'm without my weapons, I'm not concerned. Years of training with the best protectors have made me a skilled opponent. If all else fails, I always have my supernatural powers to help me kick this guy's ass.

I clear my throat and remain motionless.

"Your ability to state the obvious is mind-blowing."

The stranger releases a dark chuckle, unnerving me. I shiver in response, and my slight grin falls. My lips press together in annoyance at my reaction to something as simple as his enthralling laughter. It's like silk.

Cool.

Sensual.

Designed to pull you in and entrance you.

"I guess I missed the *clothing optional* portion of the Academy's handbook," he counters.

My stomach clenches in response as his velvety voice drifts over my exposed skin, caressing it. I swallow, in an attempt to keep myself in check and my tone even.

It is an epic failure.

"Something to work on, then." My voice is shaky.

"What's that?"

"Reading."

"Reading?"

"A prerequisite if you'll be attending the Academy."

A beat of silence passes between us before he speaks.

"Is nudity a habitual behavior of yours?" he questions, with an amused lilt to his tone.

At the sound of his deep voice, I roll onto my stomach, lift my gaze, and meet his curious expression.

He's breathtaking, in a dark and unrefined manner, if you're into that sort of thing. By the way my breathing has become erratic and my heart rate is spiraling out of control, I guess I'm into it.

"Yes," I reply.

A knowing smirk appears on his full lips. "Nice ass," he compliments, while his stare runs the length of me.

I don't shy away from his open perusal. I'm comfortable with my curves. Self-assurance comes with my title.

His eyes roam across my body, leaving imprints everywhere they go. I blush uncharacteristically at his heated intensity. My poise cracks as raw desire slithers inside me, crawling into the crevices, choking me.

Confused by the way my body is responding to him, I pinch my brows. He tilts his head to the side, watching my reaction. There's something captivating about the way he's looking at me. He's drawn to me, but can't figure out why.

I notice his self-confidence start to fade. Taking advantage of the fact that he's lost in his own thoughts, my focus shifts to his mouth, and I stare at a tiny, sexy scar on his upper lip. His breathing is smooth and soft.

Unlike me, with my unsolicited need to have him whisper dirty things to me, he seems unaffected. Cool and calm. Eerily controlled.

The stranger runs both of his large hands through his caramel hair, pushing the long pieces on top back in a sleek and sexy manner. The rain has soaked every perfect strand, and they keep attaching themselves to his sun-kissed face. It's almost as if they never want to let go.

I narrow my eyes at the wisps. They're eliciting a pang of jealousy within me. For some unexplainable reason, I feel an overwhelming sense of ownership over him. It's me who should be the one to touch his slightly scruffy, chiseled face—not those pieces of hair.

Wait, that isn't right. I don't even know him.

I scrutinize his thick eyebrows and attempt to compose myself. On most guys a brow piercing looks ridiculous. On him, it looks menacing and wild.

And hot.

So very, very hot.

I drop my gaze to the silver and hematite rings adorning his fingers. Like mine, every finger with the exception of his pinky is covered with them. I blink away the idea that our hands match, and instead concentrate on his broad chest, hidden under a white thermal.

The thin cotton is drenched, allowing me to take in his sculpted body. A pendant sits under his shirt, dangling from a black leather rope, which hangs from his neck.

Annoyingly, I can't make out what it is.

I sigh internally as my eyes trail over his rolled-up sleeves. They're pulled up to his elbows, showing off the leather-and-chain bracelets he's wearing on each wrist. At the sight of the familiar adornments, all my internal alarms go off, and something inside of me sinks. I attempt to hide the awareness that has fallen across my expression, and instead fixate on his worn jeans and heavy boots, while planning my escape.

This guy reeks of danger, and trouble. The air of cockiness he emanates is one I grew up with. It matches my father's and uncles'.

It all means this hot specimen is one hundred percent off-limits, and being near him is like being near a bullet that you never saw coming. It wounds you so quickly and deeply that you bleed out without even knowing you've been hit.

I meet his powerful cognac glare and a shaky breath escapes me. I'm startled by the way he's staring at me.

Like I'm all he's longed for.

A light chill brushes through me. I'm not accustomed to someone looking at me and seeing just me, not my bloodline. I need to get a grip on my erratic emotions.

Standing, I put my entire unclothed body on display, hoping to throw him off balance. Pushing some of my damp hair behind my ear, I lift a challenging eyebrow at him, daring him not to look at me.

Unfazed, he holds my gaze with an unwavering stare. A silent pause beats between us.

Who is this guy?

"Are you done assessing me?" he asks.

"You're a protector?" I point to the shaded Celtic tattoo on his right forearm.

The symbol binds him to the Spiritual Assembly of Protectors, allowing him to accept divine assignments.

Of course he's a protector—he's here at the Academy.

Why can't I think clearly around him?

The stranger's expression falls, as if my accusation hurt him somehow. He doesn't say anything, but dips his chin in response, confirming my theory.

I take a step back, empathetic to the heavy burden protectors carry. Nervously, my fingers find and play with my own piece of protector jewelry. The silver bracelet sits on my left wrist and is intricately designed with flowers and vines around the band, hiding my smaller, identical Assembly tattoo.

My aunt Eve gifted the bracelet to me for my eighteenth birthday. It was something her deceased mother Elizabeth, a jewelry designer, had made for her. Aunt Eve had the emeralds, my healing stone, added so they hang off the sides in a pretty and feminine manner. A small watch face was set on top in the hope that I would become more responsible about time management.

Not one of my strong suits.

Along with rules, motivation, education—anyway, you get the point.

It's crucial that all gargoyles wear something containing their healing stone.

The mineral rejuvenates us, increases our powers, and heightens our restorative abilities.

It's a necessary evil in my book. I despise the leather bands my family wear. They feel more like handcuffs to me than required protector accessories.

"Tristan," he says, in a way that slices through me.

Another unwelcome shiver crosses my skin at the sound of his voice.

"Serena," I reply thinly.

Tristan's pointed look drops and travels over my body in a palpable manner, as he becomes intimately acquainted once again with my every curve.

"Are you always so . . . welcoming, Serena?"

When his eyes finally meet mine, my brow arches.

"Only to those I like."

"So you like me then?" He attempts to hide his smile.

I hold him with a glare. "Don't flatter yourself."

Tristan cocks his head and crosses his arms over his chest. My focus strays to the streams of rain dripping off his face. He steps closer to me, so close that I trap a breath he's exhaled in my lungs, when the bare portion of his arm brushes my own.

Why am I so reactive to him?

Slowly he bends down, piercing me with an amused expression. "And here I was, completely impressed with myself that I had a beautiful girl naked—and wet— within five minutes of meeting her," he seduces.

"That a record for you?" I quip.

I offer a shy grin, unable to stop myself.

"It would seem so."

"Maybe you're just having an off year," I surmise.

Tristan stares at me with an obvious sadness that stretches over us. "You have no idea just how off."

My eyes trace his lips. I start to speak, but he abruptly cuts me off when his hands lift to my face, cupping my cheeks. I stop breathing and my eyes widen at the unexpected motion.

At his touch, a warmth runs through my veins, igniting something foreign within me. His thumb lightly brushes a drop of rain off my bottom lip, and I watch with a rapidly beating heart as he brings the thumb to his mouth and sucks the bead of water off, watching me the entire time.

"It's been . . . interesting meeting you, Serena."

My name sounds like a test on his lips.

He releases my face and takes a step back, roughly sliding his hands into the front pockets of his soaked jeans.

I swallow, regarding him for a moment longer.

"You too, Tristan."

"See you around, raindrop."

STOLAS

THE DARK SOUL SERIES

Silence envelops the room as my reflection peers back at me from the windowpane. The bright sun feels warm on my face, but the air surrounding me is chilly.

A deep shiver rolls through my body as I stare vacantly at the outside world.

"There is no reason this has to be difficult, Miss Annandale."

Startled by the voice, I blink rapidly and pull my stare away from the dark figure hiding behind a snow-covered tree. An outwardly undetected quiver of fear shudders from within my soul. The figure's constant presence is the reason my mind has turned dark.

"Miss Annandale?" the inquisitive voice firmly repeats.

I exhale and slowly shift my attention to the warm,

vibrant gentleman who is assessing me with a curious expression. "I'm sorry, what did you say?" I manage.

The expensive leather groans under his weight as he sits back in his executive chair, quietly scrutinizing my disposition.

Dr. Cornelius Foster has been silently studying me since I walked through the door, fingers tented under his strong chin. It's unnerving.

Even so, I don't show my discomfort. I've learned that displaying alarm is cause for medication. And the meds only serve to darken my mind further.

I focus on the prestigious degrees and awards the good doctor proudly showcases on the rich burgundy wall behind his mahogany desk. They're impressive. *He's* impressive.

None of it matters though. He can't help me. No one can. "Let's talk about the voices. Are you still hearing them?" The voices are constant. Never ending. But that isn't what he wants to hear. The hundreds of thousands of dollars he's spent on those framed degrees won't allow the voices to still be there. What he doesn't grasp is, if years of conventional medical treatments and medication haven't helped, one hour in a Swiss "healing spa" certainly isn't going to.

I fake a smile. "They're much quieter now."

Dr. Foster dips his chin. "And the demons? Do you still see them?"

I can't help but notice how bright his crisp, button-down shirt looks against his dark chocolate skin. The white is pure. Ethereal. For a moment, I pretend he's an angel sent from Heaven to protect me from evil. The light to fight the darkness that has settled deep within the corners of my mind.

"Hope?" he prompts, using my name.

"I haven't seen one since landing in Switzerland," I lie.

Dr. Foster's brow furrows and he runs a large hand over his full beard. The gesture causes me to stare at the few strands of gray mixed in with the black. For a man in his early fifties, Cornelius Foster certainly is easy on the eyes. His features remind me of that actor, Idris Elba. Unlike the other doctors before him, he's sharp and seems to be able to read me.

Lost in thought, I suddenly realize he's now leaning on his desk in front of me, muscular arms crossed, gaze calculating.

"Hope," he commands my attention again. "You're safe here. Our patient-doctor relationship only works if you are candid during our sessions. I can't help if you don't truthfully tell me what is going on inside your head. While you are here, I expect open and honest communication. There is no judgment. I'm here to aid in your healing."

An awkward silence lingers between us.

Aid in my healing. *Is that what I'm here to do? Heal?* If it were only that easy.

It's been two years since my twenty-first birthday; for two years my mind has been haunted by visions of suffering, pain, and torture. The images are burned into my memory.

They aren't something you *heal* from. Or forget.

I squeeze my eyes closed and attempt to push them away, along with the bile that threatens to rise.

A small knock at the door breaks through our quiet standoff. "Come in," Dr. Foster answers, without taking his gaze off me. I twist my focus to the girl who slides into his office. With her

presence, a cold chill spreads through my limbs. The stranger's brown eyes are vacant. Just like mine.

She's young, around my age, and looks to be of Native American heritage. Her straight, brown hair falls to her waist and is parted down the middle. I watch as she robotically flips it over a slender shoulder. The gesture is odd—forced even. There's no feeling behind it. It's almost as if someone programmed her to blink, breathe, and move every few seconds as a way for her to appear human.

"Hope, this is Lore," Dr. Foster says by way of introduction. "She'll be your suitemate during your stay here at Shadowbrook." I frown. "Suitemate? I thought my parents requested a private suite?"

The psychiatrist smirks. "Human nature thrives on community. I believe it's healthy to be social. Having a suitemate will be beneficial to your healing. You'll see."

I don't answer him, as I once again meet Lore's unresponsive expression.

"We're done for the day." Dr. Foster walks around and sits behind his desk. "Lore will show you around the grounds, and help to get you settled in. I'll see you tomorrow afternoon for our weekly private session."

Relieved at the dismissal, I stand and face my new room- mate. She's silent as she opens the door and waits for me to walk through. Maybe Lore doesn't speak. I can understand the desire to remain quiet and keep people at arm's length. Especially in a place like this.

As I pass by her to walk through the doorway, I watch as the inky shadows swirl around her aura. At the sight, my breath hitches. No air moves in or out of my lungs.

Annoyed with my lack of movement, she huffs and steps around me into the hallway, leaving me no choice but to follow at a quick pace.

The sound of a robotic movement pulls me from the shadowy path my mind is wandering down. My gaze lifts and locks onto a small lens with a flashing red light.

"Cameras?" I confirm.

"They're everywhere," Lore says flatly, without a

look back. My gaze jumps around, taking in each of the small devices as

we continue to walk down the hallway. The heels of our shoes echo as we step on the elegant hardwood floors.

Shadowbrook feels like a five-star resort. People are relax- ing everywhere—sprinkled around inviting velvet chaises and chairs. They're reading, writing, and using tablets in a mundane manner, as if this is a hotel and they're simply guests enjoying their vacation.

It's all so . . . normal.

Unsettling.

Lore and I step into a large open room with vaulted ceilings.

There is a full wall of windows on one side over-looking the retreat grounds and snow-covered moun-tains, and a baby grand piano on the other side, in front of a roaring fireplace and shelves of books.

The room is warm and cozy, filled with oversized couches and chairs. The walls, furniture, and accents are decorated in shades of tranquil grayish-blues and dark browns. Game tables are set up, and a gigantic glass chandelier hangs from the middle of the room.

I feel my throat tighten a little at the thought of how much like home this room feels.

I miss Connecticut, my friends, my parents, and my life—be- fore it all fell apart.

"Do you like it?" Lore asks, uninterested in my answer.

"It's like a modern Swiss chalet." I exhale. "What's not to like?" "This is the game and lounge area," Lore continues monotonously. "Where you come to play games . . . and lounge." She speaks slowly, as if I wouldn't understand.

Is this girl serious? By the blank expression settled across her stunning features, it appears she is. "I can see that," I respond, unable to keep the edge out of my voice.

She ignores me and I follow her quietly as she guides me through more hallways, until we come to a set of double glass doors. We step closer, and with a whoosh, they slide open to reveal a dining hall. The smell of coffee and baked goods assaults me, conjuring up images of my hometown coffee shop, where I'm currently wishing I was, reading a book.

"The dining hall is open twenty-four hours for all of your nutritional needs."

"Nutritional needs," I parrot.

Lore rolls her eyes and focuses on the empty room.

"Where are the trays and food windows?"

Her cold glare swings back to me and her brows pinch. "There are servers who take your request and bring it to you once it has been prepared to your liking by our chefs. When you are done, hired staff will remove your used cutlery, china, and glassware for washing."

"So, no KP duty?" I quip.

The last facility I was at required every resident to lend a hand in the kitchen.

Lore's expression turns sour. "We are here to heal, not do dishes. This isn't prison."

Speechless, I simply stand there.

It's obvious she's never experienced a *real* mental health facility. I remain quiet during the tour of the library, outdoor meditation area, spa, and indoor fitness center. At the end, she leads us to our room, which turns out to be a penthouse suite. It has a common area, kitchenette, and two hallways—each leading to a large bedroom on either side of the apartment, with its own private bathroom. It's very elegant.

"The kitchen is stocked with basic needs. Water, fruit, and the like." Her eyes scan the length of me. "No knives though. If you're planning to commit suicide, you'll need to break a mirror and slit your wrists. Or tie sheets together and hang yourself."

"I'll keep that in mind," I mutter.

After pointing out which room is mine, my suitemate disappears without another word. Alone, I release a deep breath and notice my bags have already been placed neatly on the carpeted floor. My gaze drifts over the luxurious, king-size bed.

There are no hospital sheets here. The white cotton material is without a doubt Egyptian, and a minimum of fifteen hundred thread count. My eyes roam, searching for the restraints, but I come up empty. All that decorate the bed are taupe and steel- blue bolster pillows and fine linens. I look around my luxurious hotel-like surroundings.

"What is this place?" I whisper into the emptiness.

Twisting around, I drop into a wingback chair and trail my focus over the rest of the room. Mirrored side tables flank the large bed, decorated with lamps, vases of fresh cream flowers, and stone Buddha statues. A velvet-cushioned storage bench sits at the end of the bed, most likely holding extra pillows and blankets. It's all so elegant and formal.

An oval glass desk and leather chair have been placed in front of the window, positioned to overlook the meditation gardens.

"No knives, but there sure as hell is a whole lot of glass," I say to myself.

My attention drops to the circular side table next to the chair. It's decorated with a silver tray holding two glasses, bottles of high-end water, and multiple pill and vitamin containers. A medication schedule outlining when to take the tablets has been handwritten on elegant stationery, along with a printed calendar of my sessions and treatments.

I pick up one of the orange bottles and read the label. A prescription for anti-psychotic medication stares back at me. I shake the full container before returning it to its place.

"Home sweet home."

Standing, I grab my bags and start to unpack. It takes me all of ten minutes to place the few possessions I was permitted to bring into the built-ins located in the walk-in closet. After I'm organized, I waste another forty minutes thoroughly enjoying the rain showerhead in my private bathroom, before getting out and wiping away the beads of water.

Since I wasn't allowed to bring my hair dryer, I squeeze my long, dark strands with a fluffy towel, hoping it will absorb most of the moisture. After a few attempts, I scowl at the clumps and waves forming, and give up, hanging the wet towel on the rack.

Walking to the window, I study the grounds covered in a heavy layer of fresh snow. My stare follows the uphill lines of the breathtaking Swiss Alps. The snow-covered mountains are picturesque. If I wasn't being confined, it would be like living in a postcard.

Just when I start to relax, I'm hit with a sudden burst of cold air.

I tense, as a familiar pair of lavish black leather dress shoes stops in front of me, setting off the goose bumps on my arms. I know the drill; I don't look at him.

Instead, I inhale deeply and my heart pounds wildly in my chest as I hover over an abyss of fear.

"Not now, please," I exhale, hoping the voices and visions will retreat.

"I've found you," he murmurs, leaning in to place his lips at my ear. "You can run, but you can't hide, little one."

I continue to ignore him and focus on the expensive wing-tip shoes.

Reaching out, he gently touches my hair, letting it spill through his fingers. "You were blonde a few months ago. No?" he asks in a deep masculine voice. "This color suits you. He will be pleased." He moans harshly.

Moistening my lips, I snap my head to the side, pulling my hair out of his hand.

Strong, warm fingers grasp my chin, forcing me to remain still. "The time has come for you to abandon all *hope*."

I lose my breath at his familiar words. Even though it's not the first time he's visited, his warning causes my fear to rise to absurd levels. Attempting to control my panic, I squeeze my eyes closed.

When they reopen, I look around frantically, but the demon is gone.

Trying to calm my heart rate, I pull in deep breaths and talk myself down, reminding myself he wasn't real —he was just a vision. One that keeps haunting me.

When my nerves settle a bit, I turn back to the window, hoping the scenery will keep my anxiety levels even.

I look around the grounds for anything suspicious, but see nothing out of the ordinary, until my drifting gaze stops on a dark form straddling one of the lounge chairs near the pond. The ache of fright is still present in my chest; I pull the sleeves down protectively on my sleeping thermal and curl my fingers around the material to help ground me.

After a few moments of gawking at the figure outlined in shadows, I realize it's a man.

Seeing no swirling aura around him, I relax.

Human.

Not demon.

I release a long, grateful breath and let go of my sleeves. I'm just about to step away from the window when he reaches

into the pocket of his jacket. Transfixed, I watch as he pulls out something black. *A crayon maybe?* A few seconds later, he bends his tall frame forward, and mindlessly works his hand over a sketch pad, leaving traces of charcoal with each stroke. Drawn to his swift movements, I follow each shady line marring the pure white paper. I'm too far away to make out what he's sketching, but the intensity with which he draws captivates me.

The rising silver moon highlights his raven hair. It's shaggy on top, and cropped around his neck. Stylish.

Sexy even. I notice thick silver rings on each of his middle fingers.

From this viewpoint, it's hard to see his face, but I'm able to make out the sharp angles of his jawline.

The stranger snaps his body back and studies the work on his paper, giving me a fuller view of his face. I lean forward to get a clearer look, hitting my forehead against the glass.

"Crap!" I rub my forehead, not realizing how close I'd moved toward the window.

It's almost as if he's luring me in.

Needing a reprieve from his pull, I twist to grab a bottle of water, but something stops me. Every cell in my body awakens as my gaze slowly shifts back to the window and slams into an intense, emerald-green gaze. The color is so lush and vivid, my heart skips a beat.

I become entranced, swept away with one look. No air moves in or out of my lungs as I hold my breath. A shiver runs bone deep, and my world tilts as everything but him fades.

He looks at me not as though I'm crazy, like most people do, but as if he's fascinated by me. Intrigued even.

I'm hit with a sense of déjà vu when his verdant eyes widen in recognition. Overwhelmed, I grab both sides of the heavy silk drapes and yank them shut. The abrupt motion ceases my trance, allowing me to finally take in air.

Struggling, I search my memories for a spark, trying to re- member where I've seen him, but come up with nothing. I shiver at the echo of his stare, feeling his gaze still in my bones.

I stumble over to the orange bottles on the side table. With a shaky hand, I pick up the medication and take the tablets and vitamins as prescribed by Dr. Foster. I convince myself my mind is playing tricks on me again.

I crawl into bed, and it's not long before the medication causes my lids to become heavy. I steel myself, ready for the nightmares I know will plague me throughout the night.

Like every night for the past two years, just as I fall asleep, my dreams turn against me when a familiar deep voice whispers, "*Lasciate ogne speranze.*"

"Abandon all hope," I mutter, as I slip into the darkness of my mind.

ACKNOWLEDGMENTS

There are so many people to thank. It truly does take an incredible team to be able to pull off publishing a novel. So, if you'll indulge me . . . **To my husband and daughter**, thank you for loving me and sharing your time with the characters I write and being understanding of my deadlines. It's because of your love and support that I have embarked on this journey. I am forever grateful to you both. **Hang Le at By Hang Le**, thank you for your friendship, your beauty (both inside and out), and years of creative partnership. This cover—I can't even. Together, we've done some pretty special things over the years, but this cover takes them all. **Liz Ferry at Per Se Editing**, what's left to say? You are truly amazing. Without you, these stories would not exist. At least, not the beautiful way they do. Thank you for *everything*. **Colleen Oppenheim**, I adore you. **Sarah**

Hershman, and the team at Hershman Rights Management, thank you. Kiki Chatfield, Colleen Oppenheim, Tiffany Hernandez, and the entire Next Step PR, team thank you all so much for all your hard work and dedication. A HUGE thank you to Randi's Rebels. I have the best reader group a girl could ask for. You keep me sane when I need it, provide me with endless book recommendations, and fill my days with man candy and laughs. Rebels Rock! Sara Dustin, over the years, you've held my hand, wiped the tears, and warned me not to get wrapped up in my Lincoln. Even though I've never listened, I've always heard you. And, to my Lincoln, just know the ifs still linger. Thanks to my family and friends—I love you all. To the readers, as always, thank you for reading my stories. Thank you for continuing to take chances on me and the stories I write. Thank you for trusting me with your imagination. I'm honored to be part of your literary world.

ABOUT THE AUTHOR

Randi Cooley Wilson is an award-nominated, bestselling author of **The Revelation Series**, **The Royal Protector Academy Novels**, **The Dark Soul Trilogy** and the upcoming **Knightress Series**. Randi's books have been featured on *Good Morning America*, *British Glamour Magazine*, *USA Today*, and in the Emmy's Gifting Suite. Her books range in genre, and include contemporary romance, urban/high fantasy, and paranormal romance, for both young adult and adult readers. Randi makes stuff up, devours romance books, drinks lots of wine and coffee, and has a slight addiction to bracelets. She resides in Massachusetts with her daughter and husband and their fur-baby, Coco Chanel.

Visit **randicooleywilson.com** for more information about Randi or her books and projects.

Or via social media outlets:

0757

Made in the USA
Middletown, DE
12 January 2019